The Bee Book

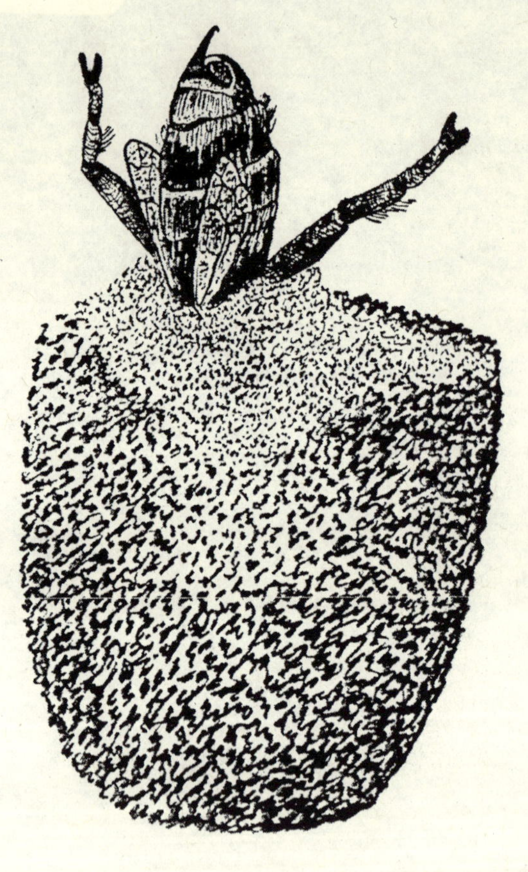

The Bee Book

Ann Rosenberg

INVISIBLE PUBLISHING
Halifax | Fredericton | Picton

Originally published by The Coach House Press (Toronto, ON) in 1981 and seen through the Press by bpNichol.

Library and Archives Canada Cataloguing in Publication

Title: The bee book / Ann Rosenberg.

Names: Rosenberg, Ann, 1940-2018, author | Schmaltz, Eric, 1988- writer of introduction | Cain, Stephen, 1970- writer of introduction

Description: Series statement: Throwback books ; 7 | Originally published in 1981. | With a new introduction by Eric Schmaltz and Stephen Cain.
Identifiers: Canadiana (print) 20250244381
Identifiers: Canadiana (ebook) 2025024439X
Identifiers: ISBN 9781778430794 (softcover)
Identifiers: ISBN 9781778430800 (EPUB)

Subjects: LCGFT: Bildungsromans | LCGFT: Fiction.

Classification: LCC PS8585.O78 B43 2025 | DDC C818/.54—dc23

Throwback Books Series Editor: Bart Vautour
Art Direction: Megan Fildes

Invisible Publishing is committed to protecting our natural environment. As part of our efforts, both the cover and interior of this book are printed on acid-free 100% post-consumer recycled fibres.

Printed and bound in Canada.

Invisible Publishing | Halifax, Fredericton, & Picton
www.invisiblepublishing.com

Published with the generous assistance of the Canada Council for the Arts, the Ontario Arts Council, and the Government of Canada.

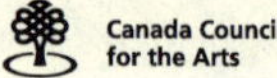

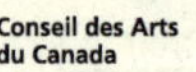

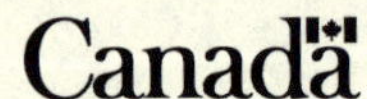

Contents

Introduction i

Preface 7

Learning the Dances 19

The Worker 33

The Drone 53

Becoming Queen 79

The Virgin Becomes the Bride 107

The Nuptial Flight 131

Propolis, Venom & Other Substances 155

New Queens & Drones 167

The Queen 173

Introduction

by Stephen Cain and Eric Schmaltz

When *The Bee Book* appeared in Canadian bookstores in 1981 there was literally nothing like it. Comprising impassioned prose interspersed with hand-drawn illustrations, musical scores, photographs, diagrams, and concrete poetry, the book was both visually and narratively dazzling. Yet, despite its originality, it also represented the culmination of various trends that had been building in North America over the previous two decades, including Second Wave feminism and the experimental, border-blurring activities of women in the visual and conceptual arts.

Ann Rosenberg's career as an artist, writer, editor, and curator flourished in British Columbia, where she was a founding member of Capilano College's Art History department and where she served as Visual Media Editor at the related arts journal *The Capilano Review* from 1974–1986. The art and writing scene in Vancouver during that period was particularly fruitful: innovative arts collectives like Image Bank collected and distributed photos through postal networks, groups like N.E. Thing Company were creating mock corporate advertising and faux industrial projects, and performance artists like Kate Craig (Lady Brute), as well as pop-art feminist mail artists like Anna Banana, produced innovative work through the 1970s and into the 1980s. Poet Judith Copithorne's work across Vancouver's artistic communities from the 1960s onwards—dancing with Helen Goodwin's TheCo group, publishing far-out hand-drawn visual poems, and working with artist-run centres like Sound Gallery and Intermedia—opened the doors for the wider inclusion of women in the scene. Outside of Vancouver, Joyce Wieland had been creating textile art and experimental films with a decidedly feminist perspective. Wieland's historic *True Patriot Love* (1971) made her the first living woman artist to hold a solo exhibition in the National Gallery of Canada. Incorporating paintings, drawings, video, baked goods, quilts, and chickens, Wieland's show was a mixed-media, tongue-in-cheek love letter to Canada that brought together postmodern irony, multimedia, and feminist practice. Rosenberg would have been aware of these experimental artists through her work with Capilano College and *Review*.

Even outside of Rosenberg's immediate circle, there were various literary projects percolating under the surface that may have influenced *The Bee Book*. A series of poems that Sylvia Plath composed just before her death in 1963 focused on bees, hives, and their relation to gender, while in California Kathy Acker was at work on *Blood and Guts in High School*, a novel that, like Rosenberg's, deals with adolescent turmoil and sexuality and that also incorporates hand-drawn dream maps, graphics, found material, and collaged texts (Acker's novel was drafted by 1978 but was not published until 1984, three years after *The Bee Book*).

Like innovative feminist art, poetry, and fiction, political and sociological feminist writing was at its zenith while Rosenberg was a young adult. Betty Friedan's *The Feminine Mystique* (1963) had exposed the entrapment and unhappiness of many marriages and suggested that women's emancipation, or at least some level of fulfilment, could only be found outside the conventional nuclear family. Later popular feminist non-fiction such as Germaine Greer's *The Female Eunuch* (1970) added the repression of female sexuality to its critique of marital and domestic life while the collectively authored *Our Bodies, Ourselves* (1970) became a best-selling manual for health, reproductive rights, and bodily autonomy.

First-time readers of *The Bee Book* may find its visual components and generic multiplicity disorienting. Is it a bildungsroman? Is it an erotic tale? A story of unrequited love? A modern fable? A mythological exploration of gender construction? A scientific treatise? An artbook? A comedy of manners? A guide to the secret lives of bees? A simple answer might be: all of the above and more. But within this polygeneric form, one overarching tone is that of satire.

As in classic satire, Rosenberg uses potentially allegorical names (Habella Cire, Matthias Harp, Solomon/ Saul Hartig, Father della Bono, Tim Consul, Sister Eulalia) in contrast to the banal Fred Smith, and archetypal situations (puberty, school days, frustrated marriage and haphazard child-rearing) in order to critique dominant social constructs and postulate possible correctives. Sometimes that satire misfires (as in the mock-Italian dialect of the waiter Gino) but when Rosenberg is on target, her wit is apparent and her critique of heterosexual and patriarchal conventions of marriage—or of the sterile lives of celibate, perhaps virginal, schoolteachers and nuns—can be devastating.

One of the high-marks of Rosenberg's satire occurs in the series of scenes dramatizing the meeting of Habella's and Fred's parents and the wedding shower. The latter is particularly comic and cutting, sending up the pretensions of middle-class suburbia, generational conflict between women, pop science marriage manuals, and even the politics of women smoking, all overseen by the harridan Aunt Lucinda. Matthias's imagined lecture on the mating rituals of bees also has strong satiric elements as he interposes several sexist jokes into his talk, demonstrating that even "objective" discourses like science are coloured by gendered assumptions and prejudices, anticipating a critique that Margaret Atwood would also make with the "Historical Notes" section of *The Handmaid's Tale* published four years later.

As a novel following the concerns of Second Wave feminism, with its attention to the female body (menstruation, birth control, childbirth), as well as the gender scripts of heterosexual courtship, sexual initiation, and marriage, one might wonder if Rosenberg's protagonist represents gender essentialism. Yet it could be argued that Rosenberg—through Habella's actions and desires—seeks to move beyond binary categories of masculinity and femininity and actually approaches the concerns of Third Wave, or more contemporary, feminism. Throughout the novel, Habella is fascinated not only by the fluid gender characteristics of bees (the asexual worker bees, the male drones, and the choices the queen makes in fertilizing eggs into either males or females) but also those creatures deemed hermaphrodites, such as snails and slugs. Attention to possible intersexuality is also paralleled by Habella's romantic, albeit platonic, relationship with the gay character Matthias. That Habella and Matthias apparently desire each other throughout the novel, yet cannot bring themselves to physically communicate that passion, demonstrates that libidinal desire crosses heteronormative formations and exists along a spectrum.

Following Habella as she grapples with her restricted sense of sexuality, *The Bee Book* unfolds through a series of interconnected vignettes that capture her evolving understanding of human intimacy and connection. While there are moments in the novel that might prompt readers to turn away in discomfort from Habella's youthful encounters, the novel as a whole demands the reader's gaze. Its nine sections are each driven by narrative prose, punctuated by visual media that are integral to the novel's tale, including technical drawings of bees and human anatomy, surrealist drawings of human figures, photographs of cityscapes and beach scenes, diagrammed bee dances, a musical score for a *sarabande*, and typographic arrangements that imitate physical objects—waves, lips, genitalia, and so on. This visual imagery is hardly supplementary to the text; rather, it is central to Habella's story.

Nearly every page of *The Bee Book* integrates a new visual element, and flipping through the book often feels like clicking through television channels. In this way, *The Bee Book* is spectacular in at least two senses of the word. On the one hand, the novel is impressive in its construction, rife with eye-catching visual media and expressive prose. On the other hand, the novel draws our attention to the spectacle of media itself, and in particular, its hyper-sexualization and exploitation of women in television, film, and advertising. Given the feminist purview of Rosenberg's work and the historical context within which she was writing, *The Bee Book* also responds to the depiction of women in visual culture. Rosenberg reorients our attention away from the woman as the subject of the male gaze to instead centre on Habella's self-determined development. Through the integration of multimedia elements, the text reclaims visual representations of women, foregrounding Habella's exploration of her own identity, desire, and autonomy.

While the inclusion of visual media in *The Bee Book* may surprise some readers, the visual components are not postmodern gimmicks: they are integral to the construction and meaning of the novel and in Rosenberg's search for a form that reflects and enhances her content. Just as Habella strives to transcend gender constructions and boundaries throughout the novel, Rosenberg seeks new forms that break from the linear, masculine trajectory of conventional fiction. This is perhaps most clear at the novel's conclusion, where Habella's last scene is not directly narrativized, but is instead depicted through a series of photographs. Whether Habella manages to liberate herself from her domestic situation or not, at the very least we witness Rosenberg's escape from the confines of textuality and her move to semiotic freedom.

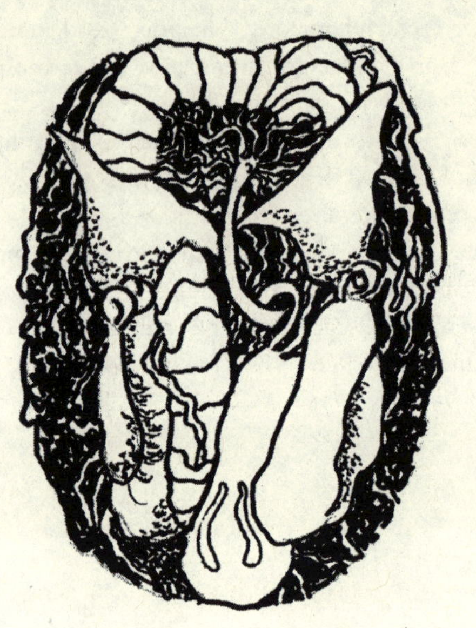

Preface

Her hair was auburn;
her face, lively.
She was the first (in our circle)
to read Levi-Strauss.

I am familiar only with the English translation of *Du Miel aux Cendres, From Honey to Ashes,* which she, of course, read in the original French (the title has Poignance now); it was useful for the notes it contained on Brazilian bees – the stingless Meliponida which, when angry, fastens itself in countless numbers onto a hapless victim in order to suck his secretions and earn the name *lambe olhos* (lick eyes); the delectable honey of the Trigona bee known in São Paulo as *vamo nos embora* (off-we-go) because it makes you drunk; the honey gathering rituals celebrated by shuffling dances that ended in death-through-exhaustion for some. Whereas I was thankful for the information, Habella perused the poetry.

From *Honey to Ashes* offered her the pleasure of this legend:

> In the olden times bees' nests and honey were very plentiful in the bush and there was one man in particular who had earned quite a reputation for discovering their whereabouts. One day while chopping into a hollow tree in order to extract honey from it he heard a voice calling, 'Take care! You're cutting me!' Opening the tree very carefully, he discovered a beautiful young woman who was called Maba (honey), who was thus Honey-Mother or the Spirit of the Honey. She was quite nude and he asked her to be his wife. She consented on condition that he never mention her name.

I didn't care for the diagrams in Levi-Strauss but Habella thought they were useful for our purposes and summarized the findings of our joint experiment by substituting into them data about the behaviour of bees. Whereas he brought science to mythology she, as determinedly, wished to infuse mythology into the structures of science. We graduated *magna cum laude.* These are our thesis conclusions:

	ACTIVELY	of a worker	works	without reward	DIES
WORKER	in the company				
	PASSIVELY	of a queen	feeds	without reward	DIES
	PASSIVELY	of a worker	feeds	without reward	DIES
DRONE	in the company				
	ACTIVELY	of a queen	flies	DIES	
	ACTIVELY	of a drone	flies	BREEDS	without reward
QUEEN	in the company				
	PASSIVELY	of a worker	feeds	DIES	
				breeds	

It was amazing to me that she saw all patterns as alike, that everything could condense into nothing. Perhaps that's why she never developed a passion for fact, although she supplied half the data for our work. Undoubtedly it explains why she preferred the realm of her imagination where the patterns offered by reality could occasionally be shattered or embellished.

What were the facts of our experiments in Apiary? 20,000 bees in a colony contained within glass walls (20,019 to be exact, but this varied from day to day) where one was a full queen, fifty were drones; the rest tireless workers; 6000 larvae on average, four queens maturing. We would watch and number, number and count until our eyes throbbed the measure of fatigue, until the glass glazed over with our breaths obscuring the enlightenment that comes from the observation of habits and customs. What we wished to discover was the precise relationship between the will of the colony in its constant drive towards perpetuation more long lived, more tenacious than that of any individual within it and the generative urge of the queens and drones. Could a colony prepare the conditions for a redundant mating? Could a mating produce no fruit? Could there be a queen with stunted instinct? For further details please consult Harp and Cire's 'Investigations into the Problem of Hive Abnormalities,' *The New Scientist*, (Tacoma, Washington), volume 45, February, 1964. It will interest you to know that Habella struggled to free her prose contributions to our study from the taint of the imagination and the sin of passionate involvement. This document shows how she purged her thesis notes of her identification with the bees in our colony:

June 5, 1962

The hive is ~~meditative~~ quiet now. ~~My companion~~ Harp is ~~asleep~~ off duty. Workers 401–4 approach chambers XVO–4506–12 to give the ~~unborn~~ maturing full females ~~Royal Jelly~~ pyroprotozentone. To these ~~princesses~~ they feed more than the ~~typical~~ .00012 micrograms of the substance composed and refined from nectar. One is ~~comely~~ a fine ~~biological~~ specimen, with unusually long antennae, ~~undoubtedly designated to become the next queen~~. Workers 2,509–13 feed the ~~princes~~ maturing males .00586 micrograms of bee bread. All will be ready for ~~mating~~ generative activity on June 9 if our calculations based upon the affects of feeding upon sexual maturity are correct. We expect to record a microscopic increase in food intake over the next four nights of $\frac{.00012^{5}}{.0034906} \times \frac{\text{Queens}}{\text{Drones}}$ which is accounted for by the relatively greater size the drone must achieve to properly perform his sexual function. In this brood there will be no drone as handsome equal to the one that escaped the perameters of our experiment last summer.

The part of 'Investigations ...' which may have contributed to her final illness, I quote in full:

In order to demonstrate that the sexual habits of the bee colony were less than ideal, depending upon a casual encounter in the air between *female* x and *male* y, we invented the equipment to perform the first artificial insemination of the queen bee. On June 9, 1962 at 11.573 hours (at the precise moment near noon when, in nature, bees prefer to couple), we sacrificed the male by tearing off his genitals. As they still throbbed with life we plunged them into the spread vulva of the female who was placed upsidedown in a special foam (see figures 1-5). It is unnecessary to add that high productivity and perfect breeding was the result of this laboratory performed union.

Habella cried when we finished (understandable because of the pressure) and said, 'This act is against nature.' 'True,' I countered, 'But if instinct reigns there will be errors in our science.'

It was more natural to Habella to invent than to measure and record. One wonderful example of her wit grew out of the desire to provide the script for a family who had to tell their bees they were about to move. According to bee-keeper custom all major changes affecting the bees' sense of ease must be prepared for or they will, perhaps, swarm in rebellion.

The Text (1)

BEE-KEEPER: Ahem, Bees?

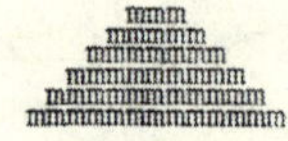

BEES: Hmmmmmnh?

BEE-KEEPER: Sorry, but me and the missus got to move!

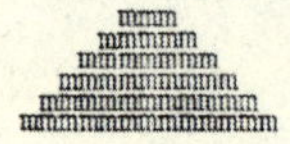

BEES: We'll help you.

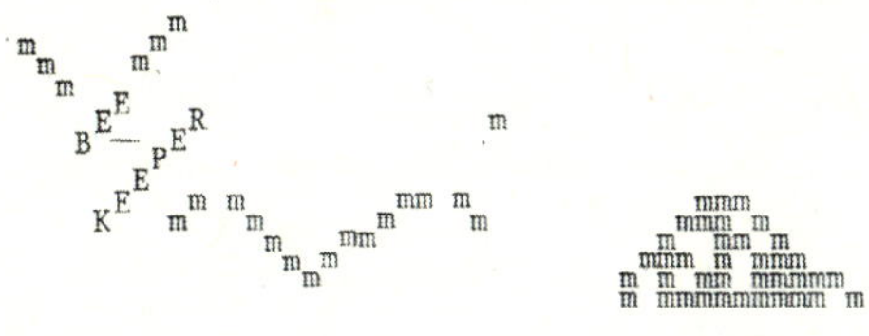

The Text (2)

BEE-KEEPER: Ahem, Bees?

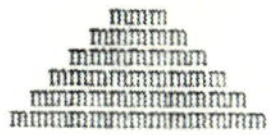

BEES: Uuuuuunnh?

BEE-KEEPER: Sorry, but me and the missus got to move!

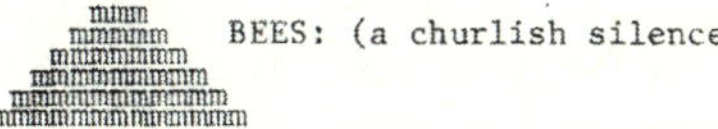

BEE-KEEPER: Don't tell <u>me</u> how to plan my life!

BEES: (a churlish silence)

Although she studied Natural Science, she was familiar with literature, film, linguistics and mythology. This set her apart from others in a generation of students still convinced that rote learning and single discipline training was education. I don't mean to imply that Habella was a student rebel; she always did what was expected of her, yet she could be counted upon to fly over the barriers. While she was by no means a political activist, she spoke well for the *politics of self* which she articulated as 'the right of the individual to live as imaginative a life as society would allow.' As you shall see, her thought and deeds achieved freedom in some measure (although the cost was great) and one can only speculate about what she might become.

Did I love her? Most certainly. I pose this question in order to answer it in terms I can control. She was my alter ego, my only love. It is crucial to know that we were extraordinarily compatible in the pursuit of the exquisite (not the precious) and the witty (if possible). This was an outgrowth of the same attention to detail that allowed us to excel as scientists, in everything we did. We were, on the one hand, computers programmed towards verbal concision and excision; on the other, we were poets. Words brought to us pain as finely honed as that which results from a golden needle inserted into the eyelid's skin or a pleasure as suffused with all-redeeming warmth as that which *is* the moment of 'Roargasm' (as we called it). We were as finely tuned to each other's messages as are the workers in the hive.

'Habella, under what conditions would you sleep with a baboon?'

'Under the same conditions that I would sleep with you.'

'What are they?'

'No crackers in bed and only in the missionary position.'

'But Habella, the baboon is not religious.'

'Neither are you.'

'But Habella, baboons don't eat crackers in bed.'

'But you do!'

or, more seriously....

'Habella, this far?'

'No, too far.'

'Too far for what we need?'

'Yes.'

'But how much must I move, then?'

'As far as the distance that separates "arrogance" from "assurance."'

'Then, this much?'

'Almost, but to the right.'

'This much?'

'Perfect! .1265 mm.'

'We're perfect.'

'Yes.'

'Let's live together, please.'

'No.'

'Why?'

'You're homosexual.'

As I reinsert myself into her vision, under her steady grey gaze, I hear myself whisper, 'eiderdowns of mist billowing;' I listen to her counter-voice, 'blue-veined leaves are scarlet with the shame of dying' – our *War of Murmurs,* loving, so lethal to my soul. She put no emotional value upon the relationship we had. I was an aberrant, estranged from the common tribe. She dismissed me then as unnecessary to her destiny. Closed me off. Shut the doors. I was a sex-less co-worker in the Queen's service. Androgyne. No threat. Excision / Concision.

We were, I insist, perfectly mated (genitals aside). I confessed to her my first sexual encounter. She was (to put it politely as I can) uninterested. Cold, unmoved by the confidence, she was blinkered by her belief in only those matings that perpetuate the human race – the dark side, oh surely, of the teachings of Natural Science. I relieved myself from the emotional stress her rejection caused by accepting a job I did not want from the Parks Board in Kamloops. There for several years I prepared antitoxin from bee venom. In June, 1977, I returned to Vancouver to pursue her.

Just the year before, Paul had entered her imagination. She became consciously obsessed with the notion of metaphysical love, in particular the Renaissance form of it which gave all kinds of distinctions to *venus.* She wrote me that Venus Celeste was divine love, that Venus Erotica was bestial love. She was restructuring the myths, taking her maternity into account:

HABELLA AND NARCISSUS

The boy, by chance, had wandered away in the silver forest. He cried, 'Come here! Where are you?' She called, 'Where are you?' He pled, 'Come here, let us meet!' Her heart rose into her throat. She sobbed, 'Let us meet!'

Never again would she reply more willingly to any sound. She came forth to throw her arms around the youth she loved, but he fled from her shouting, 'Away, with these embraces! I would die before I would have you touch me! Her only answer was, 'I would have you touch me.'

Thus scorned, she concealed herself evermore, yet this love remained rooted in her, sapping her will, thinning her voice, making it echo the fragments.

They called: 'Are you happy, Mother?'

She responded: 'Happy Mother.'

They asked: 'What do you need? Is there anything you want?'
She sighed: 'Anything you want.'
Her voice will soon fly on alone;
Her soul is turning into stone.

She included a drawing with the myth.

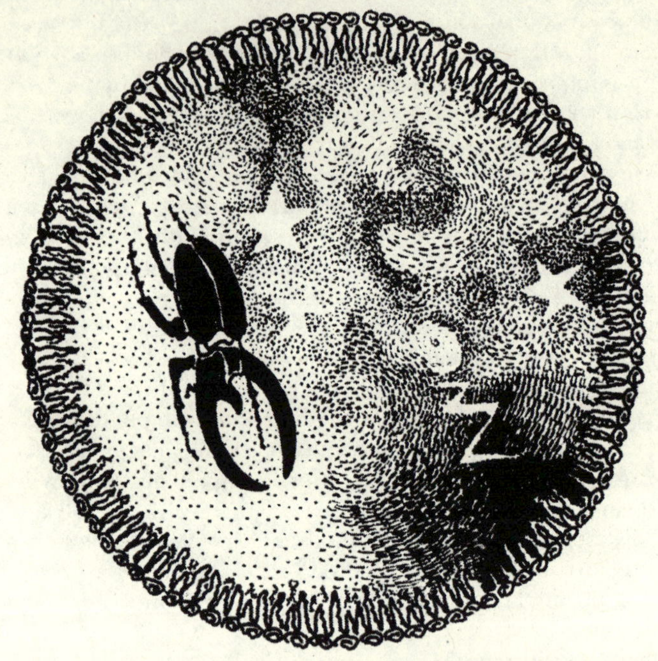

Soon afterwards, I received this memo:

=================

to: MATTHIAS HARP
from: HABELLA CIRE
date: January, 1977

FOR YOUR IMMEDIATE ATTENTION: I am back in Squamish where I started my own normal hive and though the bees are very far away, I do recall them.

Do you still love me? Of course you do. Your movements are as regulated as a watch by its dial; your vestments itch to the bee-keepers' smoke.

I have been measuring my children 1-2-3-4; I've been enumerating my loves and their kinds: Amor Platonicus (You); Amor Ineruditus (Fred); Amori Humani (Mom and Dad); Amori Innocenti (the children); Friend (Renata); God (Paul); Beast (Habella).

It's January. I need chains. I interview a bee-keeper called Jim.

Jim: 'Sure, I keep bees, kept 'em ever since I waz a kid.'

Habella: 'Was it a test to overcome your fear?'

Jim: 'Naw, never knew why I kept 'em.'

Habella: 'Do you get stung often?'

Jim: 'Sure do. Got a real angry hive, know what I mean? Christ, one of my hives is angry all the time, I mean the whole goddam time. It's the queen, ya know, passin' the hostility on to her children. There's thousands of them mad bees out there in my fields. I don't think there's many that would keep them.'

Habella: 'Then, why do you keep them?'

Jim: 'It's pure escape, can forget everything else. Unwind. Relax. See the Queen Bee. I mean, I just wouldn't give up my nasty hive. And doya know somethin'? I'd rather have a hostile bee than an angry customer. Ya can swat bees. Anyway, I really get off on the drones, just bombing around up there like a buncha guys on the loose on a Saturday night, just out *lookin for it.*

And doya wanna know somethin' else? I think there are more crazy households than abnormal hives.

Hey Jack? Got this lady's chains ready?

Good.

Fun talking toya. Seeya around. That'll be ten bucks fifty each.'

================

The next day, a parody of 'For Idleness and Mischief' arrived. I destroyed it in my shock. If my mind serves me correctly, it was as follows:

How doth the aging Habella
Reprove each sunny flower?
She gathers ironies all day
And sulks within her bower.

How wilfully she's built her cell
And tarnished her red flax
And sweetly tricks just everyone
With the echoed words she smacks.

Five months later, I received a final letter more perplexing than all else. It read:

Dear Matthias,
Once when we were together, the sun rouged your eyes amber, exciting the filaments into a ruddy dance. You kissed my lips and laced your fingers through my hair. Desire flickered across your face as softly as clouds smoke the summer grass. You didn't catch my involuntary breath. It could not exhale, 'I love you,' before ashes scattered in my mouth. The moment fled with its fire. I expected another.

It came in a different form. You sat beside me in alabaster, your hands silent in your lap unless they leapt up to express a mudhra to highlight your sermon. To say you spoke to me, is a desecration of your eloquence on this and other occasions. I do not remember the words, but you illustrated my emotions keenly. The sun threw shadows over the edges of your face and your eyes became brown rocks beneath a glacial pool. The second fire was a fire of ice, articulating the mists of feeling. It simmered slowly; I was speechless as before.

On that afternoon so brilliant with light, I wished to bring your body into incandescence with my tongue, to ignite your ivory feet with the electricity of my hair, but it was impossible, my darling, to invent the adoration of your spirit.

I offer you now these lucid words. I will taste a metaphysical passion. I can't live out the similes of the normal wife.

Tomorrow, I fly to Africa.

Habella

In the time that's intervened, I've tried to understand why she didn't love me when I was ready. We just don't know what constitutes chemical attraction. What is the element that elevates like to love? Is it the equivalent to

$$\frac{Myc}{41h \pm pr^2 \times H_5O}$$

that is known to bring all male fruitflies from a three acre area to mate? Or is it more like the related substance

$$\frac{MRd}{53h \pm 31m^6}$$

that repels all fruitflies regardless of sex? Is it produced by I:I, eye to eye, demanding and fulfilling mutual satisfaction? Or does it generate and dissipate *unconsciously* in the gonads?

There are more things to add in the way of explanation. There are many things she would not touch or eat. She enjoyed only honey made by bees who fed on honeysuckle; she would never touch bees that were sticky or damp. When I knew her, she was as clean in the laboratory as a bee is in the nest. She was a person who did not enjoy physical contact unless it was very light, almost absent. I've seen her quiver after a brisk handshake or a firm, mother-given kiss.

I present my memory of her as clearly as I can. These stories, so carefully assembled, edited and amended by Renata Schwenk with my help, you will read with less sadness than I. I leave it to you to decipher her and them.

Matthias Harp,
Vancouver, June, 1980

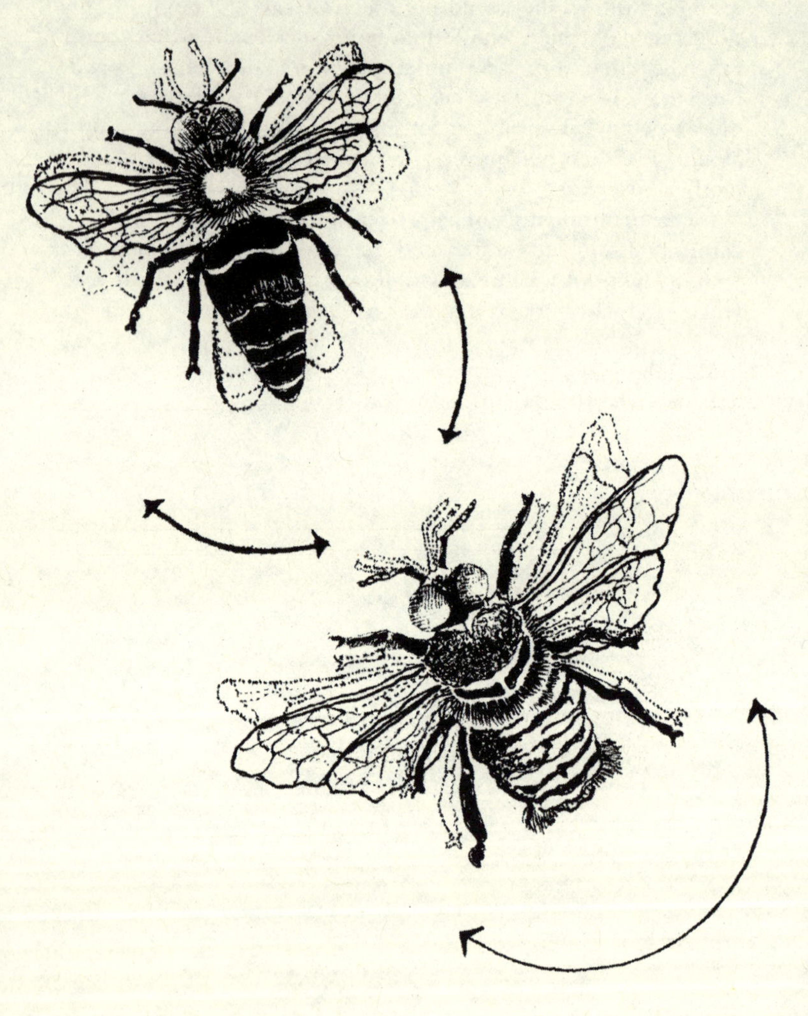

Learning the Dances

SARABANDE

You warned me about the blood but never about the mucus. The mucus first, oh mother.

It poured from me a disgusting treacle, sepia and slimy, the Saturday evening of my ninth birthday. It fell from me a thin, persistent gruel, gluing delicate labia to immaculate pants. It stuck, it streamed steaming in the unexpected October orange heat; it drooled, it pooled, threatening the pink nylon tulle dress you had sewn me for my first recital in the Old Royal Conservatory. It corroded my flesh, coruscating there brown diamonds of pain (so that I could not sit down on the way to the concert)

memory voice:

'No time to change,' you said.

'But mother, I'm uncomfortable.'

'There's no more time to spend in the bathroom,' you said.

'I'm trying to get ready,' I cried.

But it would not stop, I could not make it stop so I hung, suspended soon over the front seat near you, over you, stifling the questions I dared not ask, succumbing to the treble inundations of brown flood, nausea, and fear that lapped over my consciousness and menaced the pink dress with the proof of a functioning I did not yet understand, that inundated the clear sad notes of the *Sarabande* I was about to play before an audience of relatives and friends with blurring blood.

I could not let you down; I could not make it stop coming down. I could not stop it changing note to flood:

So that, my mother, as we reached the place, that arena where the young are expected to display the benefits of careful parenting, I could not perform for you, for my father, for myself: I was so overtaken by the murkiness, the delta-muddiness of the first symbol of womanhood that blood rushed to my cheeks and it was red unlike the rich mahogany that flowed from me as ancient and alien as Nile mud. Oh meniscus of premature maturity, we should have been celebrating you (concert cancelled) somewhere else, just mother and I.

memory voice:
'Please don't wiggle as we drive,' you said.

'But mother, I'm uncomfortable,' I said.

'Well, you're nervous. That's expected. Sit down, your father can't see as he drives!'

'I can't mother. I *can't.* I have a pain ...'

I could never have told you that I would fail that night to be what you expected. The girl with the right touch, the child with the magic touch was drowning in inundations older and wiser than herself yet she could not say, 'Please. Please we must go home!' The pulses overtook her so that *Sarabande* became:

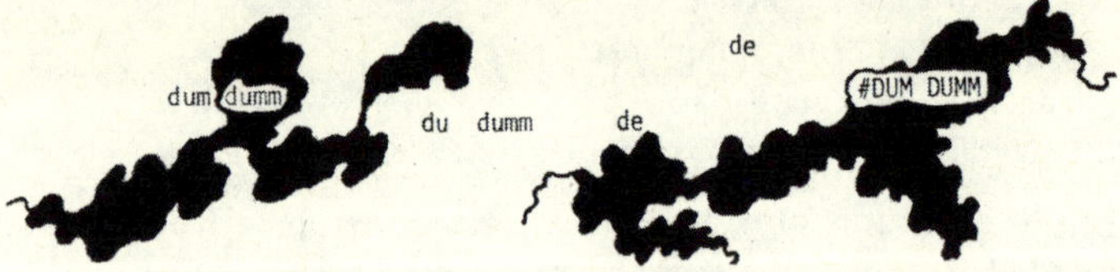

The pulses took over so that there was no I *to speak* – so generalized now into a formless, noteless dumbing that was a *priming* like the acceleration from neap tide to spring. So that I did not begin to know, so that I did not begin to comprehend what happened until I stood in my twelfth summer before the Pacific beach watching the tide magnify itself under the summer moon in three / four time

thrump thrump thrump, thruump THRUMP THRUMP THRRUUMMP. The music erased, then, was less important than the eloquent code that elided the chords.

That : dum dumm de dum dumm dum dumm de dum dumm de

beat and flowed into the climax of

da #de da de DAH de da DUMM DUMM

da

It was not so much a note-forgetting as a remembering of primal ebb and flow.

We should have danced, my mother, in a primitive hut where we two would have been banished in filth among the thatch to be apart and a part of the wisdom of women. But instead we were estranged at the moment when I was becoming you: first, seat barrier in between; next, gentle father in audience. You would only know my failure never my triumph on that Saturday of my ninth birthday when brown-stained and burning I would forget the black chords that would play the dance its proper form. I would play my own B-Minor complaint, for you warned me about the blood, mother, but never about the mucus. You told me that one day I would find a stain, vermilion or scarlet, and I would know then I had become mature. But not you, and not that little book on the *facts of life* you gave me said that *mud was terror.* Not you and not the book that equated human reproduction to the ovulations of chickens and the copulations of dogs whispered anything about the confusion, the agony, the sweat of the moment when a thread of umber slime would force its blackness through the pink fist at the top of my cervix, a sharper and surer rape than that which the surgeon's needle inflicts upon the swollen duct of an eye. Your duty done, by word and book, you were unanswering of all unasked questions, except to say (much later) that you hoped that I would not suffer as you had, hunched in pain over a bucket of water rinsing out the menstrual blood.

Wave nausea now (in remembrance). Wave nausea then staining pink to brown; submitting ideal nylon ('It drips dry,' you said) to murky putrescence which attacked its fibre with weak acid as fragrant and persistent as the wax that had been lapped over the Conservatory floor for one hundred years, as pungent as the milk that had turned sour the moment it touched my lips before we left in the car, before the embarrassment that painted your cheeks carmine. But the blood that brought you colour was the same pigment that combined in me to make the mucus brown and unfamiliar to a child as blood. The mucus that you never, *never* told me about as I turned nine and *let you down.*

Nausea seeping over me, straining from the pink cells the memory of the brown notes so that I played

with my blood.

COURANTE

On Friday afternoons, my mother, I would be at the Gerrard Street Library looking through the books on Biology and Natural Science, searching for the answers:

memory voice:

'No little girl!' she smiled, 'that book doesn't *do* out on a children's card.'

'But it's not for me – my aunt told me to get this Bee Keeper's guide for my uncle,' said I, producing the right card.

'I see, little girl, I see,' (and surely she did).

I would retreat into my aunt's spare room to pursue Reproductive Organs, admiring the drawings and the mysterious labels they carried: seminal sacs, yellow saccules, ovaries, oviducts rolling over my silent tongue. But more than the words, the figures had the power to pull me into the twists and turns of the vasa deferentia as my eye fell from the testes, and into the ovaries I swam to count seeds more numerous than stars. For I was running, mother, obedient to the current, always ahead of the clock you had in mind for me, the metronome to discipline my beats, so that while you were concentrating on my periods (which had been evident to you since I became nine and a half), I was racing heart-sick *from* the first palpitations of love.

Male Organs of Drone, much magnified.

a. Testes	e. Common Duct
bb. Vasa deferentia	fg. Ejaculatory duct
cc. Seminal sacs	h. Penis
d. Glandular sacs	i. Yellow saccules

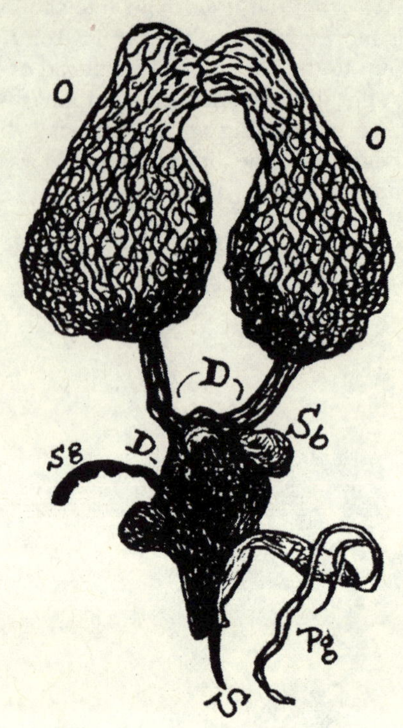

Female Organs, magnified, from Leukart.

O. Ovaries

DD. Oviducts

Sb. Spermatheca

Pb. Poison sac

Pg. Poison glands

Sg. Sting glands

S. Sting

The Bee Keeper's Guide; or Manual of Apiary, A. J. Cook, Lansing Michigan, 1888.

The *Sarabande* was stately compared to the complex *Courante* which followed:

It did not begin in water (though it should have), but it ended there. It began in the passageway between the living and dining space in his carefully appointed home – his wife, who worked as an interior decorator, had painted the walls white, so uncharacteristic of the time – when he kissed me with his tongue and ran his hand over my curving thighs. I turned pink in my white dress as he led me to the piano, bidding me to play and I did play the *Courante* that I knew while his hands massaged my shoulders and his voice breathed:

'You are my special girl, I love you.'

I played the notes with the passionate energy I felt and beads of sweat coursed down my sides and drops of perspiration formed on my brow, aphrodisiac, no doubt, to a man of his nature. And as we were often in the same company there were a hundred other little proofs of his interest in me that my tendency to confuse symbols already confused for love. One day, by the lake, I was rubbing his shoulder blades and they jutted out suddenly, as he changed position, in the configuration of wings.

'You are an angel,' I cried.

'The opposite,' he said.

It was years before I knew about *The Fall of Lucifer,* and even if I had, I wouldn't have believed, so much I accounted the approval of a few stolen kisses and intimate murmurings, so much I misunderstood the feelings that I had. I did flirt; I did wriggle; I did seek him out. I did flatter; I did wheedle (oh, *'uncle'* x, do come!); I did blossom into the bud that he knew I was until the game grew menacing as it did, once, in the water.

We were there, together, wife and parents watching in a pellucid pool, water wrapping round us like a silken scarf, water floating us to surface, water cooling.

'Swim under my legs,' you said (and I did).

voice memory: 'She really is a good swimmer for her age.'

'He really likes children, pity there were none.' 'Yes, one of those sad things – we tried but we couldn't ...'

'Swim under my legs again,' you said (and I did).

'Swim under my legs again,' you said (and I did only this time you clenched me with your knees and held me there so I felt something like a finger floating over my spine).

'Swim under my legs again,' you said (and I did but this time with fear and you ejaculated over me a sticky fluid and I arose red-faced and gasping from the water).

voice memory: 'Are you alright? Better come in now.'

'Yes, I'm O.K., just a little water up my nose. I want to go home now. Thanks for the swim.'

Memory of dissections: memory of fish bladders floating in water. Memory of the *testes* of bees. The taste of fear growing fur in my mouth. The remembrance of fear overtaking my brain, invading my cerebral cortex with a pool of yellow slime that could not be washed out.

So mucus again, my mother, the viscid fluid; medium for begetting came to me first in a current as prematurely as the flux of blood, years and years before you thought I would be threatened by it, years and years before I was ready to receive it or to comprehend it:

> The spermatheca can easily be seen by unaided vision and by crushing it on the slide glass, by compressing it with a thin glass cover, the difference between the contained fluid in the virgin and in the impregnated queen is very evident, even with low power. In the latter it is more viscid and yellow and the vesicle is more distended. By the use of high power, the active spermatozoa or sperm cells become visible. But if the queen has not truly mated, the yellow fluid will fall from her body and the spermatheca will be filled with virgin secretions.

I was a virgin who was running ahead of the clock you had in mind for me, and away from love, although everything, even the music spoke about it:

DYNAMIC MARKS

Term	Abbreviation or sign	Meaning
pianissimo	pp,ppp	very soft
piano	p	soft
mezzo piano	mp	moderately soft
mezzo forte	mf	moderately loud
forte	f	loud
fortissimo	ff,fff	very loud
forte piano	fp	loud, then soft
sforzando, sforzato	sf, sfz	sharply accented
forzando, forzato	fz	sharply accented
crescendo	cres., cresc.	gradually louder
decrescendo	decr., decresc.	gradually softer
diminuendo	dim., dimin.	gradually softer

although everything, even the music gave me practice in it, and especially the signs for it so that I began to see that there was a connection between the:

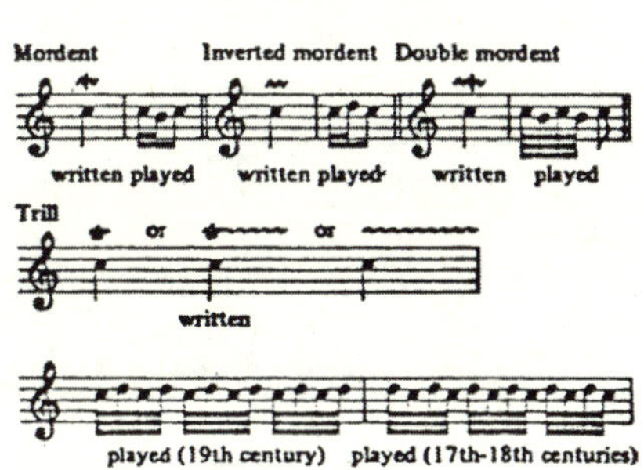

and the:

and even the:

With the event in the swimming pool, I was unable to articulate to myself a reason why this ornamentation was better than honesty. For I was running, mother, *au courante,* so fast, so blindly that I fell into the trap of mixing everything together in order to explain the simple factor called: *Lust.* That he lusted for me was important and (evident) and a cause of fear (in me): that he lusted (at all) was a factor of him, as the lack of *lust*

Lust n. & v.i. 1 (Bibl., theol.) sensuous appetite regarded as sinful; animal desire for sexual indulgence, lascivious passion, whence – *'ful* a., *ful*ness n.; passionate enjoyment or desire *or* (– of *battle, conquest, accumulation, applause*) ...

would become a factor of me. I think we both knew, my mother, that the definition was correct when it equated – and violence. (But we would never discuss it; we could never discuss it.)

What were the dreams then? I could tell you those, in safety. There were dreams of walking over a stile (which you kindly explained to me was a bridge between the fields) and after you did tell me, the *stile* grew into a cage large enough to contain the energy of cougars who nipped my ankles as I did cross 'to the other side.' I did wake nightly, screaming, and you did tell me (without much conviction) there was 'nothing to fear;' I did invent, nightly, the dances that would see me cross in minor peril. (You did not know that I crossed nightly the passage of the virgin into bride with fear as my attendant, dry mouthed and tossing, sweat-browed and writhing, for at the other side I had to chose between my father – chiselfaced, with the wondrous eyes of principled slate and he-of-the-brown-eyes with a face of yeast – in other words between honour and passion.) The second dream, I suppose, was more typical for an adolescent: Christ would come, shining and eighteen, to lead me to a life of purity. You said, 'How nice.' I asked, 'What are purity and passion?' You said, 'Look them up in a dictionary.' I said, 'But mother, P-R is *missing*.' You said, 'Father has an eye out for bargains – the dictionary is incomplete, just do without the definitions.'

Yes, you were there, my mother, behind me (doing your best) but I always wanted to know more than you could tell me. I was running ahead at a rate you did not expect, and the dictionary was short of the correct examples so that when I confessed the swimming pool incident I could not look up the word *'roué'* you shouted before you burst into tears. I could not look at you as I told you; I could not look at him again; I could not look *him* up. And though I was learning the rhythms, the dances and the currents, I was forgetting how to swim.

CONCRETE

It did not begin in water; it didn't end there. But it began by water at a cottage on a placid lake. By then I knew that:

roue (roo'a), n. Debauchée, rake. (F.p.p. of *rouer* break on wheel, = one deserving this)
= rake, n. Dissipated or immoral man of fashion

but I could not have provided so easy a definition for the word *boy* because I had never *seen* one.

You were elegant and brown; you never wore your shirt. You dissipated the leaves with a rake and I watched you from under veiled eyes pretending to read scores by John Cage, although the life of my mind interested you not at all. You seemed to like me and you would stand looming over me, legs an inverted 'v', lean and leaning on your rake. You would say very little and what you said was not important. How I felt *was*.

I would be looking at your body with a visible hunger, especially where you disappeared into your jeans, tracing there with my eyes the patterns of your fine brown hair, wondering what the patterns were I did not see. (It was not confused with down-cast modesty.) You read me very well and we met daily by the side of the garden. And sometimes we would swim.

I refused to swim between your legs, but you had other games in mind. We were good swimmers, you and I, and sometimes it was fun. We would race each other and you would always win by *just enough.* We would say 'our hearts were racing' and they were. We were good swimmers, you and I, and sometimes it was violent. You would take me by the ankles and hurl me into the water head first and once I hit my head upon a rock so that I certainly became as frightened of you, suddenly, as I had been of the *man.* But now *lust* was working in me, sending me home from you with legs covered with slime and a dry mouth filled with desire. You were fourteen and I was ten. Ten, and racing towards the love I'll never understand. And you were there, mother, seeing it all, worrying about me, trying to regulate the metronome, slow it down. 'Don't look at Ned like that,' you said; 'Like what?' I asked. 'As you do.' you said. 'Why?' I asked. 'Just don't!'

The usual diversions did not help. Cage with his drums of car hubs, songs of silence, was just another way of progressing. It did not help me that I knew what *Nachtanz* was, the 'after-dance,' the name used for a variety of fast dances; it did not help me that I knew that Cage would be more important to me than Bach, that Cage would concretize my dance, my music, as Pierre Schaeffer had done before him; *musique concrète* (my zek'kon kret') French first, American later. It did not help me that I knew the score

because I could not play it, I could only *think* it. It did not help me that I knew that bees danced most intricately when they were imparting information about the things that were far away, that their dances were accompanied by songs made by their wings at measurable frequencies, *hectares* quivering in A flat or B minor. I only knew that I was flying, nerves jittering, to a first encounter. So that the day it happened, I was prepared. You took my hand and led me to a secret place. My body screamed:

You were brown and lean and the conversation was difficult and through the pauses (frequent), I heard the:

dddddddd- thruuuum, ddddddd-thruuuum, d-d-d-d thruuuu uum, D-D-D-D

(of the mating grouse and the)

phew, phew, phew, dedededede, pnew pnew pnew

(of the birds)

but most of all, I heard the *thunder* of my heart in my throat.

Dry mouthed now, and desperate to know, I sat on the knoll with my arms wrapped round my ankles. Sitting near you but not touching you. I hoped for a kiss as gentle as my father's and as chaste. I did not wish to speak to you because you were not adept at speaking. But I wanted to *know* you and, at ten, I was ready.

You said, after a long pause, a musical rest – 'Do you know what boys and girls do?'

'No,' I said.

'Do you want to *see*?'

'No, no, NO!' I said, but that was a lie. You had failed me by not knowing how to reach me.

And I was running, running, mother, out of the quiet of the forest, out of its green and impassive eye, out of its verdant privacy, right back to you, mother, where I confessed (as always) my fear that you could not deal with, you could only prevent my encounters with roués and boys who carried rakes, for I was running ahead of the schedule you had in mind for me, running with the currents I did not understand so that they could not carry me, so that I could not obey the pulses although I understood them, so that I could not dance the dances before I was ready and even if I knew them I could not play them. The more distant and abstract they were the more I liked them; the closer and easier they were the more I failed them and they me. For I was running ahead of the clock, mother, and though I knew how to dance I had no suitable partner; although I knew how to swim, I swam in fear.

You were wonderful, my mother, when you said I would go to a girls' school far away to protect me (from myself and them).

The Worker

She was a speck on the grey horizon of no more consequence than an insect and, like an insect, she enlarged herself through uncertain movements.

She crossed the broken pavement of St. Paul's school to enter under the pediment marked GIRLS. I could see:

a gaunt head topped by an untidy bun;
a slight hump between her narrow shoulders;
a dowdy dress fluttering about her ankles;
two shopping bags grasped in claw-like hands.

I was sitting demurely under GIRLS in my new tunic and blouse and when she reached me her face broke into a smile composed of yellow overcrowded teeth.

She did not speak and I was glad, for I would have been obliged to answer, pleasantly.

Had I not, after all, been sent to this old brick school to learn Catholicism and manners?

Had I not dreamt of hearing ecclesiastical wisdom whispered

from the mouths of nuns whom I would call Mother and Sister?

This stooped crone had no place in my fantasy of the perfectly redundant spiritual education of a twelve-year-old Atheist.

(I rubbed my thighs together less for warmth than for reassurance.)

On that brisk September morning fate declared that I and twenty other grade six students would be called from segregated files to occupy her classroom. She came as the clock struck nine to lead us in a recitation of 'Our Father Who Art in Heaven.' All heads bowed before the plain wooden cross that dominated the room.

With that same cheerful smile that marked her first acknowledgment of me, she introduced herself as Miss Josie Kelly and instructed each of us to rise and give our names. And to each of us she commented warmly, remembering a 'delicate mother,' an 'amusing brother' or an 'amazing cousin'.

The fact that there were six 'C' names in the class pleased her so much that I can give her exegesis of the associations they carried and suggest the pupil's reaction to her words.

Jenny *Constable.* Aren't you lucky to have the name of the first English painter to take the appearance of nature seriously. He would have loved the park this morning.

(Jenny became the best landscape artist in the class.)

Jim *Constantine.* You bear the name of the first Christianized Roman Emperor. Before him, they used to throw us to the lions for practising our faith.

(The boy who was skinny and retiring stiffened his spine with pride.)

Tim *Consul.* This is wonderful. Another name from ancient Rome. Consuls and proconsuls will figure in this morning's Religion lesson. You will help me.

(Tim, who was fat, blushed red at the prospect of participation.)

Mary *Constant,* constant Mary. Constancy is the virtue of the Blessed Virgin Mother. You were named with pious hope, my child.

(Mary smiled broadly because she knew Miss Kelly had spoken truth.)

John *Conway* gave her little to seize upon.

Mine, Habella *Cire,* gave rise to a remark upon the nice mixture of Spanish and French blood my name implied. My 'bright eyes' told her I would be helpful in her lesson on the Language of the Bees. Although I regretted still not having a nun as teacher, I was certainly prepared to pay attention to the instructions of Miss Kelly.

At half past nine promptly we had our first lesson in Religion. Because it was the first, because it was the area in which I knew I would be the most sensitive, I can recall in detail its form.

She began by rummaging through the contents of the shopping bags she had deposited on her desk as she entered the classroom. She placed before us:

several copies of a Latin Reader,

a framed engraving of a man in armour who looked as though he were hailing a cab,

a silver coin,

a sheet,

a golden safety pin,

two dozen ripe figs,

a crown of laurel leaves;

(I was mistaken that the bags contained books alone).

She summoned Tim Consul to the front of the room and lovingly began a transformation of his person:

First she drew the sheet with great skill about him, her gnarled fingers pulling and tugging until it took on the shape of a toga and could submit to the discipline of the pin.

Next, while offering an explanation of the nature and meaning of laurel crowns in the Mediterranean culture, she encircled his head with the lacquer-green leaves.

Then, after the class had touched it during her explication of the importance Roman Tribute would have in the life and parables of Christ, she pressed the silver ducat into Tim's moist hand.

So dressed and dignified as Consul, the boy stood firm as a Citizen of Rome.

The Latin texts were distributed and shared. Each child read from the Journals of Julius Caesar, adoptive father to the Augustus who ruled the Roman Empire at the time of Jesus' birth. And as the engraving of the figure of Augustus was circulated, she gave a cogent explanation of Roman polytheism focussed upon the Eros who clutched at his leg. She gave us the succulent, seed-filled figs to sweeten our play at recess time.

I am compelled to recount the lesson in which I took part. At the beginning of that hour, as usual, Miss Kelly displayed the relics appropriate to the subject. These she chose for the Language of the Bees:

a natural hive,
a specimen of Worker, Drone and Queen,
a taperecording of bee song,
a bee-keeper's net,
a jar of honeycomb honey.

At the appropriate moment, I entered in the garb of the Queen Bee which I, being something of a sculptress, had fabricated (appropriately) out of papier mâché daubed over chicken wire. The ingenious device masked my normal body parts. From my enlarged abdomen I ejected, at regular intervals, small eggs to the amazement of all. My wings were an artifice of amber gauze; my feelers, fabricated from willing wire. Forty hands and forty eyes explored my transmuted self. Then at Miss Kelly's signal, the day's monitor produced the quiet hum of a hive at rest. She bid me lie prone facing the class to pose to her, as Worker, a series of predesigned questions.

'What is the first duty of a Worker?' I asked.

'To revere the Queen who is the object of all energy and the source of continuance' she said.

'What are the manifestations of this reverence, my teacher?'

'The workers will serve you, oh Queen, from the moment of your birth as an egg, feeding, stroking and nudging you into adulthood. They will create you as Queen to mate with an outsider at their choosing so that you will return triumphant as Widowed Bride filled with the seed of a city.

'Some Workers, my Queen, will continue to serve you when your first fertility has overcrowded the hive. They will follow you rather than obey a young successor; they will abandon willingly 10,000 finished chambers, a treasure of honey and pollen and the incubating young. They will flow after you as continuous substance trickling themselves into a ball to roast on the branch of your selection. Boiling and broiling there as though on a hidden spoon until in the heat one Worker has transubstantiated her honey into a waxen toffee.

'This Worker will extract from beneath her rings of horn the molten wax. She will plane it, extend it, knead it with her saliva. She will mould it into the keystone of the dome of your new town and when she has finished another will take the place beside her, and another and another will follow in this task until there be Royal cells, cells designated for Drones, cells to serve the Workers' slumber and storage.

'Then the Alchemy will begin anew. They will usher you into a pristine vault and you will deposit into a pearly hexagon the first egg of the new colony. Your attendants will curtsy before you. When a slight spasm signals that your body has fulfilled its role, one of your impotent daughters will throw her arms about you and whisper, 'Congratulations.' You will arise and move to the next place of birthing, leaving behind an everlengthening chain of bluish beads that your infertile sisters will feed and tend to maturity in the sex of their selection.'

My eyes were gleaming when I asked the unexpected question, 'What happens when it is time for us to die?'

'As living things we must die and not having souls there is no chance for an Afterlife. But Queens and sometimes even Workers manage to live beyond their apparent usefulness at some hidden corner of the hive. I don't know which end is more cruel: to die on the sting of your kind or to linger without the hub of social order.'

On the sound track, suddenly there was the whine of bees in rage.

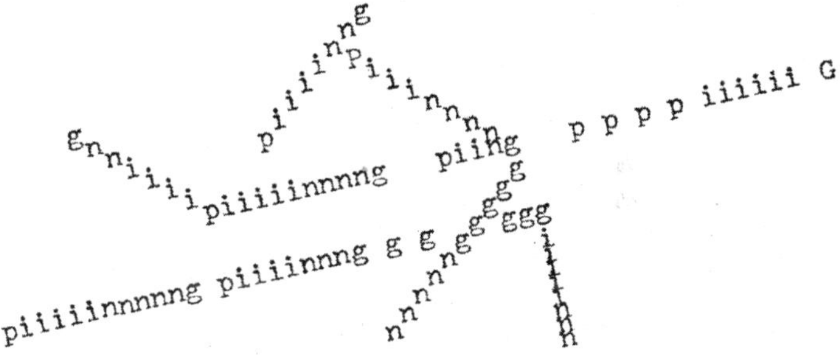

So frightened was Constantine that he put on the bee-keeper's veil and that caused laughter to relieve the tension. The students rolled up into a ball with me at their centre, pulling and tugging on my swollen body so that eggs, more and more eggs spilled over the newly waxed tiles. We ate up the jar of golden honey, crunching on the comb like cannibals. This lesson so delighted our teacher that to each she gave a glimmering star

Under the influence of St. Paul's' Miss Kelly, I attempted to become Catholic. I read the Catechism in order to be one with my classmates. My progress was watched by a kindly, rotund priest whose breath usually smelled of wine and onions. His name was Father della Bono.

Through him I learned to pray for indulgence to the Holy Queen, Mother of Mercy and to cry out as a poor banished child of Eve. I bartered my goodness for a glimpse of her precious womb's fruit. O clement, O loving, O sweet Virgin Mary. I memorized the responses to prescribed questions.

LESSON 16

88. *What is the first commandment of God?*
The first commandment of God is: I am the Lord thy God; thou shalt not have strange gods before Me.

89. *What are we commanded by the first commandment?*
By the first commandment we are commanded to offer to God alone the supreme worship that is due him.

90. *How do we worship God?*
We worship God by acts of faith, hope and charity, and by adoring Him and praying to Him.

91. *How does the Catholic sin against faith?*
A Catholic sins against faith by not believing what God has revealed and by taking part in non-Catholic worship.

92. *What are the sins against hope?*
The sins against hope are presumption and despair.

And from these laws of God I was to take words and supply them to the blanks: We must offer to God the _____ that is due him; We worship God by acts of _____, _____, and _____. Or I was to take other words that I was supplied and give them back to the sentences from which they had been rudely snatched. For the words that follow, the *Baltimore Catechism* reserved a place:

believe	fortune-telling	non-Catholics
charms	God	ourselves
faith	love	trust

Please, my children, give them back to the phrases where they belong.

1. F_____ obliges us to make efforts to find out what God has made known.
2. A Cathoic sins against faith by taking part in a n_____ C_____ religious worship.
3. The first commandment forbids the use of c_____ and f_____.

I was also encouraged to pass moral judgement on others, yet I did not care to censure Tim for the neglect of his religious homework, nor did I wish to report to my confessor that I believed in fortune-tellers as much as I believed in everything else. Habella would remain a non-believer among the many who *ad te clamamus, exsules filii Evae.*

My parents saved me from admitting that I could not oblige my friends, my priest and my teacher. They had to move to another city and so I left St. Paul's. With her customary generosity, Miss Kelly arranged a farewell party for me in her apartment, close by the school. Her rooms were filled with books, simple sturdy furniture, nature study objects and plants. We feasted on caraway seed cake with honey and lemon tea.

I cried when I left her, because I supposed we would never meet again.

At age twenty-four, I returned to the city of my birth as a graduate in Natural Science with a special interest in Apiary. I set up housekeeping with a girlfriend in the Manhattan Apartments. Apart from having four high-ceilinged rooms at a cheap rent, the feature that delighted us more than the ancient cage elevator and the

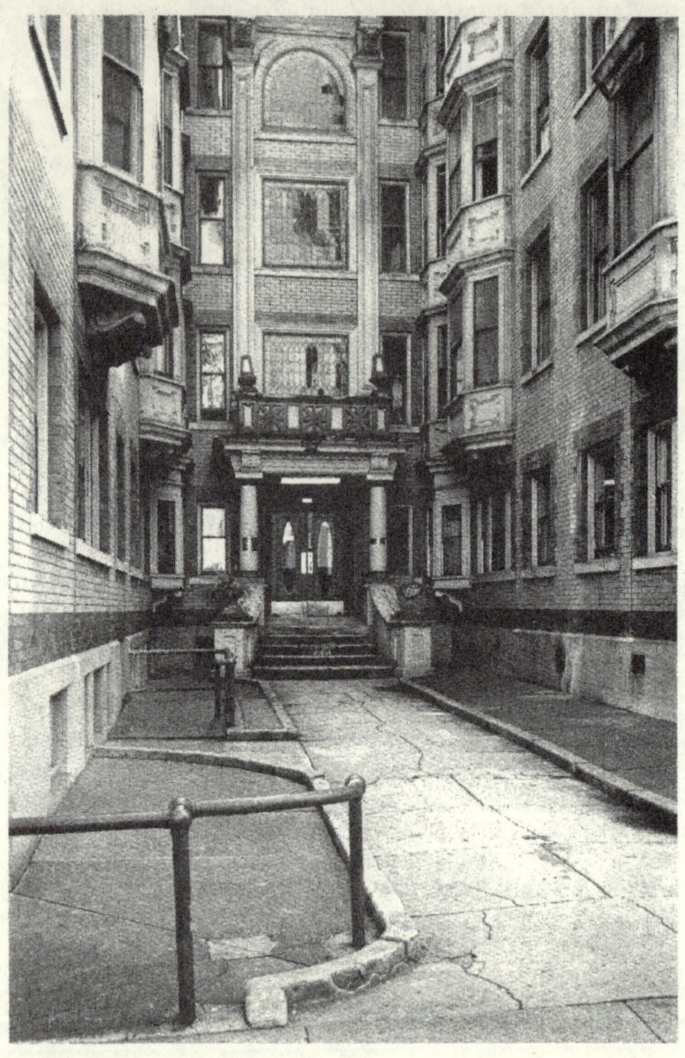

stamped tin walls was the fact that the Manhattan had a garbage chute. It was wonderful to toss bags of refuse down five stories, *thuunk,* into a waiting incinerator. It was proof that architects Parr and Fee whose slogan was '*Utilitas* is our Motto and Revenue our Aim,' really knew their business.

One day I followed the bent form of an elderly woman to the smelly door of the chute. Her crooked feet shuffled and her hands gripped firmly onto the handles of two shopping bags. As she turned towards me, her task complete, I saw that I was face to face with Miss Kelly.

'Habella!' she cried, 'you've grown into just the young lady I expected. Come and see my flat.'

I followed her slowly along the narrow corridor and she opened the door to an almost empty suite. I did not need to ask where the furniture, the books and the natural history objects had gone, but I did venture to ask about the absence of living things.

'Where are your plants? Don't you miss them?'

'Yes, Habella, I do. But when you're old, it takes all of your time just to keep yourself alive.'

In the year that I lived there, my friend Renata and I often visited this old woman. She suffered her poverty and her many serious afflictions with grace. We would laugh and talk together about almost every subject. What I missed in her conversation more acutely than I missed her plants was that playful erudition that made her such an extraordinary teacher in the past. It took all of her energy now to communicate the essential.

In our meetings together she told us of her childhood: how it was to grow up as a poor daughter of an Irish immigrant family in turn-of-the-century Montreal; how and by what arduous means her parents had given her an education before sending her to work to support the family. She told us of her brother and sisters. Her only brother, a priest, had died 'of Catholic politics' in the Basilica; her pretty sister had died of the 'forbidden love of a Greek Orthodox' man; another sister had become a nun and lived in California and a final sister who was born 'good but simple,' took shelter in Trois Rivières.

She regaled us with the exploits of Tim Consul who had become a civil rights lawyer and she introduced into our lives roly poly, dependable Father della Bono.

It was her custom to leave open the door at all times so she would not have to 'drag her old bones to answer it'.

Once my friend and I entered her flat so quietly that we became unintentional witnesses of a private ceremony: Miss Kelly on her knees before Father della Bono, receiving Holy Communion on the golden anniversary of her mother's death. The good Father intoned:

Who shall find a valiant woman? Far and from
the utmost coasts is the price of her
The heart of her husband trusteth in her and
he shall have no need of her spoils
She hath put out her hand to strong things and
her fingers have taken hold of the spindle
She hath opened her hand to the needy and
stretched out her hand to the poor
She hath opened her mouth to wisdom and the
law of clemency is on her tongue ...

from the Mass 'Cognovi', Common of a Holy Woman not a Martyr, and together they offered this plea to the Virgin Mother:

Speciousus forma prae filiis hominum:
(Thou art beautiful above the sons of men)
difusa est gratia in labiis tuis
(grace is poured abroad in thy lips)
Alleluia, alleluia, alleluia, alleluia.
Post Partum, Virgo, inviolata permansisti:
(After childbirth thou didst remain a virgin)
Dei Genitrix, intercede pro nobis.
(O Mother of God, intercede for us)
Alleluia, alleluia, alleluia, alleluia.

her crackling voice joining ardently with his own.

When the Mass was over he helped her rise and kissed gently her almost bald head; she kissed with equal gentleness his fat small hands. When she turned in our direction her face was transfigured by love. I knew that she had not heeded the stern words of St. Theresa of Avila that I had learned as a child. ('Let us not allow our will to be the slave of any, Sisters, save of Him Who bought it with his Blood.')

We had been brought into the presence of a pure and incandescent love, passing between the Father and his child, and a moment of perfect intimacy between man and woman. This love made his eyes glisten with Wisdom and set her seventy-six-year-old heart on Fire. We left as quietly as we had come.

At the end of the first year of our reacquaintance, Miss Kelly was surviving well. She took in boarders to supplement her income and ran a newspaper clipping service from her flat. She thanked God daily that her mind, eyes and ears were clear. When I married at the end of that year and when my friend took a job in New York she celebrated with us and to each of us gave a shopping bag full of mementoes. After that my visits to her became more occasional and, perhaps for that reason, more extraordinary.

One day she greeted me with troubled eyes. She had had a most distressing communication from her sister, the Californian nun. She gave me this letter to read with the warning that the language was a little 'extravagant,' and the mood, 'overexcited.'

November, 1966.

Dear Josie,

In my nunnery, I was a great tree casting its own shadow of destruction. I gathered to me the branches of young students to sing and play, so much so that the root of the order became myself.

I suffered, perhaps, the Sin of Vanity forbidden by Our Precious Mother. I have told you often of the plots against my well-being, yes even my life. You remember the time they all took the vow of silence against me in order to chastise my ears for being so anxious to hear the sound of voices. You recall, dear sister, how I was the only person to get food poisoning following Christmas turkey. Now, Josie, they have gone too far.

A week ago, after vespers, I fell asleep before my harpsicord. I felt the sharp jab of a needle in my arm and the cruel and rough removal of my Habit. I was wrapped in a blanket and dragged into a car. It was God's mercy that I lost all consciousness.

I awoke in nausea to find myself in a train beside a stranger in a nurse's uniform. She told me, grimly, that I was being taken to hospital for a rest and a cure for paranoia. She said if I cried out she would stab my arm with a shot of morphine.

In thirty hours we arrived at this distressing place. Yes, dear sister, I have been committed by my Order which acts in lieu of family. There is nothing to be done, save prayer.

My Blessing upon you,
Sister Eulalia at the Institute of Health, Minneapolis.
P.S. I'm not mad.

This letter, as my only fact, led me to believe that the Sisters of

Sacred Mercy had committed, to say the least, a grave injustice. From that moment on, for several years, sister Eulalia, her woes and her letters, dominated our infrequent conversations.

Her letters were always true to form. They began invariably with some religious metaphor with Eulalia at its centre:

'I am like unto the Virgin Martyred in Innocence;
I am the Penitent with the Stripes of Suffering
Written on my Flesh;
I am the Beggarwoman who is locked within the Gates.'

In the middle of each there was some allusion to wrongs having been committed against Eulalia's person:

'My window, left mysteriously open, has given me a malevolent flu;
the pills that were intended to assuage my asthma were usless placebos;
they do whispering against me in the dining hall.'

They ended without fail on some note of passive resignation:

'I pray for the forgiveness of the Sisters of Sacred Mercy;
I submit myself to the Gentle Will of Jesus Christ;
I trust that in the afterlife All will be Revealed.'

Even Miss Kelly admitted that her 'poor, dear Sister' had always been rather 'intractable' and not liked by others, yet this was insufficient reason for lifelong incarceration.

Taking matters into her own frail hands, this woman who was so weak that she could no longer venture into the streets conspired with the just Tim Consul, a plan for the release of unfortunate Eulalia.

Four years after the first unhappy letter had come, I received an unexpected early morning call from Josie. In a voice frayed with fatigue and frantic with worry, she communicated this short, breath-fractured message as though on teletype:

HAB	JUSTAM	CAL	LINGTO
SAY	BE TAK	ING	ATRAIN
MON	WAN	TED	YOU TO
KNOWTHAT	YOU	MAY	HAVETO
PHONEAND	FINDME	NOT	AND
WORRYAND	CALLUP	THE	POL
ICE ?OH	YES	YOU	ARE
THE CLE	VER	ONE	IAM
TAK ING	THEMON	DAYGNW	AND
IAM GOIN	GOTOAH	MINNES	OTA

I sat down on the floor, my hands covering my eyes; in my mind I saw her floating over a varied landscape, her old wings whirring, her scrawny body rubbed thin of hair.

She stretched the twelve thousand bristles of her alert antennae to the wind and followed, uncertainly, a small sweet memory of another that lingered in her olfactory hollows and in the three-lobed wonder of her third eye.

One mile, two, a hundred, a thousand without

pause, she propelled her fragile body beyond exhaustion into the fevered ecstasy known only to saints.

Suddenly she fell from the sky before a particular locked flower and with infinite patience, she opened its petals. Inside was a creature as abused as herself. She led it to a wintry hive. A week passed and on the eighth day, the expected phone call came. Could I meet Sister Eulalia?

In my fancy Eulalia had achieved a specific form. She would be pale and thin, her face a wise orb of experience. She would speak in parables and fables. She would murmur her thanks in a gracious voice. My heart quickened as I reached Miss Kelly's room. Beside her hunched a nun in grey and white Habit, sunglasses concealing her cunning eyes.

'Hello Sister Eulalia.' I extended my hand.

She pushed it aside and asked in a dry accusatory rasp:

'Why do the young girls wear their skirts so short?'

She continued with a diatribe against the contemporary Habit which had risen, according to her, 'obscenely above the ankles,' but not, she hastened to add, as high as my skirts. These she judged to be an 'offence to God.'

(Oh Eulalia, namesake of a maiden Virgin who died by fire at the desire of Diocletian in the year 304 or 384. Oh Eulalia whose fore-bearer was otherwise known as Aulazia, Ollala and Eulaupia, someone should cut out your evil-speaking tongue.)

The schoolgirl respect I had for Miss Kelly forbade any display of the anger that arose within me. So with a shawl draped over my offending knees, I listened and nodded. Eulalia, in any event, was speaking to herself.

'That Josie,' she continued, 'she would never *commit* herself. When I became a Novice, I begged her to join me, you know, but she was stubborn, thought it better to stay home with our parents. When I was young, I travelled to Rome to kneel before the feet of Pius. What a thrill to see St. Peter's and in Jerusalem I walked the Via Dolorosa. What a hot day *that* was. I had to drink that awful, germy Mineral Water.

'To wear the Habit of the Sisters of Sacred Mercy was my joy. These veils of the Bride of Christ symbolize my rejection of the profane world and all vanities (she touched them, coquettishly), even Josie would have looked good in this Habit. She always was the plain one, had a stoop even as a child. And you would have travelled *free*, Josie.

'This was Josie's only trip, apart from her coming here after our loving parents' deaths (she added almost as an afterthought), all the way to Minneapolis, Minnesota! She arrived half dead, poor thing, and *demanded* to see me, right there at the desk. Some fellow, ah, Tim, Tim Consul had arranged for me to be released. I suppose it was a miracle of sorts. But who was that lawyer you were with? Didn't like him. Jewish. Pushy. Chewed gum in front of me. In the Convent we got boys to kneel on corn kernels for that offence; nowadays I suppose they practice Modern Psychology. We used to teach them manners pretty quick.

'Well I suppose you expect to know what my plans are. I'm taking the plane to California tomorrow. I guess you think I should keep Josie company in this filthy climate. *Never.* It would be nice for her to have me around, after all her trouble. But ...

'I'm going home to California. California here I come, just where I got started from.'

This last piece of information she sang in a quavering voice, and despite the musical interlude, Eulalia was by no means finished.

'They'll be pleased to have me back. I was a great teacher. Used to get little boys and girls to play note perfect. Rapped their knuckles if they didn't; gave them candy if they did. I never handed food around for no reason. There was no room for self-expression, just discipline, discipline. Submit yourself to my will, I'd say, just like I submit to God's will. I won lots of state festivals, brought glory to the Sisters of Sacred Mercy and just look how they thanked me.

'Josie tells me you're a teacher, Habel, ah, Bella. Hah! Your name is from the same place as my *Sister* name. We're both from sunny Spain, sisters under good old SOL. Sol sisters, hah, hah, hah. (She laughed uproariously at her own joke.) Josie says you teach art films now, but you used to teach science. What films are fit to teach, dear? The list of *permitted* films gets shorter every year, but then you have no Catholic conscience. Aren't you afraid, my child, that Hell's Fire will lick around those naked knees? What does your husband think of that get up? Doesn't he blush to go on the street with you, the men leering up your skirts? Alright Josie (catching Miss Kelly's angry eyes), she's *your* friend. Just a little joke.'

'Habella can only stay a while. She just wanted to meet you. Her husband needs the car at four o'clock and she has to go home to nurse her babe. She is....'

'Huumph, bet he has to beg for it. Women aren't as homeloving as they used to be. It's a shame, a crying shame. Suckle your babe, do you? Thought as much. I suppose the bottle isn't good enough for an earth mother.'

I arose, tears in my eyes. Not because of the insults of this garrulous nun, but because Josie's voice had been permanently torn by the rigors of that journey. Eulalia, otherwise known as Ollala, a grey and sour Bride of Christ, was returning to the Sisters of Sacred Mercy with venom on her tongue. It was a good try, dear sisters, but the Minnesota solution was not the final one.

Within days of her return to a touching reunion you arranged, oh wondrous beings, a permanent place of rest for your Sister, Eulalia. She was tranferred from the Order to a wing of the Carmelita Hospital designed especially for retired nuns, financed out of god knows what complex guilt by a man called Hymie Lieberman. With this shelter Eulalia was as content as she knew how to be. She had won the 'Rest that God in His Wisdom provides for the Pure in Heart.'

After the departure of Eulalia, Miss Kelly's health and emotional well-being deteriorated rapidly. Her hands drew into themselves like claws and her spine thrust her head pitifully forward. Her friend, the jovial Father, was taken from her. She took his death stoically and without tears and somehow her lively mind and generous spirit allowed her to look towards the future.

On her eighty-fourth birthday, she called me to her side to give me some important news. When her palsied hands had delivered the last morsel of cake to her mouth, she felt prepared to make her announcement.

'H   abella, you r   emember that I told y   ou that I had three sisters and that l   ittle sister was, well, ahhh n   ot v   ery clever but a sw   eet and gentle s   oul. She is co   ming tomorrow on a plane from M   ontre   al. Tim the d   ear b   oy arranged it. Oh y   ou w   ill l   ove Agnes. It w   ill be f   ine to h   ave s   omeone to t   alk to. I w   ill f   eel useful a   gain.

In due course I was ushered into the visitor's room and found a tiny, tiny withered woman quietly fondling her beads and sighing with the faintest of voices:

'Hail Mary full of grace! the Lord is with thee; blessed is the fruit of thy womb, Jesus. Holy Mary, Mother of God, pray for us sinners now and at the hour of our death ...

'Hail Mary full of grace! the Lord is with thee; blessed is the fruit of thy womb, Jesus. Holy Mary, Mother of God ...'

She was like one of those minute insects who buzz upon the clover. She had no means for storing pollen but fed directly from the flower. She was completely at the mercy of fate in this flat which shone bright in the sunlight.

She interrupted her meditations and with a sweet smile she turned to me and said:

'Pray for us sinners now and at the hour of our Death.'

The burdens of family life and professional responsibilities prevented me from taking care of the well-being of my friend and her eighty-year-old sister, but perhaps these are offered as excuses for a typically human indifference. There were only three more encounters with Miss Kelly and in the first, having entered with the same quietness that allowed me so many years ago to witness her ecstasy at private mass, I overheard this phone call.

'Y   es, that's r   ight. I w   ant a half a p   ound of t   ea, 4 large c   ans of o   range juice, and ahh, a package of b   iscuits, 3 dozen e   ggs, s   ome b   ack b   acon, 4 t   ins of Spam and 6 l   arge boxes of t   oilet p   aper, the k   ind you have on s   ale at W   oodwards. Y   ou w   ill deliver my or   der, John Conway, y   ou al   ways w   ere such a h   elp.'

. . .

'Oh, H   abella, didn't h   ear you c   ome in.'

'Wow,' I said tactlessly. 'That's enough paper to last a year.'

'No, d ear, it will only l ast a m onth. Agnes is in continent. She j ust gets up f or meals.'

'Josie, maybe you should consider a change, perhaps there are homes ...'

'Don't you d are s uggest it, Hab ella. While I st ill h ave breath, I w ill look af ter us. I w ill never leave this place. I w ill die in m y own w ay and in m y o wn good time.'

Her emerald eyes blazed and she raised to me a desperate fist that did not threaten our next meeting. At *this* time, however, her mind was showing the same sort of tears that had rent her voice and into her conversation oozed references to things that I thought she had forgotten. Her words and mine mingled in the cloying smell of decaying air.

'Habella, wh ere is your t unic, n aughty thing. Y ou c an't c ome to St. P aul's in str eet cl othes. F ather della B ono, c ome look a t this s illy g irl who f orgot to put on h er uni form! What sh all we d o w ith her? And y ou're late, l ate f or c atechism *again* and I b et y ou h ave f orgot ten your responses. Wh at, m y ch ild does the S ixth C ommand ment for bid?'

'The Sixth Commandment forbids all impurity and immodesty in words, looks and deeds, whether alone or with others,' I answered.

'So y ou do r emember, Habel la. Y ou w ould h ave made s uch a m arvel lous C atholic, despite what Eul al ia s aid about those skirts of y ours. S he al ways sees the w orst in others, c an't help h erself. You w ere always s uch a Qu een, dressed in g auzy w ings. T he W orkers will al ways s erve y ou, j ust l ike I s erve f rail Agnes. She's b een pray-ing th at y ou w ould c ome, so quiet a nd n ice, n ot l ike the o ther one wh o l ives i n C al i forn ia.

After M in neap ol is, I w as n ever the same. J ust tu rned into a s illy o ld bug, b arely a ble to b uzz ar ound th is pl ace, w ings fu ll of h oles

B u z z Z Z u b s s S
B u z z Buzzzz z Z Z s
Z sszzuubbb u
z z u B z z ..
B u z z

Although I smiled at her self-parody, I added with seriousness an invitation for her to move. She dismissed me gently.

'I know, I kn ow, Eulalia al ways said I was stubborn. K iss Agnes be fore you go.'

Before it happened, dreams disturbed my sleep. Tremors heralded the approach of a recurrent nightmare.

I saw her lying immobile on her bed, eyes probing the air, the air charged with fear.

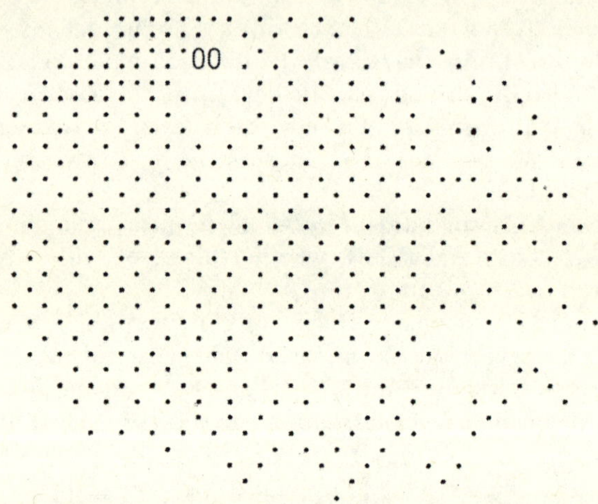

There was a knock at the door.

A masculine voice cried out: 'Miss Kelly, open the door. I'm here to – you.'

A dreadful silence followed.

With incredible slowness she arose, naked. She crawled to the door; her extremities were f i b r i l l a t i n g . She opened the door by dragging herself erect on its handle. The young man gasped at the sight. She said:

'L eave me a lone. I m ust l ook after Agnes. We e at, we sl eep. Wh at more is th ere to do?'

The young man ran

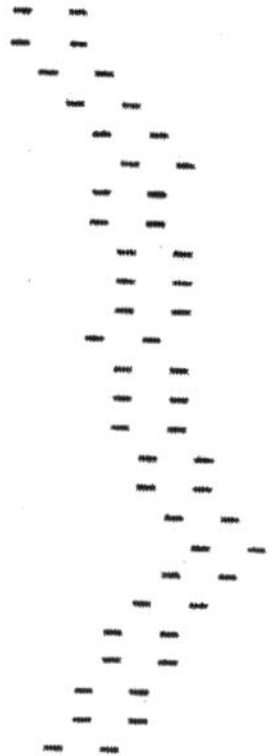

into the cage-like elevator.

Then I had a phonecall from a woman who lived in the Manhattan Apartments.

'Habella Cire? This is a friend of Miss Kelly's. Just calling to say that Agnes died peacefully in her sleep last night and that Miss Kelly has been taken to hospital. Not a moment too soon, I'd say. Things were pretty dreadful near the end. She used to wander the corridors naked and had to be helped into her flat. Her mind was rambling, you know, but no one had the authority to remove her and her sister. Funny, no one would dare though the social workers did try. She was asking for you. She's at St. Paul's, the hospital beside that old school.'

I left immediately, my heart as heavy as my guilt. I found her room and when I entered she was sleeping. With her twisted hands, she clutched the white starched sheets that trembled with her breathing and the customary nervous pulses of her form. Her face, surprisingly, was not much older nor more worn than when I first met her.

She opened her eyes and smiled her wonderful, crooked smile.

'Ahh, H abella. Kn ew you'd come. Good to see you.'

(The brief care had improved her voice.)

'Agnes h as gone and I will f ollow soon. Pretty difficult at the end, c ould h ardly manage. And poor Tim, turned Judas at the last. He used to send th ose Social W ork fellows, and I used to answer the door without my clothes on. That scared them off.'

She was laughing and I laughed too, with tears running down my face. Then she pulled a small paper bag from under the bed linen. Inside there was a small religious medallion.

'Thought you might change your mind,' she said.

'No, I can't,' I answered. 'You have taught me more than any church.'

She seemed to understand. Two days later she was dead.

I did not attend the Requiem Mass sung in her honour by the black-garbed order of St. Joseph. She remained in my mind as the Worker who did not outlive her usefulness, the one who never committed the sins of presumption and despair.

The Drone

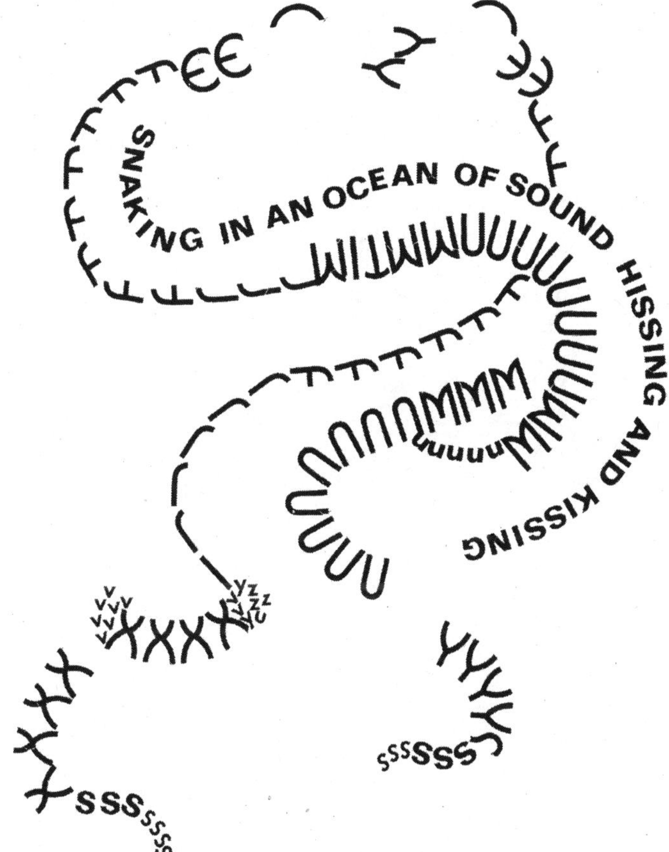

They met by chance at Pharaoh's and rubbed and dubbed to a contemporary rock tune. Into each other's ears they hummed and moaned the prescribed ineptitudes of first meetings.

What's shurname? Hunmnuhmmmmmm? Mmmmmmmm?

H A B E L L A .

Whatsures? Mmmm? Mmmm?

Solomon.

What do you do, w i s e k i n g?

I'm an Egyptologist, what do you do?

I teach Natural Science.

That's s o o n i c e, s o o g o o d, Mnmnmnm, Mnmnmm, Hold me tight, Bella, Hold me tight. I *want* you.

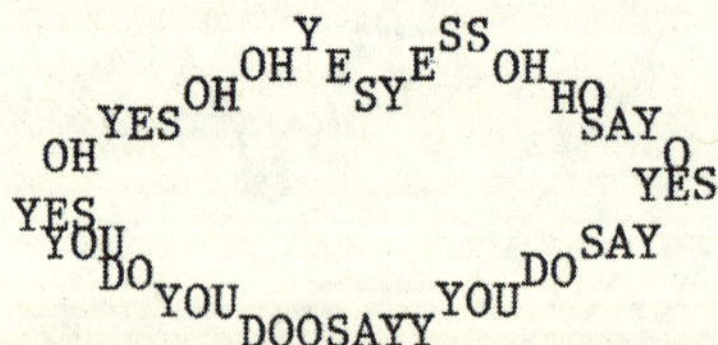

Come h o m e please come h o m e with m e e.

O OO
ON N N NO
ON ON OO NO
ON NOO
ON
O OH
NON NON
NO OH
NO NO
NO ON
N O O O
O N N

(She equivocated.)

(His snake fell, rejected from the moist spot between her legs and dejected, he pushed forth an invitation between his teeth.)

Then let's meet tomorrow at three at the Golden Door.

She awoke with the following vestiges of their meeting imprinted on her flesh:

a golden hair from his beard,
a delicate rash wherever his beard had rubbed her,
a brazen hair from his waist,
the garlic-musk odor of his sweat,
a pool of untasted honey
(between her legs).

She tried to recall the feel of their clothes cloying, their fingers fingering and amused herself with a recreation of Solomon's Trial of the Artificial Flower.

She was Sheba, radiant and wise, clothed in brocades and anointed in the perfume of cloves. She stood within a garden dignified with cypresses and yew. Cicadas celebrated her lord's coming.

sicasawsawsaw ciccaseeeseeeseee sicasawsawsaw
sicsicaseesee ciccasawsawsawaw sicaseeseesee

(Their ululation ceased.)

She curtsied before him and placed the flower of her manufacture beside a real flower of its kind. They glistened, together, in the sunlight on a marble podium, petals spread, stamens and pistils waving, succulent nectar shining, scent ascending.

Solomon examined each of them, his brow furrowed in thought. They challenged all his senses. His face was crinkled with amusement when he took her slender hands in his and said:

Dear Lady, you have tricked me, but I think I know now how to discover the true flower. Benjamin (he turned a languid eye to his servant), fetch from the hive some bees in a glass. They will test each for truth for they are experts.

(The King and Queen and their retinues refreshed the crystal air with laughter as they awaited the *proving*.)

In due course Benjamin returned, servile and scurrying. He released over the flowers the bees' intelligence.

Buzz, Buzz, Buzz, Mmm, Mmm, Mmm, Buzz, Buzz, Buzz. They

nuzzled and sucked the correct blossom.

Sheba fell upon her knees and kissed Solomon's feet, so grateful was she for this display of his Wisdom and the chorus of cicadas began anew, as though by a secret signal.

Solomon led her, then, into his informal garden and after a lunch of pomegranates and wine, he condescended to 'tell her all her questions' and (mysteriously) he revealed to her 'nothing that was not hid from him.' Flashing her a white-toothed smile, he made this confession:

The rumours are true. I have loved many women from among the Egyptians, Moabites, Ammonites, Edomites, Zidonians and Hittites and I worry that they will beguile me into the worship of idols, but please understand, dear lady, that I know the difference between good women and bad, just as I know how to distinguish real flowers from false. I don't see women always as sensuous snares, they are also (occasionally) for me embodiments of Compassionate Wisdom. I am proud that what I have written in Chapter 31 of Proverbs has become the basis for the Catholic Mass 'Cognovi', Common of the Holy Woman not a Martyr.

Then holding her close, he sang in a smoky contralto the poetry that had brought the downfall of one thousand sisters.

My beloved put in his hand by the hole of
the door and my bowels were moved for him
I rose up to open to my beloved and my hands
dripped with myrrh, and my fingers with
sweet smelling myrrh, upon the handles of
the lock
I opened to my beloved; but my beloved had
withdrawn himself and was gone.

In thanks for these intimacies, Sheba cast off her precious garments and communicated to her beloved 'all that was in her heart.'

Although this vision should have warned her, she went to the Golden Door Cafe. She was caught by his beauty:
his eyes were the eyes of doves;
his cheeks above his beard were like beds of spices;
his strong hands glimmered with rings set in beryl;
his transparent shirt was unbuttoned
(to his waist).

His words, fitly spoken, were to her ears 'like apples of gold set in pictures of silver.'

'The ancient Egyptians were hedonists,' he said. 'They'd say, '"Come on, set singing before thy face. Increase yet more the delights thou hast, follow thy inclination and thy profit. Do thy desires upon earth and trouble not thy heart until the day of lamentation come to thee.' Nice sentiments. Quite unlike the ones you learn from your subject, I suspect.'

'I guess only the Drones have a life approaching the one you describe as ideal,' she replied. 'They are fed by the hive until they grow fat, furry and fit. They are expected to spend their summer days searching for a Queen to lay and if they do, they'll die for that pleasure and if they don't the hive will kill them as winter comes. But while they live, they're happy and free and single minded in pursuit of pleasure ...'

'You talk about bees as though they were people ...'

'I know they're not, yet their lives have an instinctual clarity that ours lack. Their motives are never confused by thought. They live and love efficiently and I envy that.'

'Surely our desires are no less clear and obvious. Let's take the afternoon to talk and go back dancing this evening. Afterwards we'll have a little wine at my place ...'

(Into her mind flashed images of dancing bees which she drew to his great fascination on a napkin)

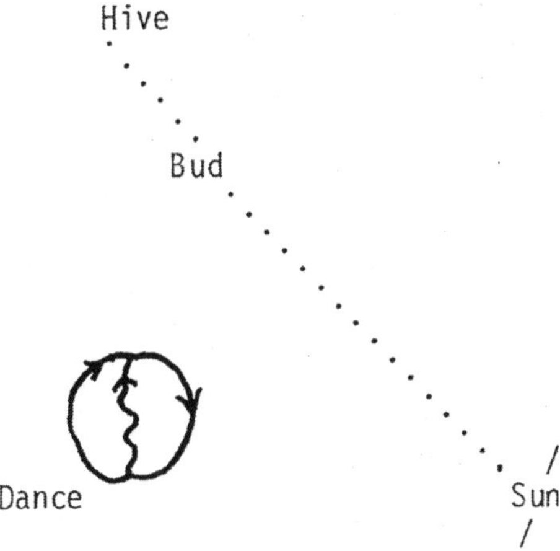

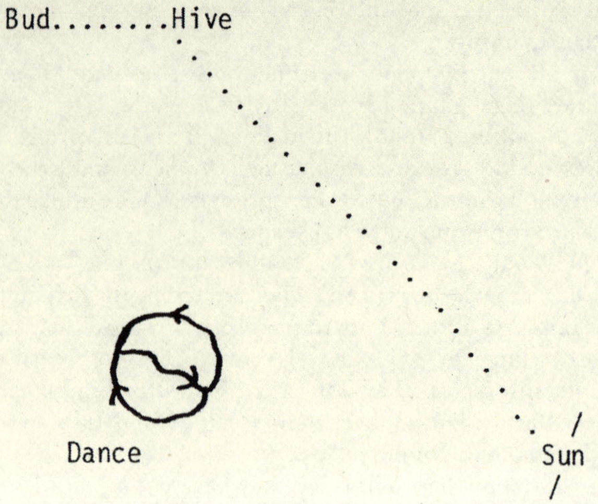

Bud........Hive

Dance

Sun

(This she followed with a diagram of the nature of the dance).

Stages suggestive of the *shuffle* as practiced by bees when foraging.

(This he countered with the Egyptian pictographs and ideographs he thought she'd like to know.)

a bee

SELKIS: the scorpion goddess.

SESHAT: the goddess of writing

SETH: the god of storms and violence.

(With these diagrams he challenged her mind. She began to *love* him.)

She flew to the dance on sprightly feet and this time the music was more suggestive than before:

UUHHHHH HUUHHHH UUHHHHH HUUHHHH UUHHHH HUHHH
MMMMAHHHH MMMMAHHHH MMMMAHHHH MMMMAHHHH MMMMAHHHHH

o o
o oooooooo m m m m oooooooo o m m m m oh oh oh ohh
o oooooooo m m m m m o oo m m m m m

m m m m m m m o o o o o H H H H H
m m m m m m o o o o o o A A A A A A OOOOHHHHH

MMMMAHHHH MMMMAHHHH MMMMAHHHH MMMMAHHHH MMMMAHHHHH
UUHHHHH HUHUHHHH UUHHHHH HUUHHHH UUHHHH HUHHH

They clung together drugged by mutual desire. Her normally open face was closed in lust: face unnaturally flushed, eyes slanted and shut, skin stretched taut over bone, body hair erect. She rubbed herself upon him in the darkness and his body quickened to hers. As they walked home the tension between them amplified to an unbearable hum that she tried to break with words.

'Will I like your place?'

'You will never get used to it.'

'Why? Won't I like your style?'

'My style and tastes always change.'

'What style do you like now?'

'Gentle, compliant and forgetful.'

'Surely you don't want people to forget you!'

'Yes I do, that's all I want.'

His hand in hers did something to reassure her. It did not betray his inner panic as each phrase stung his conscience and elicited from him an evasive reply. If only they could have flown from the dance floor into bed.

In his house shone:

candelabra of brass and gold;

objects enriched with carnelian, turquoise and lapis lazuli.

A falcon with wooden wings outstretched hovered over his bed.

He led her under this canopy with facile blandishments and unloosed her garments with practiced hands.

'Let me kiss you with the kisses of my mouth for my love is better than wine; thy breasts are like two young roes that are twins, which feed among the lilies.'

'The hair on your chest is golden wire spun into fleece,' she sighed.

(It startled him, a little, to have someone reply in kind.)

'The hair on your head is like russet silk cascading over a rock,' he murmured.

'You are my prince with hair of yellow fire,' she crooned in earnest.

His breath became ragged and, suddenly, he pushed his finger through her petals to discover honey.

'Habella,' he begged, 'You're ready. Come on, come on!'

'Wait, wait, Please talk to me, stroke me some more ...'

'It surprises me that this isn't easy,' he said in a tight voice.

'Don't be angry, please help me ...'

(He nibbled on her breasts as if he were enjoying them, addressing them carefully with his lips, eyeing them as though they were novelties which indeed they were.)

'ASTARTE BREASTS,' he pronounced with forced glee, 'INTERESTING.'

(She giggled and kissed him with a passionate trust.)

(His hands travelled over her like wings over water and once again they met no resistance, but he was no longer friendly nor was he concerned with her pleasure.)

'Huh, huh, huh, mmmm, mmm, mmm, huh, huh, huh,
ooo, ooo, ooo, mmmm, ,,,, mmm, ooo, ooo, ooo,
huh, huh, huh, mmmm, mmm, mmm, ooo, ooo, ooo ...'

'Please, please, please,' she cried.

'Open to me,' he commanded.

'I can't,' she sobbed but ...

'Huunh, huunh, huunh,' was the sign of her co-operation and

'Huunh, huunh, huunh,' was the sign of his disgust.

(He pushed her knees up and then apart. He knelt between them and said with a laugh:

'Last offer, m'dear. Do I do it or not?'

'Please yes, I can't help it, I'm frightened ...'

'Aren't you on the pill?'

'No.'

'Well use this.'

He handed her some Spermicidal Foam.

'Huuh, huunh, huuh, mmmm, mmm, mmmm, Huuh, Huunh, huuh,

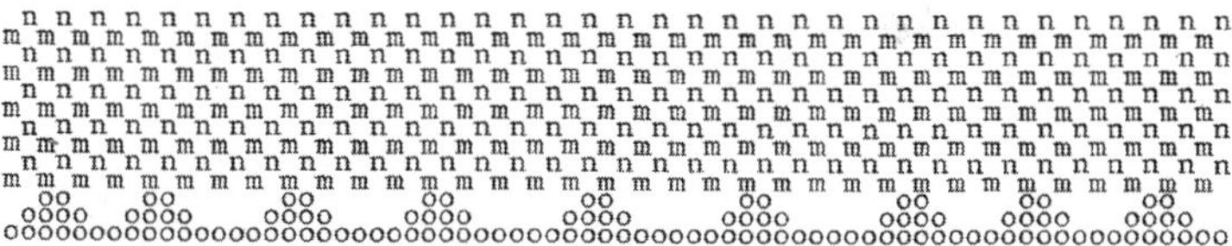

(They moved together towards the mindless bliss of the cells that humans call

Orgasm.)

'It *does* hurt, you're my first.'

'It'll be so much better next time, you'll see. Dry your tears, get some sleep. I'll call you tomorrow. I like you, my little bee, You'll feel better in the morning.'

(He made her some lemon tea, dressed her gently and, as she left he kissed her cheek.)

She went home with  for eyes.

Of course he never called and all she knew about him was that his name was Solomon. She was, naturally, very hurt because she thought that they had a lot in common and his open blue-eyed face seemed one to trust. She was only slightly less distressed when her *flowers, O lacrima Virginae* arrived on time to stain her bed.

Her classes suffered and so did her research. She took refuge in talking like a text book opened anywhere:

In 1956 Dr. L. Seifer carried out interesting experiments that showed bees do not simply need pure water, but also water containing salt, ammonia, etc. In the test, drinking bowls were filled respectively with pure water and water containing 0.25 percent ammonium, 0.05 percent vinegar, and 0.80 percent common salt. Over a measured period the bowl containing salt water was visited by 2546 bees, that with the pure water by 1510, that with the ammonia water by 1186. It can thus be concluded that bees need salt and beekeepers who care for their winged friends should supply them with salt water. If we consider the observation of Serbinov (1913), Zander (1927), and others, that the illnesses affecting bees (foul brood) are in most cases passed on through water, we can see that a good, convenient drinking bowl is an extremely important and necessary item in any modern and well-equipped apiary.

Or she would have an irrational response. A slide of the Queen bee (see illustration ensuing) triggered this poetic tirade:

She prostrated herself before the image and cried:

'Please, please, please,' she cried.

'Open to me,' he commanded.

'I can't,' she sobbed but ...

'Huunh, huunh, huunh,' was the sign of her co-operation and

'Huunh, huunh, huunh,' was the sign of his disgust.

(He pushed her knees up and then apart. He knelt between them and said with a laugh:

'Last offer, m'dear. Do I do it or not?'

'Please yes, I can't help it, I'm frightened ...'

'Aren't you on the pill?'

'No.'

'Well use this.'

He handed her some Spermicidal Foam.

'Huuh, huunh, huuh, mmmm, mmm, mmmm, Huuh, Huunh, huuh,

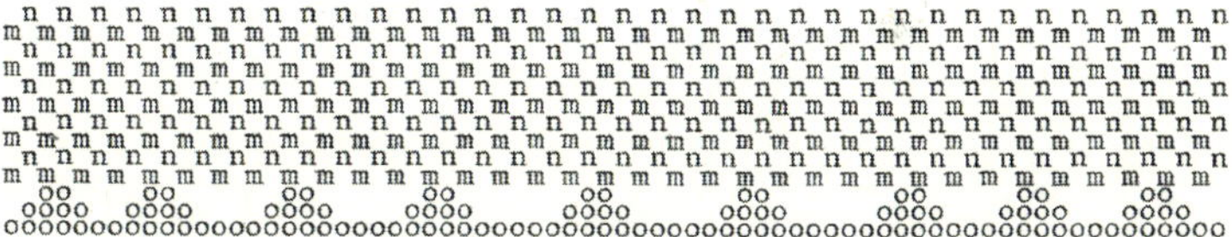

(They moved together towards the mindless bliss of the cells that humans call

Orgasm.)

'It *does* hurt, you're my first.'

'It'll be so much better next time, you'll see. Dry your tears, get some sleep. I'll call you tomorrow. I like you, my little bee, You'll feel better in the morning.'

(He made her some lemon tea, dressed her gently and, as she left he kissed her cheek.)

She went home with  for eyes.

Of course he never called and all she knew about him was that his name was Solomon. She was, naturally, very hurt because she thought that they had a lot in common and his open blue-eyed face seemed one to trust. She was only slightly less distressed when her *flowers, O lacrima Virginae* arrived on time to stain her bed.

Her classes suffered and so did her research. She took refuge in talking like a text book opened anywhere:

In 1956 Dr. L. Seifer carried out interesting experiments that showed bees do not simply need pure water, but also water containing salt, ammonia, etc. In the test, drinking bowls were filled respectively with pure water and water containing 0.25 percent ammonium, 0.05 percent vinegar, and 0.80 percent common salt. Over a measured period the bowl containing salt water was visited by 2546 bees, that with the pure water by 1510, that with the ammonia water by 1186. It can thus be concluded that bees need salt and beekeepers who care for their winged friends should supply them with salt water. If we consider the observation of Serbinov (1913), Zander (1927), and others, that the illnesses affecting bees (foul brood) are in most cases passed on through water, we can see that a good, convenient drinking bowl is an extremely important and necessary item in any modern and well-equipped apiary.

Or she would have an irrational response. A slide of the Queen bee (see illustration ensuing) triggered this poetic tirade:

She prostrated herself before the image and cried:

'Pulchritudinous Virgin! Do not go forth.

Beware, beware of the Drone Dog. He is Cerberus of the Hispid Faces:

i. one face is open like a summer peach, its seed is hard, O Virgin;

ii. one face is closed like the opium poppy, *defusum est male in labiis tuis*;

iii. one face is quizzical and diffuse, it gives no answer to the questions.

The Face of the Drone is Full of Eyes.

The Body of the Drone is Full of Wings.

The Brain of the Drone Drips

(with Cunning).

He has *one thing* on his mind.

Do not go forth, O Virgin, to that

Evil

Droning

Dog.'

(The class burst into nervous laughter.)

In front of the slide of the Queen bee prepared for artificial insemination (see illustration ensuing) she gave her final class as an instructress in Natural Science.

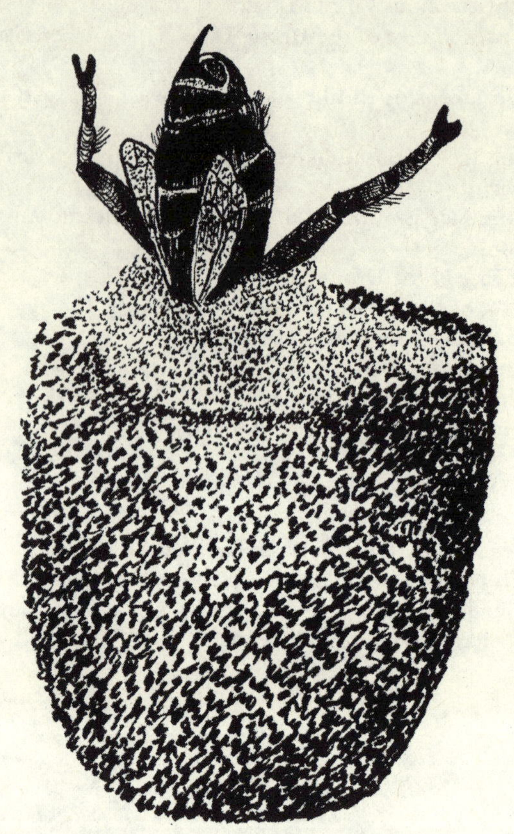

'OPEN TO ME
OPEN TO ME
OPEN TO ME
(she cried)
You are upsidedown in foam,
your legs are spread.
Post Coitum, Virgo, inviolata non permansisti
(after intercourse thou didst not remain a Virgin)

(Thou wert beautiful above the sons of men).
Poor Bee, pobrecita Habeilla,
You are only capable of stinging another
Queen.

I force you to act
contra naturam. You will
but cannot sting
Him.'
(There was no laughter.)

It was a relief for all to learn that Habella, so distracted in the last months, had embarked on a different profession.

Daily she searched for Solomon and in the sixth week her efforts were rewarded. She saw him sitting at the same table they had shared at the Golden Door in deep conversation with a lovely young girl.

She resisted the impulse to fly into the room as SELKIS, sting raised upon her head.

She entered after they had left and on the table she found hints of conversation written on the table mats:

JEREMY'S MAT

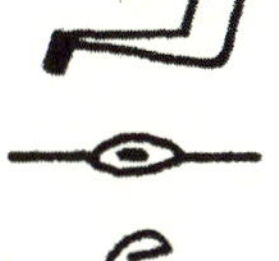

(forearm and hand) pronounced *Ayin*

(doorbolt) pronounced *'s'*

(abbreviation for quailchick) pronounced *'w'*
Come unlock my door, Chick!

VIRGINIA'S MAT

The savage man can have no desires beyond his physical wants. The only good he needs in the universe are pain and hunger. I say pain, not death for no animal can know what it is like to die; the knowledge of death and its terrors being one of the first acquisitions made by man departing from the animal state. ROUSSEAU

P.S. Let's drink to the savage man.

One thing about these messages shocked her. She approached the familiar waiter.

'Excuse me. My name is Habella. I was here with the young man who just left with a pretty girl, oh, way back in April. Only his name was not Jeremy, it was Solomon ...'

'O Santissima Madonna! Bellissima Bella. I canna immagina what he dida to you. I musta laugh, forgiva me. Male, Male, a bada man. Somebody shoulda locka him up He gathera floras lika the men, they shoota the deer. Differenta nomine, ah *namas.* Differenta disguisas. He turna his interesta in Egypta to diversas purposas. I Officini of psychiatristas and alla riveres are completa, fulla to the brima, witha distracted madonnas. Hanging woulda be too gooda for him. Male, Male animal. Finda yourself a gooda man, an honesta man. Getta married, begetta bambini. Donta wasta time remembering him.

She continued with her study of 'Solomon', with the kind waiter's help, more as an amusement than as a bitter exercise. She had only been foolish, not in any other sense, the fool. She had simply misread the signs. Only two messages on four mats, out of the many Gino saved for her, are worth reporting.

In one guise he was Aaron and seemed to give his new love at least as much warning as she had been given about his nature. He wrote in his neat hand:

Be ye ware of Ptah, Lord of Truth!
Lo, he will not overlook the deed of any man.
Refrain ye from uttering the name of Ptah falsely;
Lo, he that uttereth it falsely,
Lo, the same shall fall.
Ptah caused me to be as the dogs of the street,
He caused men and gods to mark me.

To which Flora responded:

Flowers for your honesty. No one with a face like yours could ever lie and if he did he would be guilty about it.

In the next he was Jim pretending to be Thoth, Egyptian god of wisdom and justice and asked questions like a catechist to which Kitty sensuously replied:

Thoth: 'What is the first Duty of a Woman?'
Kitty: 'To serve her master.'
Thoth: 'What are the manifestations of reverence?'
Kitty: 'She will serve his every need. Including, especially, c , and f
Thoth: 'Will she have other gods before him?'
Kitty: 'There is no god but him.'

On the night of her twenty-fifth birthday she had recovered sufficiently to celebrate with a friend the notion that in this world there are two classes of beings, the fuckers and the fuckees or, as the Old Testament more delicately put it, the *borers* and the *bored.* She had no doubt that Solomon was a boring fucker, the sort of man who would put his number into the phone book as Hugh G. Rection and wait masturbating for the results. Since her seduction she had begun to doubt the power of the word. She attempted to respond like an insect to all events in her life, her senses feeding upon the visual properties, the smells and the touches proper to each occasion.

That same evening Solomon had gone with his new friend William to read the Tarot. William had selected Sol as the subject of a sociological study examining the conscience of seducers. He had been drawn to him because of his reputation and in order to befriend him had told some judicious lies. It was a friendship fashioned by the Gods.

'Then why do you need so many women?' asked William as they approached the reader's door.

'I'm looking for the experiences that my senses enjoy. I want to lose myself in another, fall through the sky of passion. I am attracted by instinct to a fragrance, the hum of a voice, the grace of a walk, the hair on a slender arm. I will change shape anyway I can to draw a girl to me.'

'How can you change shape, surely you must be the same for everyone ...'

'No. I change shape through the words I choose. Let's suppose you're a woman and I want you. Easy. I'll just pretend that I'm interested in everything you say, everything you represent. Ah, William, I saw an article in *Esquire* the other day about the sexual attitudes of the forties. It's the funniest thing I've read for years. I'd love to read it to you, why don't you come to my place, we'll have a drink and ...'

'Ah, you're kidding me, Sol. That's just old-fashioned politeness ...'

'No. Politeness isn't what I intend, seduction *is* ... And even though I always give a note of warning the girls never listen because they're just as intent upon being seduced as I am on playing the seducer. And when it's over nothing – not even a memory of a conversation – usually remains.'

'Do you think you'll ever change?'

'I must change. I'm beginning to bore myself. Everything is too easy. Nothing matters ...'

'How can you change? You are what you are ...'

'I know. I don't know.'

They entered the house of the Tarot reader. It was filled with:

a tumble of furniture of indifferent choice;
a jumble of worthless objects;
the smell of snuffling dogs;
the pungent keenness of cockroach
(droppings).

An old woman greeted them with a face as dry and as rough as a breadcrust. She served them lemon tea from unmatched cups, and lectured them gently on the History of Tarot. To Sol's question about the meaning of the cards she gave this enigmatic reply:

That man is best who sees the truth himself;
Good too is he who hearkens to wise counsel.
But who is neither wise himself nor willing
To ponder wisdom, is not worth a straw.

Then she removed from a silken bag the heavy Tarot deck and after a suitable deliberation she unfolded before them the Wisdom of the Cards. They fell into this pattern:

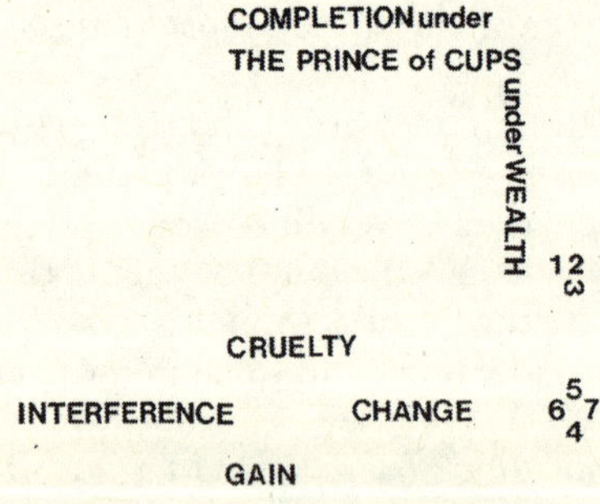

COMPLETION

She spoke the ritual of the cards:

'COMPLETION represents you, O lord of Manifested Power. Flames of ardour burn at your centre and the rams overwhelm the doves with their horns. The female element (upsidedown) hints at abuse. The PRINCE OF CUPS is likely the William who brought you. He delights in taking pure energy from the fire of others; he has no decisive actions of his own. WEALTH may impede or aid your actions in the future. Ponder the meaning of the first three cards.'

(Sol looked to William for reassurance and saw that he was pouring himself a drink without the hostess' permission.)

'Card 4 is GAIN and its spangle of coins reinforces the dilemma of the present. In this context the good fortune that GAIN normally implies is contravened by the weight that the trappings of Wealth has placed on your shoulders. It is your albatross, young man, and its ten foot wings beat about your throat. What will be ideal in your future is CRUELTY. Its nine swords drip blood and urge you to pursue a perverse idealism *or* to accept a passive martyrdom. INTERFERENCE, the 6th card, denotes a past filled with false starts and contradictions. Card 7 says CHANGE is coming.'

('Thank God, Thank God,' murmured Sol.)

'You must not yet feel relief. CHANGE seems dynamic as it is a snake turned infinitely upon itself, but the snake coils itself into *stasis*. Impeded by his nature, he is fixed upon a single goal. He may endlessly repeat the first step or he will take one step and there will never be another.'

'Perhaps the reading of this card will be tempered by your reading of another,' ventured Sol.

'Young man, the next cards have confusing messages. Many of them are upsidedown and contravene their usual meanings. Many allude to your self-certainty and innerdirectedness; some connote opulence and leadership, but their potential is thwarted by *position*. Perhaps you would like to come back when you are more sure ...'

'No, please continue. William says you are rarely available ...'

'Cards 13 and 14 indicate the *final outcome*. These cards are strong. SCIENCE bespeaks the balance between the intellectual and the moral in a situation and I think its import is the same however it is placed. Beside it stands THE DEVIL. It is also a card of balance, between bliss on the one hand and human consciousness on the other. You have drawn to yourself the most rampant sexual omen through which to manifest your desire. The goat leaps with lust upon the summits of the earth. He is Pan-Progenitor, the All-Begetter. He is mounted in front of a phallus which is the tree of life seen against the divine madness of spring. In his testes broil impulses that do not partake of reason or foresight.

Your mountain is barren.

Your horns spiral energy upwards into air.

Your want is the want of OSIRIS / HORUS.

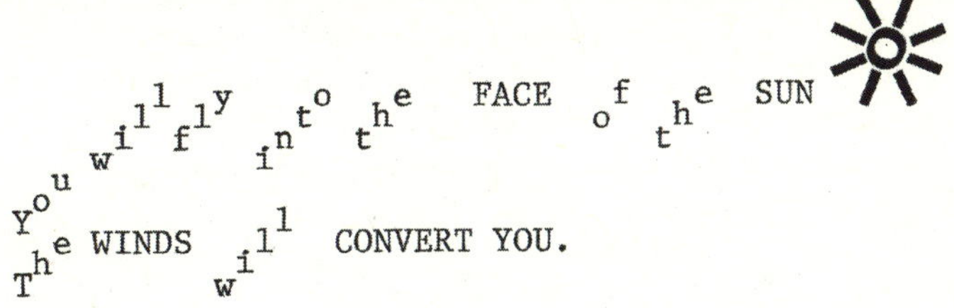

B E W A R E   O F   A I R   RUN RAM RUN.

(Her voice which had been so steady in the ordering of the service rose in a shrill scream). She fell into a faint.

William said, 'Don't bother. She always does that. See Saul. What did I tell you. Tarot's more fun that the movies. Here, take the last card. She'll never miss it when she comes around.'

Sol took the card home and the next day he looked at

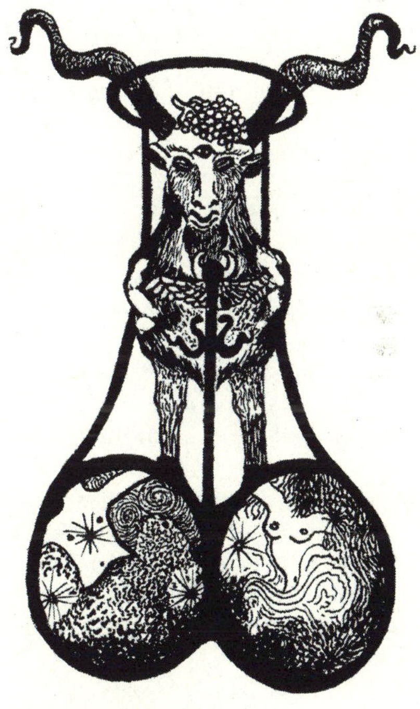

THE DEVIL

He had been unnerved by the previous evening and had kept William with him for company. The fact that the reader had taken a hysterical turn had invalidated for him the whole experience. He talked to the guest who was still in bed:

'Hey, what a nut that was. You're not the Prince of Cups. I'm not the Devil. I'm going to change in amazing ways and if I remember where the old crone lives when I finish, I'll go back and show her who's powerful. William, come on, get up! The goat's staff has wings like the ones on my bed. Hey, the sun disc and confronting snakes are two of my favorite signatures. Hey, William, damn it! The goat's third eye has just disappeared, what shall I do?'

'Burn it,' said William sleepily. 'Let's talk about your conscience.'

The next day with William for comfort, he took a trip into the mountains. His pack contained bread and water for he was determined to accomplish self-redemption. For seven days and seven nights he fasted, compelled by an inner necessity that felt for all the world like unsatisfied lust and on the seventh evening, just as the meditation books had promised, he had a vision that filled him with wonder.

Out of the clouds came a man of incredible beauty (like unto himself) with a flower for a penis. He pulled off the petals one by one, letting them float into the air. When the last had vanished, leaving him flat and naked, the man fell down dead, on the ground.

Out of the clouds came a babe of astonishing beauty who before his eyes shrank back through the successive stages of development until it became two dots., egg/sperm in the sky and vanished.

Out of the clouds came a woman of unsurpassed beauty. She writhed before him in serpentine dance as she progressed through the successive stages of decay until she blew on the wind as a handful of dust.

He went down from the mountain with ashes on his head and a phylactery of cedar and moss around his neck. About his arms he wound two snake-like branches and over his neck he placed a shawl of bark. His revelation told him to cast away his superfluous gold and women, to settle down and become a family man. The wife he had selected was Habella Cire for she was the only woman in a thousand for whom he had, fleetingly, felt a more than physical attraction.

'In the middle of our second meeting,' he explained to William, 'she said that language was "usually dishonest", that it almost never meant what it said. She said that you can scarcely expect to get the groceries you order by phone. Spoken language, then, is not nearly as pragmatic as the language of the bees where so many shuffles to the left or the right sends the worker off following the directions of her scout to just the place where the flowers are.

'Poor Habella fell into the trap I set with my language and I want to apologize for that. I think that we could love each other ...'

He phoned her on three occasions without success:

(1) Brinnng, Brinnng, Brinnng, Brinnng, Brinnng, Brinnng, (out)

(2) Bryunng, Bryunng, Bryunng, Bryunng, Bryunng, Bryunng, (busy).

(3) Sorry ... the ... line ... you ... are ... calling ... is ... not ... in ... service ... sorry ... the ... line ... you ... are ... (moved).

Later when Sol's house was almost emptied of furniture he sat before his window reading with William. A curious flutter tickled their brains. They discovered that they shared space with two worker bees.

The visitors' behavior was polite; their procedure was wondrously efficient. Their wings drummed an almost imperceptible *huummnn* as they searched diligently for an exit.

They moved parallel to the windows executing the 90 degree turns at the corner without fault. They rediscovered the window route six times in a smooth meticulous circuit. They became baffled and seemed to run formal memory tests on the avenue of approach. The larger of the two bees, momentarily, stood still in space, then neatly performed four directional probes to the North, East, South and West and moved, then, unerringly to the exact spot of her entry. Sol helped her out.

The smaller bee was, perhaps, younger or less experienced in flight outside the hive. She rested on the window and before she could begin again, Sol caught her in a glass.

He saw that she was beautiful:

her face was a mobile and inquisitive mask;
her feelers – black lines of iron – bent willfully against air;
in her amber wings throbbed veins of dark obsidian;
her abdominal stripes were as clear and precise as
Egyptian cloisonné.

(He released her into the air and that very day in order to emulate the flight of bees, he decided to take up hang gliding. The visitors in every respect seemed a wonderful

OMEN.)

That evening he said to William,

'I must tell you something important.'

'What is it?'

'I have been lying to you ever since we met.'

'Oh? How?'

'Well, I've always used different names with people and Sol or Solomon's the one I use most often. SAUL, Saul Hartig's my real name ... Hope you don't mind.'

'No trouble, it sounds the same.'

NOTE:

Habella took up hang gliding for reasons Sol would have admired. She wished to lose herself in flight, testing her eye and spirit in spontaneous motion through a fluid medium. She had become a filmmaker and film critic. Art, not science, was on her mind.

She saw herself hovering over the land as Isis, brooding over the torn form of her husband OSIRIS who for reasons no one knew history had connected with HORUS of the SOLAR DISC. HORUS / OSIRIS victim of SETH, god of the wind.

(She saw no connection whatsoever between hang gliding and the bees.)

After several weeks of separate training through which they learned the intricacies of Jesus bolts, glide ratios, spans, Hang Fives, the two novices had progressed sufficiently in the sport to be invited to take the difficult jump off Hollyburn Mountain. In anticipation of the intense camaraderie the jump was bound to generate, the instructors circulated a list of the intended gliders. Saul was overjoyed to see

HABELLA CIRE.

(Habella did not know anyone called)

SAUL HARTIG.

Saul manoeuvred his name on the list so that he would jump into the air immediately after her. He counted upon his greater weight to bring them very close together at mid flight. In his imagination he conceived a touching reunion akin to the NUPTIAL FLIGHT of bees. He visualized the prospect of this brilliant mating.

(HE) Buzz,
Buzz,
moving closer to

(SHE)

(HE) Mnnn,
Mnnn,
MNMNMNMNMNMN

MNMN
MNMNMNMNMNMN
HABELLA!

(SHE TURNS)

MNMNMN, Hey Bella,
it's Solomon. I've
flown to marry you.

(SHE SMILES)
She says, "You've
changed. You dyed
your beard."

YES. The change is
real. I'm sorry. I
love you. Give me
a sign.

(She blew him a

kikisssikikisss

He drifted down satisfied, the wind rustling his silk.

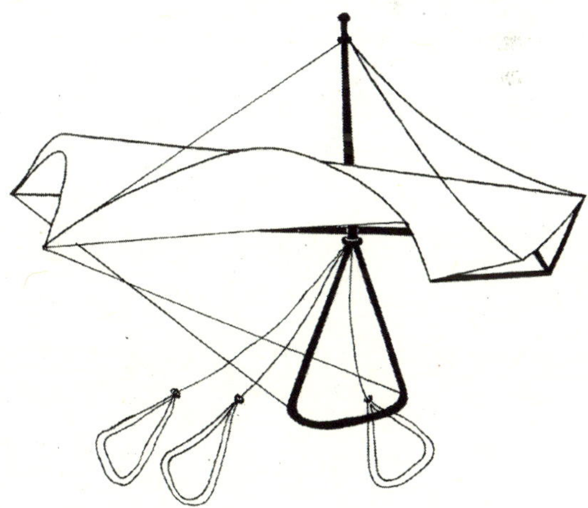

He liked the idea the day-dream contained. He made an appointment immediately to have his beard dyed back to its natural colour, brown. That would make the surprise *complete*.

On the special day, Saul rose with songs in his heart and by the time he had reached the top of the mountain they beat like thunder in his ears. He shrewdly took up position beside Habella and at the proper moment, flew into space to mate her.

But the winds that day were capricious and angry and SETH god of storms and violence (the antithesis of HORUS of the SUN) created for SOL a curious fate. As the pair began their flight they wrote in the sky the Egyptian symbol of the goddess scribe:

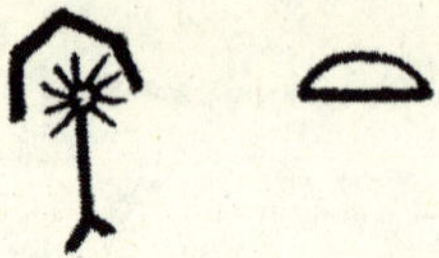

One could see immediately that something was awry. The figure of Habella was at peace with her kite as a tidy semi-circle in the sky; Sol was struggling to gain back control of his from the wind.

They moved f u r t h e r a n d f u r t h e r apart.

The critical message did not pass between them.

The spectators on English Bay saw that something was terribly wrong.

000 000 0 0 0 0 0 88 00 8 00 00 0 0000 0 08 000 0 0 0 0 0 8 0000 0 0000 0 0 0 0 0 0 0

SAID THE CROWD. An updraft had caught Sol and in hang glider's terms he

Skyed Out

He disappeared into a vacuum of air.

Three days later an obituary appeared. Saul's parents wished no publicity.

IN MEMORIAM *Saul Hartig*, a linguist with a special interest in Middle Eastern Philology, died in a freak hang-gliding accident at age 28. The body has not been found. A private service will be held at an undisclosed address. Do not send flowers. The Heart Fund would be pleased to accept gifts in his memory.

On the same page of THE SUN was an announcement of Habella Cire's engagement to the good and decent man she intended to marry.

Becoming Queen

His eyes were the eyes of a raven;
his lips curved into a gentle Buddha smile;
one fragile hand sought perpetual comfort
in the other. He drew about himself
an imagined cloak (of melancholy).

Rehearsing a speech to be given at The Vancouver Club on Saturday evening before his mirror under the eye of a bulb, he practiced the words and the gestures. He enjoyed affecting a sepulchral appearance and imagined being dressed for the occasion in his black velour suit.

He was Matthias – so named for Grünewald because his fingers writhed like those of the crucified Christ of the Eisenheim Altarpiece when he suckled his mother's breasts. She baptised him with the memory of their mutual discomfort and their relationship went down after that. *Harp* for the father who did not play one, who fled from his mother when he was six.

Before the mirror now, the expert on the sub-class Hexapoda (true insects) of the order Hymenoptera (from two Greek words meaning membrane or wings) which also includes the wasps, all ants and ichneumon-flies, the gall and saw flies – in brief, all small invertebrates segmented and winged in the proper way and with biting and sucking parts – was recalling the black anger on his face when he discovered he would be sharing his lab space with a *woman* called Habella Cire. He was bemused, however by the aptness of her name for one interested in Apiary – Bee Wax or Be Seer get-the-hell-out-of-here! Mock surprise now on his face, he recalled the jolt of pleasure he had felt when he first encountered her and so entered the arrangement to discover what it would bring. And they survived the first wars over positions of plants and other personal paraphernalia in the lab well enough to enjoy talking with each other, well enough indeed that he had asked her after the first week of their acquaintance to be his thesis partner and to celebrate they lay close, like kittens, in the lunch-time grass.

'Habella, I have to confess that ever since I was small I've only felt easy with boys ...'

'Oh, I know that just watching you with others ... I feel easy with you too because you don't endanger me. I don't have to worry, to play games with you. I can just be myself. It's almost as though you were my brother. There will be no incest, so it's simple ...'

'I don't see our relationship as sexless, entirely ... I've told you how I have memorized your face and counted the hairs on your arms ...'

'I'm not indifferent to you either, but I just feel free to look at you as I would a woman, not really to flirt but just to know. But because you're a man I am, perhaps, more curious and notice more ... Your chest on the heart-side is larger and the pulses can be counted ...'

'Jesus, you are the complete scientist – always at work!'

'Come on, Matthias, I just love seeing your chest. In woman everything is so covered up, so woefully covert ...'

'Maybe that's why they frighten me ...'

'Perhaps so. But the opposite frightens me ...'

'Habella, do you think I'll ever be a queen?'

'I hope not, Matthias, queens sometimes get stung by another.'

'But Habella, if I were a queen I could become a mother.'

'Silly boy, you are a *mother* now!'

They were *fraternal*, and he smiled broadly now, as he remembered the pleasure of that simultaneous insight; but they were not so exactly alike that it was as though she *mirrored* him. He was more rational and practical in his approach to research and he had, on the whole, a careful nature; she was the prophet, the reckless speculator and she was disposed slightly to hysterical response – together they would have made a perfect ellipse and rolled happily, Plato fashion, down the hill of life. He was certainly aware that she had given his scholarship leaven, and it was only because she could not be there, that he was dramatizing his speech before the glass. He wished that she was there to clap and cheer, to make rude remarks, to twist his rational correctness into nonsense.

They were also capable of reversing roles. This worked best when they were involved in the neutral territory of their shared research, where they had similar kinds of information to bring to an extended joke. One day they pretended to be François Huber, the 17th century Swiss blind bee researcher, and his worker-servant, François Burnens:

Burnens, peasant, count zose bees.

Oui, mon maître: un, deux, trois, quatre, cinq, six, sept, huit, neuf, dix ... j'oublie, mon maître ...

onze, ONZE, fou! Comptez, Comptez ...

douze, treize ... et cetera, et cetera ...

ET CETERA? fou! Comptez. Comptez les abeilles!

Combien must-I compte, mon maître?

O! un peu. Peut être, soixante-mille ...

Sacrement! J'suis fatigué ...

Comptez, Fou! comptez ...;

and on another they pretended to be Conrad Lorenz arguing with Karl von Frisch, two Germanic titans screaming:

Der geez sind nicht so agrezziv dem beez.

Nein, die beez sind nicht so agrezziv dem geez.

Jah, ich denke, jah.

Nein, ich denke Nein.

Jah, sie sind zo.

Nein, sie sind nicht so.

Die beez sind nicht upgehonken alle damn nacht.

Aber, die beez upgestingen and heraus gebuzzen.

Jah?

Nein?

Gehonken?

Gebuzzen and gestingen.

Dumm.

Nichts dumm.

Their office was decorated with bee trivia and bee jokes. The chief jewel was this drawing of a 12th century German hive.

They were so remarkably harmonious at work and at leisure that Matthias knew that many wished that for her sake he could change his sexual preferences. His eyes shut tight in the recollection of the fragrance, or aura, that drew him close to her so that he would linger to examine all her qualities. It was the same pleasant feeling that led to arousal and release when he discovered an interesting man and he knew that while she admired him, enjoyed his conversation, his appearance, while she willingly spent more time with him than with anyone else, he was for her quite *neutral.* He knew that when sometimes in the dark he would seek her hand and she would hold his warmly, that when occasionally they would fall asleep beside each other and tempt each other with words, that the only thing counted as significant between the sexes would never occur between them.

In his deepest pessimism when he stood as now, naked before his private mirror, bulb-eye staring down, he was the Burnens who patiently counted the blessings Habella could not see, enumerating to her *soixante-mille* virtues or he was Huber, exacting from his servant the feeling he could not produce within himself for he had most certainly used her in his work and, whenever he could, engaged her in tasks that required her greater imagination. It was she, not he, who was *inventing* the text of the *BEE NOVICE TEXTBOOK* he was producing for the schools and in his imagination he recalled the eloquence of her words and the bold simplicity of her drawings as she traced the cycle of the queen from egg to imago:

On the first day of June a bluish translucent egg fell from the hips of the Old Queen into a pristine waxen cell. It was bathed repeatedly by the mysterious substance formed in the forehead glands of six day old workers. It lay quiet, like a comma, a pause between, two possibilities.

On the second day it stood up exclaiming surprise at its own life, erect under the hundreds of Royal Jelly gifts showered down by different workers celebrating their sixth day of life. On the third day, similarly washed, it knew that at the very least, it would become a larva.

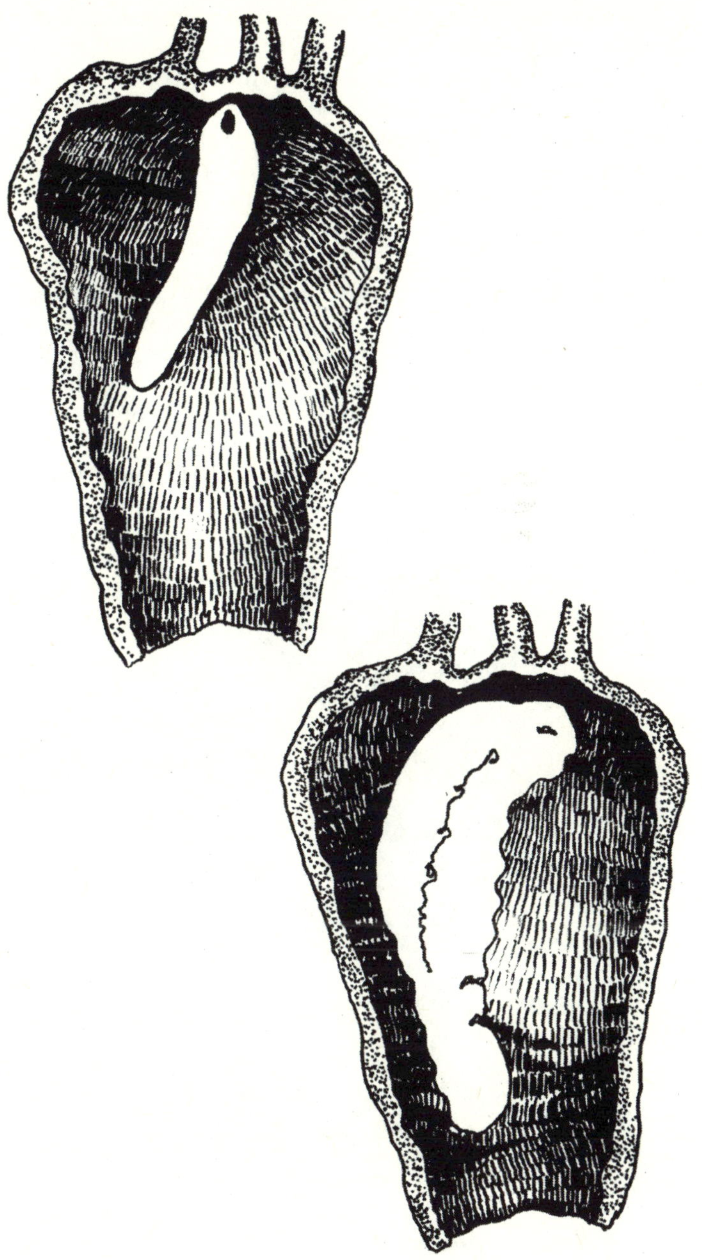

The fourth day was critical. The nurses did not bring the bee bread or nectar that would have predestined the larva to a sexless life of unceasing toil. Once more the six-day-olds arrived with gifts of Royal Jelly. And on the fifth day, after a final regal repast, the larva's skin split for the last time. She wiggled herself into the shape of a comma and became *very* still. The worker architects struggled to cover the increasing scale of her calligraphy by constructing over her head a thimble-like dome that proclaimed her queenly status to the entire hive.

On the sixth day she spun herself a silken cloak inside her peaceful dome and when her spinning was finished her spinning glands obediently vanished. On the seventh day her eyes grew large and black and her body now divided into head, thorax and abdomen. Around her spread the delicate beginnings of antennae and legs. No longer a comma, she was the noun *bee*, a milkglass figurine as turbid and as cold as glacial ice. On the eighth day her abdomen grew long, refined by a vicious downcurving sting. On the ninth she was perfect. On the

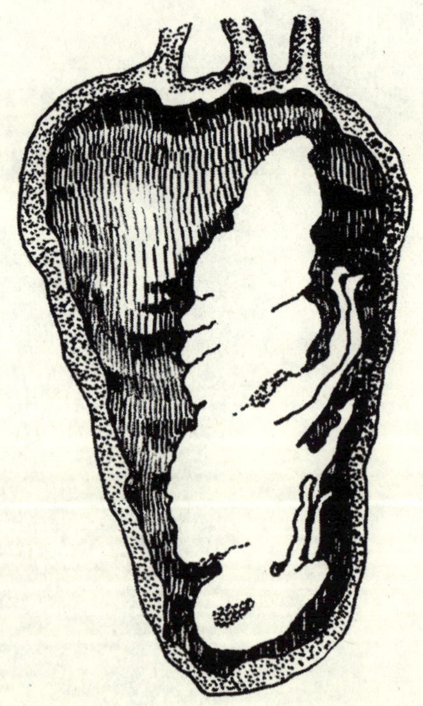

sixteenth, she animated herself and her sharp jaws broke through the wax two black marks resembling periods, the termination surely, of a joyless childhood.

On the same day the weather was fine; the hive fell unnaturally silent. Then, sounding a swarm note, the strong young workers streamed impetuously from the hive until they alit by common consensus, on the branch of a nearby tree with the Old Queen as ruler. Within, the New Queen tore her waxen *domus* to pieces and emerged with a high shrill

Hhhhhhhhhhhhhhiiiiiiiiiiii

that was her battle song to any remaining queen who had the will to fight her. Her jaws sank in to subdue another's flesh to thrusts of her stinging. The new queen ripped the remaining domes to shards of wax and put to sword all the nearly developed females. She was pleased to let the Old Queen follow the swarm. She prepared for her own Nuptial Flight.

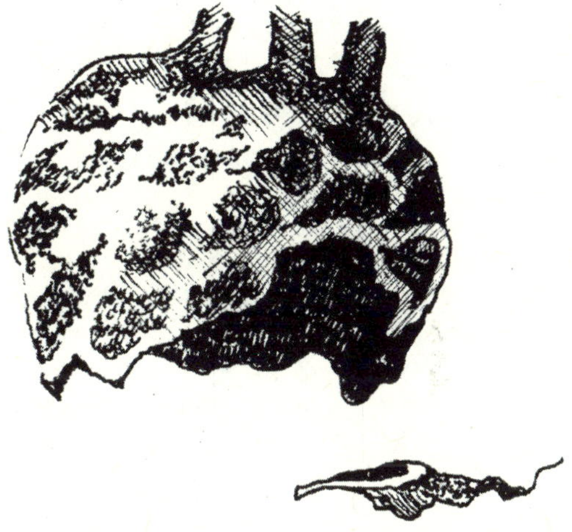

At times like that when she had lived up to his expectations, he would praise her warmly:

'That's good, Habella, that's great! Now what are you going to do about the drones in this little book that will make our fortunes?'

'You deal with the drones, you understand them better!'

And soon she was crying and a confession could be discovered between sobs:

'Damn it, damn it. I I'm so ashamed. I I gave up my virginity to someone I I'll p probably never see again. I I j just lost my head ... my mother would kill me ...'

'Don't let your mother know and nothing's lost if you aren't pregnant. Besides, I've been telling you for a long time you should lose your head once in a while and live a little ... Come on, let's see you smile. You're the one who cries when we inseminate the queen, fussing around about loss of instinct. For once you've acted upon yours. We should be having a drink to celebrate. Anyway you know that queens sometimes meet drones, as shown by the white thread, and yet are not impregnated. The spermatozoa did not yet reach the spermatheca and in such cases a second and perhaps a third mating is required. Huber was the first to prove that impregnation always takes place on the wing.'

'I was on wing, there was a white thread: don't text-book talk me, Matthias – I've read them all, now I've done it all. I just don't understand how I forgot my instinct of self-preservation. He seduced me by his words, as much as by anything else ... If I act on whim again it will be to enter a life-long relationship. You just don't understand!'

'*Thinking,* surely, will have something to do with a choice like that!'

'No. Instinct will make the choice and the logic will be in following the pattern ...'

He winced as he remembered how she had flounced out of the room and slammed the door. That was only a short while ago and so the memory was fresh. *He touched the dark circles under his eyes and wondered if he should tie his long hair back when he was giving the lecture,* but this was a simple diversion against the more recent encounters with Habella.

In the last three weeks of term he had noticed that her behavior had become increasingly strained. She was incoherent, for example, when asked to recount her nightly observations and there were rumours about an embarrassing breakdown during her last class. As he fingered his eyebrows, he wondered if they would ever finish the thesis they were writing jointly. The bees had been silent as she cleared out her desk in the laboratory. He had shifted his weight from buttock to buttock, afraid to break through the sullen air. She had turned to him bitterly and said:

'Now you know I have no control over myself – undoubtedly you've heard about my hysterical outburst!'

'Yes, I did hear, or course, but one mistake doesn't destroy eight months of work ...'

'Oh? One mistake can destroy a lifetime. It does. It can. I'll never teach Natural Science again!'

'Yes you will, one way or another, you will. You're programmed to ... what are your plans?'

'To take up hang gliding, make movies and get married as soon as possible ...'

'But Habella, you're afraid of heights!'

'Well, I'll learn not to be.'

'But Habella, you've only made one movie.'

'Then, I'll make more.'

'Habella, forgive me, you told me you are afraid of men.'

'But I'm not afraid of marriage.'

'Don't rush into things, you need a rest. Stay with me for awhile.'

'I can't; you're not what I want. But thank you, I'll keep in touch. And Matthias, don't worry about the thesis, you know I believe in commitments.'

The bees grumbled in their cells then and Matthias began to practice now his oratory before a mirror.

In the hive, ladies and gentlemen, the future state of the bee is determined by feeding to an amazing extent. If the fertilized egg deposited by the queen in its cell is fed exclusively on royal jelly the egg will metamorphose into a new queen; if on the other hand the fertilized egg is fed bee bread and nectar after its third day of life, it will become a sexless female or worker. The creation of the male is a different story. The queen at certain times of the year (or before she has mated) lays unfertilized eggs at will that regardless of feeding become the drones who will vie for the privilege of fathering the new generations of workers and queens. So the male bee, then, like Christ, is created through *parthenogenesis* and the drone was used as the proof of the virginity of Mary in the 18th century.

In the human hive, as you know, there is no such easy method for producing males, females and intersexual beings. The feeding the foetus receives in the womb of its mother (unless contaminated by radiation or other toxic substances) has no effect upon the gender of offspring, neither can the human mother before mating, or after all the semen she contains has been utilized (or at any moment in between), produce males at will by the simple act of constricting the opening of her spermatheca, for the human mother has none *(a pause, for laughter).* In the majority of cases, the sexing of the bee-offspring is obvious for in addition to the gross physical differences, and I show you here comparative drawings executed by my colleague Habella Cire,

where it is clear that the worker is the smallest and most delicate; that the drone is the hairiest and fattest, and that the queen has a most delicate waistline and the most elegant proportions so that one could say she is wonderfully wrought or, in street language, 'stacked' *(pause for laughter),* it is in their smaller distinctions that the differences are the most interesting:

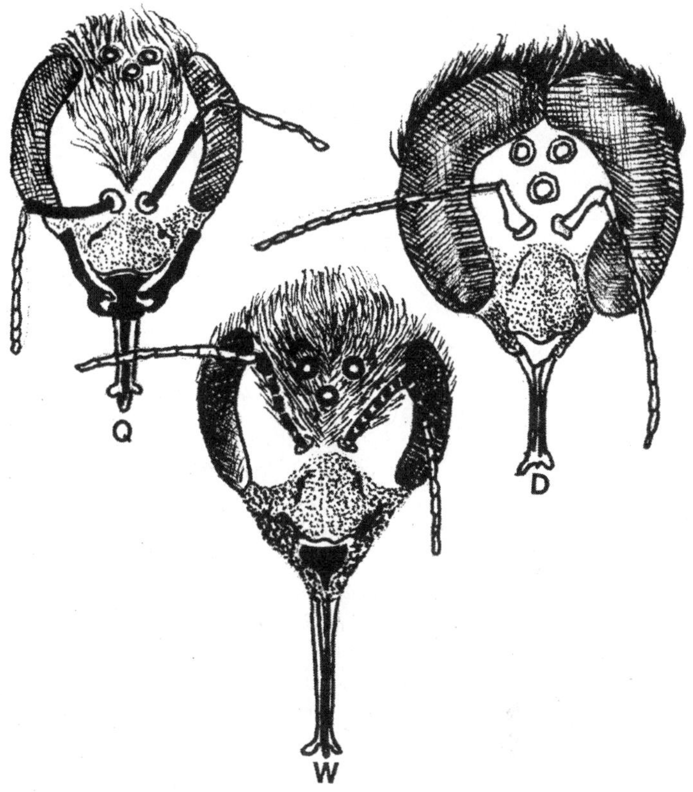

In humans, it must be noted, while the males and females are easy to identify, it is very difficult to identify the intersexual beings, unless they take on a bizarre hermaphroditic form at an early age. In humankind, moreover, it is impossible to determine from appearance alone who is sexually active, who is sexually inactive, and this is a mercy *(pause for laughter)*.

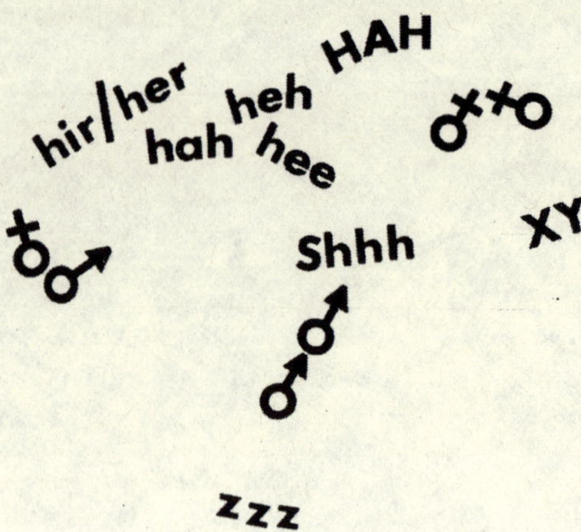

What we must wonder about, what we must ask about in this age when the behavior of animals is being studied in order to help us comprehend (among other things) the habit of humans singly, in couples, or in groups, is whether the bees' sexual behavior is *instinctual or learned.* What we must wonder about is how we ourselves become *sexual* creatures by considering the lives of the bees.

In the hive, ladies and gentlemen, sex is a privilege of only the full males and the females and upon successful union the future of the hive depends. It is significant that no one teaches the bee to mate – the instinct is within them, they know the time and the place. The male bee is not only deprived of a father, but also of an exemplar, for all males die upon achieving union, their obsidian penises torn from excited bodies and in any event all sex acts take place so high in the air that they have never in nature been witnessed except by the 'couples' that perform them. But nature equips the drone with everything he needs: extraordinarily developed eyes, marvellously strong wings, 30,000 pore plates on each antenna to draw him to the target of fragrant pheromones exuded by the ripe queen and a tracheal-bronchial system that must be filled with air before he can hope to ejaculate, before he can hope to properly penetrate the spermatheca of the queen. He will die in sexual agony for the sake of his race or he will miss out entirely the one activity for which he is especially programmed and equipped. His attractiveness has nothing to do with it;

his ability to be *attracted does,* as I will later demonstrate *(a pause for gasps);* his *lust* has more to do with it than anything else, for I have known, in my brief career as an entomologist with a special interest in bees, some remarkably lazy or 'laid back' drones who would rather be in the hive getting stuffed than in the air, *stuffing* (if you will forgive my crudeness).

The queen is a different matter. She invariably *outlives* her sexual experiences. (There are recorded cases where the queen, all spermatozoa elided from her spermatheca, has mated more than once.) But she fails to induct her daughters into the *mysteries,* perhaps because she is, like Winnie-the-Pooh 'of small brain', hence suited to the task of endless egg-production – oh feminists forgive me *(pause for laughter)* – and while she may *see* the consequence of mating all about her and knows from her first instant of life which rivals-in-their-cells to destroy, she is left to obey an inner urge that she will never refuse and she will lay subsequently (on average) 1000 eggs a day eight months of the year producing between 720,000 to 1,200,000 eggs in a three to five year life without complaint, without a decent holiday in the Barbados *(pause for laughter)* and in return for food, adequate shelter and some regular stroking. But she will never tell her daughters how it's done or *why* it's done at all because she will flee the hive when they are becoming her and she will do it before they were or where they cannot see it, so she is no more the model of sexual behavior for the next generation than is the unfortunate drone.

The workers, of course, have no sex life at all that we would recognize. But I wonder if they do not lead more fully *sensual* and satisfactory lives. After a day of rest, they begin to behave in a totally *productive* manner: first as nurses, later as builders, food processers, guards, queen's-maids, and finally until they drop dead from exhaustion, as pollen and nectar gatherers. They are taxed to the limit of their intelligence and adaptability every moment. They touch, stroke, nuzzle, suck, dance and sing, dine and sting – in short they lead lives 1000 percent more interesting than those of the dull drones and passive queens and certainly they are stroked, rubbed, and stimulated more often than you or I, but perhaps I should simply speak for myself *(a pause for laughter and an adjustment of one eyebrow)*. Further the workers are capable of learning things from each other and from the humans who have attempted to teach them and have come to understand their ways. It will surprise you to know that bees read *(a pause for the 'Ohh' of surprise that would inevitably follow)* or at least, according to Karl von Frisch, they will never confuse:

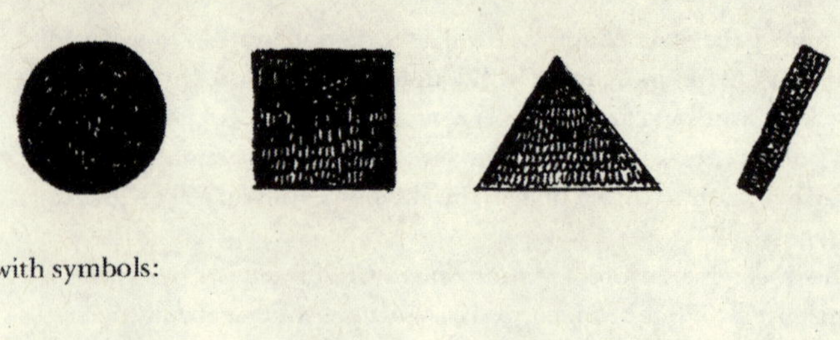

with symbols:

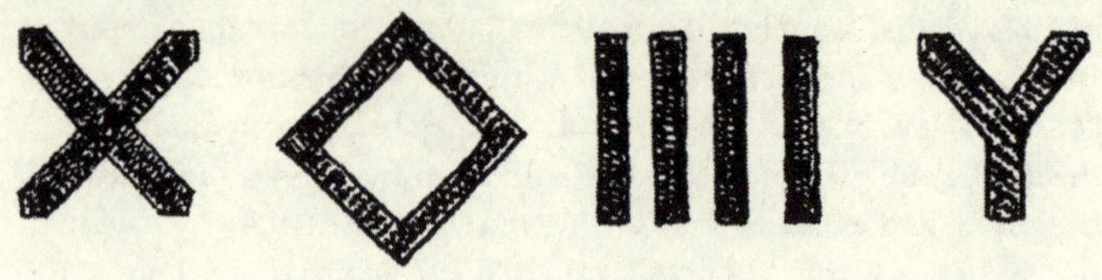

And with the same ease, they follow the radiant influence of the sun and see with their very special eyes bee violet, ultraviolet, and bee purple.

In the human hive, my friends, the male and female also note that it is customary to perpetuate the race via sexual union and even without real biological parents present and copulating (taboo in most societies), even without specific teaching (although a few couples have been amazed the *lying together,* in Biblical euphemism, just won't do the trick) the male and female learn to mate. And even if custom has confused the facts surrounding the begetting of children, attributing the mother's condition to mashed-banana ingestion, spoiled milk, a plague of warts, or spirits who invade the darkness of the hut, in a million thickets, in a million dwellings for several million years the penis of the mature male has nevertheless penetrated the warm caverns of the female body with demonstrable success. Some highly productive members of society (of both genders) have had prodigious sexual appetites (Catherine the Great and Goethe to mention two) while others like Michelangelo and St. Theresa of Avilà have, apparently, had none at all or so little that it is not worth noting. But many people, especially those who embark on the sort of marriage that is sanctioned in Judeo-Christian tradition – and here I am perhaps, letting my homosexual preference speak *(a pause for the consternation that would follow and a minute adjustment of the hips)* – enter the union with certain sexual expectations and end up enslaved in a system that is impoverished in terms of sensual pleasure and intellectual challenge.

There are those who must choose (or dare to choose) a lifestyle in which the biological family is not *prima facie.*

Let us remember ladies and gentlemen, the lives of nuns and monks, the sexless beings of our society. Their days are regulated by cycles of work and praise, eating and sleeping, speaking and being silent. The rhythms are prescribed through custom, just as in the bee colony there are undulations in productivity, passivity, communication and receptivity of the workers. Consider the habits and the cowls; consider the simple crucifixes and the white-washed walls; consider the simple meals of wine, bread and cheese; consider the sensuality of the murmured masses and the sexuality of self-confession; consider, my friends, the beauty of a holy touch upon an arm. No children to interrupt the flow, no possessive physical relations to disappoint and build distrust. *(Remembering the touch of wool upon his arm, remembering the heat of an embrace that was forbidden and did not occur then, Matthias looked again into the mirror and found rivulets of water.)*

Let us praise the men and women who live like monks and nuns, who have the pleasure of a simple solitary meal, who can regulate their pleasures and their play, and ask yourselves what is the price of sex within the framework society decrees as marriage (*Remembering the touch of him upon his arm, remembering the empty heat of the embrace that was forbidden but did follow, he looked into the mirror and found that the tears were in his eyes.)* Let us give thanks for the altruism of the sexless worker and praise the passion of their olfactory glands as they search out flowers, not sexual objects.

It is not my business here to convince you that you are bee-like, although I have occasionally outraged my audience so much that they have swarmed out of the room, making a bee-line for the exit *(humour now recovered, he paused for a smile),* but I wish to draw attention to the thing that you have, ladies and gentlemen, that you must be the most thankful for. The bee can think and reason and communicate with incredible skill but he/she can never say the equivalent of, 'Hell, find yourself another nurse,' or, 'I think I'll be a drone for a while,' or 'I think I'll live for a while with a more primitive set of bees' – although occasionally a clever queen will mate and live with a Bombus or with a drone of the genus Xylocopa who resembles the bumble bee but is less hairy, or with a tailor bee of the genus Magachile who makes wonderful cells from variously shaped pieces of leaves or with an elegant Osmia, the brilliant Augochlora, or one of the more sober (but more numerous) Andrena, or with anyone of species of genus Apis:

SPECIES	RACES	VARIETIES
Apis Indica, Fab.	A. dorsata nigripennis, Latr.	
Apis florea, Fab.	A. dorsata bicolor, Klug.	
Apis dorsata, Fab.	A. dorsata zonata, Smith	
		Carniolan or Krainer.
	A. mellifica nigra.	Heath.
	German bee.	Austrian.
		Common black.
Apis mellifica	China bee.	
	A. mellifica Adonsoni,	
	African bee.	
	et cetera ...	

And it is interesting, my friends, that in my favorite book on bees, *The Bee-Keeper's Guide,* A. J. Cook, Michigan, July, 1888, if one compares the indices for queen and drone:

queen, 82
  barren, 97
cage for, 242 & 266
candy for, 272
cell of, 87
figure of, 80
clipping wing of, 243
development of, 90
dollar, 271
eggs of, 84
eyes of, 85
fecundity of, 86
food for, 85
glands of, 98
how reared, 233
unfertile, 236
marketing of, 328
rearing of, 233
shipping of, 272
sterile, 97
trap for, 240
young virgin easily introduced, 233

drone, 100
antennae, 102
brood of, 105
characters of, 100
copulation of, 106
destruction of, 105
figure of, 104
food of, 105
development of, 100
figure of, 101
function of, 106
how to select, 240
longevity of, 105
mating of, 106
purity of, 107
testes of, 101
trap for, 241

one finds that the very bodies of these sexual beings are equated with money, that the behavior of these creatures must be controlled through traps and special rearing. Contrarily, with the worker the financial aspect is emphasized in regard to their products and they are seen not as individuals but as a collectivity. *(A pause for an appreciation of his brilliance would be appropriate and, perhaps, a small adjustment to his long black hair; a pause for reflection on the first time he had bought a boy, all pink and steaming, at the Olympia Baths and his desperate and furtive coupling there, overcome by the sickness of desire.)*

Man can reason himself in and out of many situations; he may even change his culture and his sex unless he lives in an oppressive non-modern society and/or dwells at times of war or stress, in which times the smallest decision may not be easily accomplished. To perpetuate patterns that go against an individual's will can produce vacuity of conduct at best and at the worst, madness and self-destruction. The bee colony, dear audience, eliminates anyone or anything that impedes the established cycles and the established order. In the human colony, I challenge you to question the mainstream cycles and bid you to indulge in only those to which you are individually suited, reinventing always the *possibilities* of your life.

In the human hive, ladies and gentlemen, the sexual effectiveness of the male and the female depends upon the ability they have to attract each other; in the hive the same factor plays its role.

In my experiments I have set up three tests with queens bred in our laboratories (see diagrams ensuing). I set out three drones in boxes, or traps, near the hives where they were bred and I placed Queen 1 in a cage within easy detection of their olfactory devices. In *test A*, you will observe, all three drones proceeded towards Queen 1 as directly as they could. In *test B* I placed Queen 2 in a cage, again within the males' easy reach, and you will notice from the material contained within the diagram that the drones made what seems to have been a choice between Queen 1 and Queen 2 that had nothing to do directly with the factor of distance. Finally in *test C*, I placed Queen 1 in rivalry with Queen 3 and all the drones of the experiment moved immediately towards her cage. We must conclude, then, that she was the most alluring of the three queens just as in life we observe that, if you'll forgive me, a number of females have a lion's share of the available lovers while others have few or none and this may be based upon something as simple as the females' ability to exude an aura of willingness, *je ne sais quoi* what fragrance equivalent to that which encircles Anaïs Nin in real life, or the Chanel No. 5 of Catherine Deneuve. I did not let the males in my experiment contact any queen because then their lives would have been over. As a reward for their co-operation I returned them to the hive where they could benefit from care and feeding until autumn came and they would be put to sting by the workers. For the drone even if he is lazy, even if he too is found by the queens at large to be unattractive (a fact that I have also made experi-

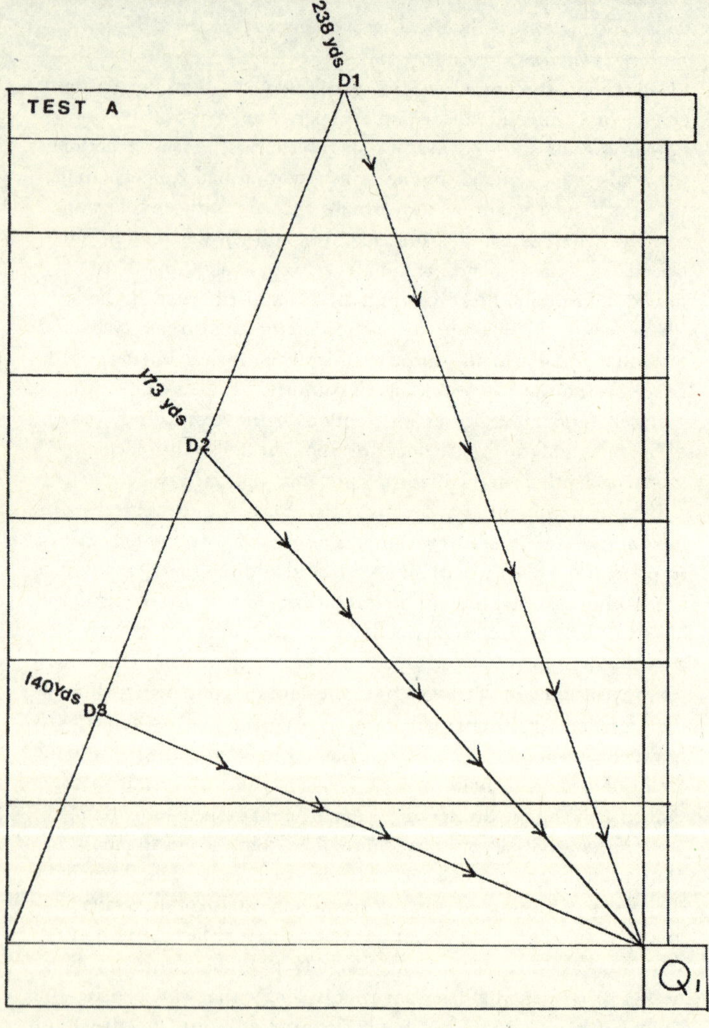

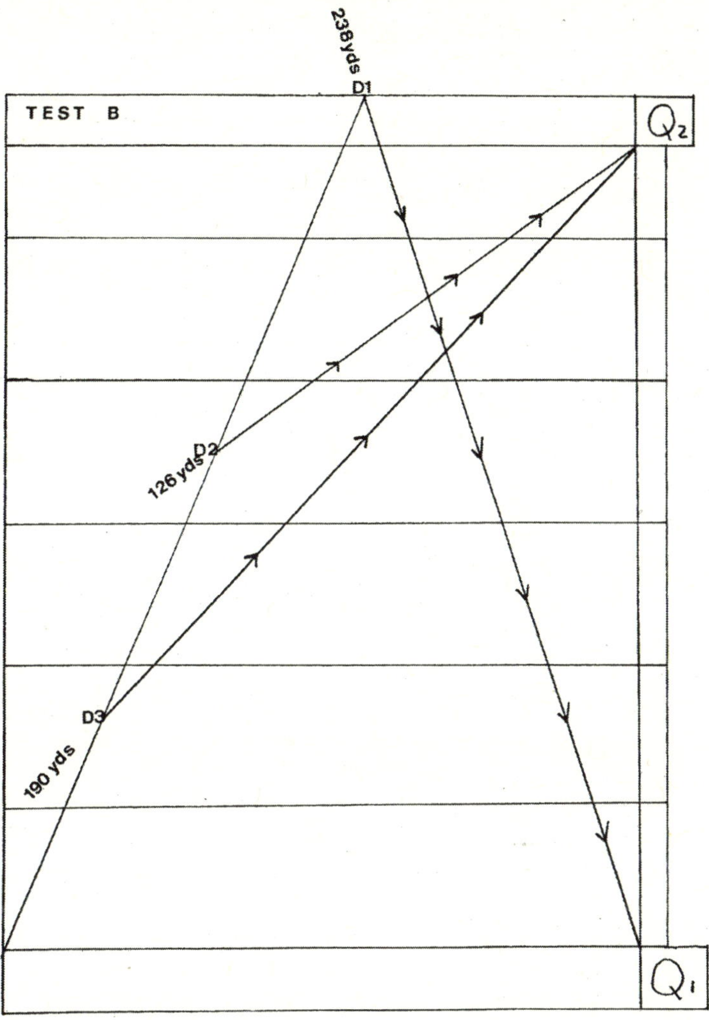

ments to prove) his life is made short and its quality defined by his masculine condition. The worker does not live long, but this sexless *she* is at the centre of everything – antennae stroker to the queen, she offers reassurance; chief architect of cells she is maker of the city; she is warrior brave and self-sacrificial. The sexless worker, oh hear, is

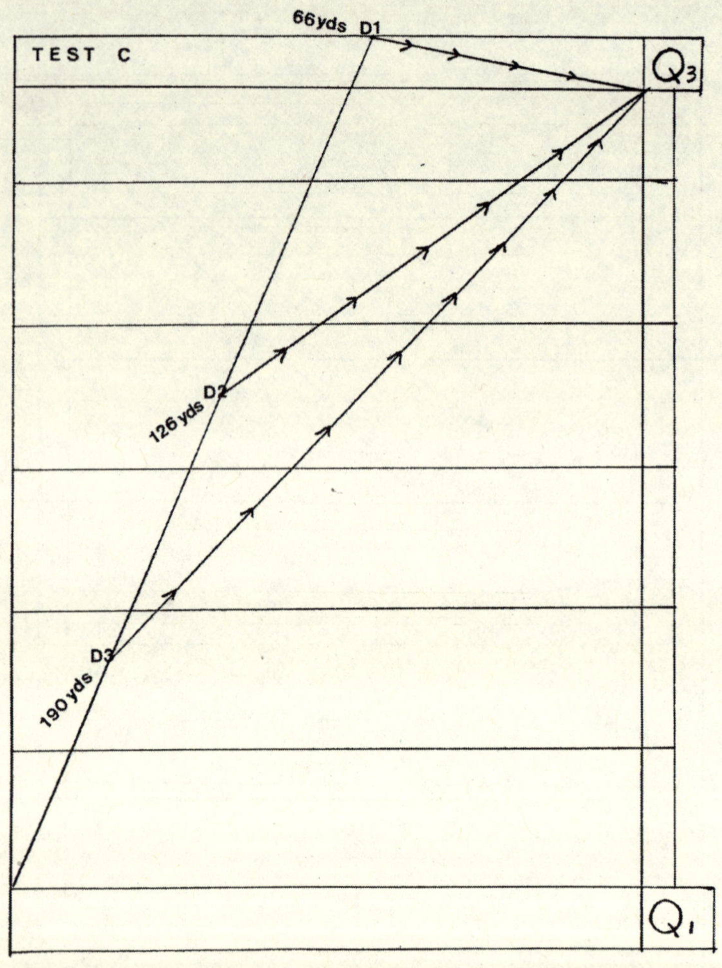

stroked and nuzzled a thousand times a day, her abdomen rubbed by a dozen workers seeking information and sustenance. She shines in the radiance of the sun as she searches with freedom and ingenuity for the nectar of a million flowers. I bid you to do the same. *(That would be the finish of the amazing speech and Matthias, shivering before his bathroom mirror, dressed, went off to meet Habella, roses in his hand.)*

After their customary short visit with Miss Kelly who lived upstairs from Habella in the Manhattan Apartments and after he had enquired about the whereabouts and health of her best friend Renata, their conversation began over halibut and salad.

'Are you feeling better now?' he tactfully enquired.

'Yes,' she said, 'I'm not pregnant.'

'Great news, Habella, I'm relieved for you, but please let me see you smile again; let me tell you a legend from the Koutomi – it should make you feel well off!'

'The Koutomi worship the magic of the stick. One day a warrior went into the woods and found a purple stick shaped exactly like an erect penis. "Oh ho,' he said, "I could use you to satisfy my wife. She makes me very tired."

"Oh no you won"t,' said the stick, "It's not that easy. If you take me off the tree, I won't be upright."

"Oh ho," said the warrior, "I could hold you while you do it.'

"Oh no," said the stick, "It's not that easy. I lack the proper water."

"Ah hah," said the warrior, "I'll make the water for you."

"He he hee," laughed the stick. "Then you'll be doing all the work and I'll be having all the fun."

'From this the Koutomi learned the meaning of laziness.'

'From this the Koutomi learned that the stick in the hand is not the same as the stick in the bush.'

'Eeck, eeyuck,' laughed Habella, 'though I'm hardly in the mood for that sort of joke, it did cheer me up.'

'But it's not a joke, Habella, it's a myth and therefore true. Come on, tell me how it was. I've always told you everything.'

'It happened so quickly, I don't know what to say except the excitement leading to it was better than the act itself, although I did get a little "Roargasm" ...'

'Hey, that's good for the first time – it suggests you aren't inhibited, however much your mother has tried ...'

'Matthias, that's not fair. Leave mother out of this. She's only trying to protect me ...'

'If you believe *that,* then *why* did you do it?'

'The music, the situation, his attractiveness – everything compelled me, maybe it was just like when you go to the steam baths, except I thought there was more between him and me. I wanted there to be more ... I need someone to be regular with ...'

'Then marriage is still on your mind, Habella.'

'Yes ...'

'Think it over ...'

'It's the only way for me ...'

'No it isn't.'

'Look, Matthias,' she insisted. 'Let me take my chances in the form I have chosen. I don't tell you how to live your life.'

'But you do disapprove of my habits and you do say what a pity it is that I'll never be someone's father. I am only saying don't rush into becoming a wife, it just won't suit you.'

'It's better than being a *queen*.'

'You'll see, Habella, you'll see that it's the same as being a queen. It's just a different pattern for the same kind of bondage. Break the patterns ...'

'Matthias, let's not talk about this any more. These are word games and I'd rather you'd tell me real word games – more myths, more myths!'

'Ok. Ok. Here are two more, the first to tease you:

'The Koutomi are related to the Suazi who view freedom as a menace. Here is the story of their first princess who knew how to ride on the backs of damsel flies until the day of her marriage to a man she thought she loved. After the wedding and the ritual sacrifice of dogs and pigs, and after the copious consumption of Kiwiwi, the couple copulated in the marriage tent. The princess said to the man she loved, "Now we have finished, I want to fly my damsel fly." "No, no," he said, "now you may only fly on me." "But I must," she said, "or the damsel flies will die of sorrow." He said, "If you fly on them, I'll die of sorrow." She said, "Then I will die so that neither you nor they will see me choose ill." "No, no," he said, "there is another way. I'll show the damsel flies you're mine and they will understand you have no choice and thus will take no offence. I will put a golden chain through your nose and tie you to the tentpost when I'm not at home." She did consent to this because where there is no choice there will be fidelity, and the damsel flies flew with the girls who were not yet prisoners of love.'

'The Suazi tribe have taken the damsel fly as a symbol of sexual dalliance. If a wife ever breaks her marriage chain she is accused of ukuki ne lamani *or "riding damsel" and she is stoned to death with coconuts.'*

'Here,' said Matthias, 'is another to please you.'

'No, please, no!' cried Habella, covering her ears.

'The Suazi also believe in male intercourse and begin the practice very young. It is a privilege to be chosen hirtutu *or initiator-of-the-boy. After the ritual sacrifice of toucans, this ancient story is told as a preface to the adolescent rite.'*

'The first boy of the second generation of the tribe was called Inuni. He kept a toucan as a friend and daily fed nuts into its scimitar bill. The elders invented the hirtutu-lemani *ceremony in tightly closed tents, chose the*

hirtutu *and called the boy to stand within the coconut circle on the day he was thirteen.* Hirtutu *who wore the mask of the wild boar to make him anonymous, thrust into the boy a ceremonial penis which covered his own and Inuni screamed in pain. His friend toucan carried him swiftly into the sky but the warriors shot down the bird and several men held the boy down so that* Hirtutu *could initiate the boy once more into* lemani. *When they were finished the boy sobbed, "Why did you kill my friend toucan, he of the brilliant feathers and saffron beak?" The men replied, "Toucan let you fly from our regular custom, he is enemy to the tribe."* (And so the adolescents submit to the rite and the toucan is put to death painfully by the tearing off of his powerful beak.)'

'Matthias,' Habella cried, 'You're very cruel.'

'No, I'm not being cruel, I'm trying to tell you to take care in choosing the customs you will follow. The Suazi, poor bastards, live in the middle of a jungle with coconuts and pigs for food and a vocabulary of fifty words to make known their needs. Here, learn the words that regulate their lives in the next five minutes!

riniki (food that walks – pigs, possums, armadillos)
trillimi (enemies that fly – toucans, insects, bats)
ukuku-ne (damsel – all evil, evil being any small infraction of tribal custom)
kiwiwi (hallucinogens, alcohol, mushrooms, smokes)
ukuku-le (un-damsel, non-damsel – all good, good being strict obedience to tribal custom)
lamani (to fly, the sexual act)
featu (all deeds involving pain or death)
beatu (all deeds involving pleasure and life sustenance)
intiti (boy or girl children)
hirtutu (initiated ones, boys after the *hirtuti-lemani*; girls after marriage)

'That's enough to give you an idea and you just string them together like little beads so that *riniki-featu* is 'kill food for supper', and if you know *ne* is *yes* and *le* is *no* you can say *leriniki-featu* or 'Don't kill food for supper' or you can make a double negative by placing together *le-intiti ne-ukuku-ne* to say 'children are not evil' or ...'

'Matthias, your cleverness is boring me. I want to talk about my feelings ...'

'No, you want me to encourage you to get married and I won't do it.'

'Please go, Matthias, I want to pack. I'm going to the island tomorrow. I'll feel better for the holiday and when I come back I promise I'll be better company.'

So home Matthias went to his quiet room, feeling more estranged from her than he had felt at any time during the year that he had known her. Feeling more strange to himself than ever before. Three days later he was delighted (at first) to receive this letter.

May 29, 1963.
Point No Point, Sooke, B.C.

Matthias my dear,
Just checked into the cabin overlooking the surf that we stayed in before. This resort is so much more magical in May than it was last September when we came with our Natural Science class. Point-No-Point, far from being the existential joke we thought it was, I know now is the precise point on the compass where I am located. In any event, this place makes the difficulties of the recent months simply vanish.

Almost immediately upon this second coming, I ran down through the gate marked 'private', descending into the labyrinths of paths as the maiden of old rushed into the maze, unsure but certain she would find the 'right way' to a perfect mating. So to the right, then, I went with the ocean's drum pounding its directive beats, down through and under the trimmed vaults of silver pine that sheltered the path, like two bodies bending towards each other endlessly in a hand-clasped-over-head gesture of celebration. Pine locking its many and delicate fingers and limbs into inextricable embrace with the limbs and fingers of shrubs – the Bearberry Honeysuckle overburdened with sticky yellow flower twins; the sturdy Hazelnut festooned with waving amber catkins; Syringa or Bridal Wreath whose grey-green leaflets brood over the buds that would become Orange Blossom in June. And to the waists of the pine-sentinels surged skirts of Salal – the Indian name generic for *plentiful shrub* – thick with leathern shiny leaves and bright at every interstice with rows of urn-shaped beads that by July would change from translucent pink to solid, edible purple fruit – Salal interwoven with a weft of spiney stems and the brazen magenta petals of the Wild Rose to perfect the garment of the marriage guard. And everywhere, Indian Paintbrush in multitudes nodded thick with scarlet at the pines' ankles.

At other points vaults of different floral composition threw up graceful arms over the path: Salmonberry intermixed with Goat's Beard (purple flower, whiskered berry and barbs thrust among pencils of white blooms) or emerald Kinnikinnick whose leaves when burned were one ingredient of an Indian smoke invaded by the wicked yellow needles of the Devil's Club, or Broom, magnificently multicoloured and pungent conjoined with the airy delicate-scented plums of Ocean Spray and the midnight lethal flowers of Deadly Nightshade. Everywhere brilliant marriages of the expected and the unexpected sang in praise of monogamy, polyandry and polygamy in sumptuous visual polyphony; everywhere the paths trimmed through the vegetation resemble the peaceful aisles of medieval churches and forced undisciplined fertile profusion into useful structure, much as the church brings restraint to the primitive polymorphous sexual urges by offering instinct the regulation of Holy Matrimony.

Further, the fragrant labyrinthine aisles offered to my ear an erotic concert, the Music of the Path: the whimpers of the crooning Wood Dove, the 'pruuummm, pruuummm, bruuummm' of grouse in percussive mating; the exhortive hoarse-voiced pleading of the coupled crows, the trills and whistles of countless other 'featherings' – expressed in high registers over the steady beat of the sea's drum and the variable droning of the foraging bees that clung like saffron oriental jewels to the lips and noses of flowers. Only in the Alder groves did the trunks whine and complain in minor as the wind pushed their heads and arms together in unwanted rubbing. Their bark bore resemblance to aging flesh, so I guess they were just too old for that kind of fun.

Anyway, Matthias, I just wanted to prove that the setting was *Primavera* with flora-virgins and fingerlocked dance, so that you would believe the miraculous could occur in this magic place. Further, you are the only one who knows the myth (and myths) I enacted in life this afternoon.

I lay naked in the sun, the surf pounding near my head and yet I heard, suddenly, a

'chop ... chop ... chop' too loud for a woodpecker.

'chop ... chop ... chop'. Again.

I knew it was someone mutilating a tree, so I rushed naked to the edge of the Alder grove and shouted: 'Stop, stop! You're cutting me!'

The noise ceased immediately and a voice called out, 'Who are you?'

I projected from my hiding place to my surprise, the words: 'Maba, Honey Mother, Spirit of the Honey.'

He replied, astonished, to my disembodied voice, 'How did you know that I search for Honey?'

To which I responded chidingly, 'Does the honey not know *danger* to its Spirit?'

Soon I felt safe enough to reveal myself to him, so stepped out naked from behind my cloak of Salal and the man gasped.

'Phew, you *are* a Honey. Can I marry you?'

'Well,' I said, remembering the condition of the South American Myth, 'You may if you never call me *that* name.'

'If not *Honey,* what shall I call you?' he asked.

'Habella,' I replied.

'Well, Habella, that's a deal. You may call me Fred.'

Anyway, I thought you might be amused by this news. I will, of course, keep you posted.

('Christ,' thought Matthias, 'She'll never learn.')
Matthias threw this letter into his drawer. Then, he decided to keep it as proof of her affection although he knew that their relationship was finished; he wished not to make a fool of himself by pursuing it now on anything other than a professional basis. 'Hirtutu-lemi trilimi-ne; le-intiti ne ukuku-ne, intiti beatune; Harpu riniki lemani-le, harpu ukuku-le,' he thought, as he flounced out the door to keep an appointment at the Chateau Gai. Rene waited him with a faultless smile. Rene from Eugene. Rene the machine.

'God, it's dark in here!' exclaimed Matthias, blinking in the smoky blackness.

'Thought you neveh come, I was gonna daynce with that spade oveh theyah,' grinned Rene.

'Knock it off, Rene, I'm really bushed, I need a friend tonight ...'

'You need a freyend, ah came to git layid. I know you're gonna give me a lotta shiyit about havin' a heaidayche, you intellectyalls are all the sayme. I suppose Habella's getting to you agayne. All I've eveh heard since I metcha is Habella, Habella, beginning to think you're not a fag, you're *bi* man, a chickshit fence-sitter. Look why don'cha put an ad in the *Georgeah Strayat*

Bi guy wants weekend fag, queens only need apply and straight chick for intellectshul talk in week handholding only, no one under I.Q. 160 need apply gd. lking not importent, vocal cords must be in good condision as must be brains.

'Ah, fuck you cayn write it better yerself. Comeon, let's dance, let's get it on!'

'No, you dance. I'll just sit around and watch. Maybe I'll feel like it in a while ...'

Rene leapt to his feet and hips bouncing, headed out into the dance floor. Unless he opens his mouth, thought Matthias, he really looks like a great find.

Having nothing better to do than to watch, Matthias made a number of diagrammatic impressions of the dance-floor activity where homosexuals, lesbians, inverts and transverts of both sexes jostled hopefully. In the centre of this hive was a Queen, outrageously dressed in tight pink pants and a silver afro wig. Around his eyes glinted a milky way of stars and towards him as though drawn like insects to a light, moved the bodies of the dancers. And just as in the dances of bees the closer to the recipient of the communication they were, the more intense the ass-

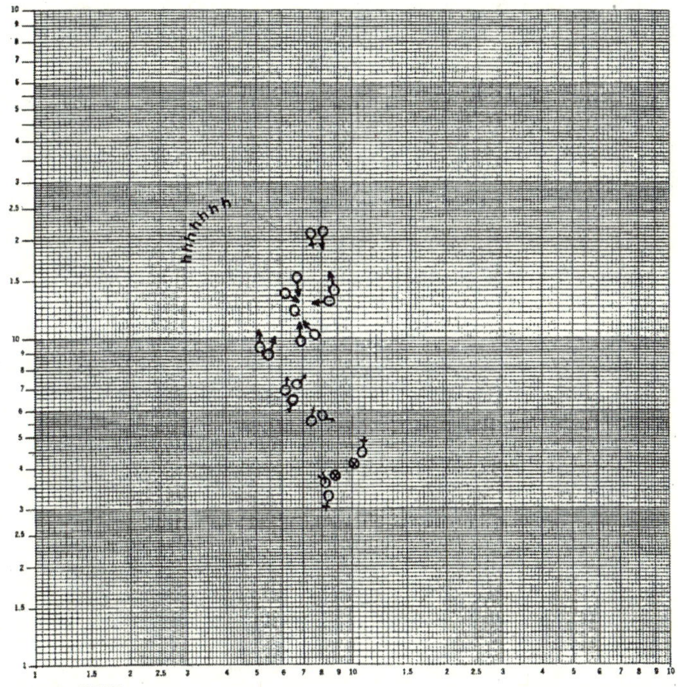

wiggling that accomplished the dance. The band, as always, was *fabulous*.

The moment after Rene insinuated himself into the embrace of the AFRO-QUEEN – hip grinding against hip, thigh rubbing against thigh – Matthias experienced a gentle conversion much like the one his biblical namesake had in the inn. He knew what he must do and would write Habella about it. Meanwhile he would move directly to Kamloops to take the only job he had been offered.

May 30, 1963.
Point No Point, Sooke, B.C.

Here I am again, sooner than I expected. It's 2 a.m. and Fred's just gone back to Jordan River where he is running some soil tests. We had lunch, supper and midnight snack together. He asked me if I wanted to make love and I said since we're to be married soon, let's wait.

So we are going to do it the old-fashioned way and for old fashioned reasons, like having children right away. He's the only person that I've met who thinks as I do that marriage will work if one understands its forms and conditions. So we will be embarking upon something like an arranged marriage, except that nature and fate conspired here – not dowry-mongering parents and because we don't know each other, we'll probably not bore each other. Besides he's really good-looking and very nice – a perfect specimen – and you know how much faith I have in solid breeding and even temperament. And as I have told you at 24 I'm ready to settle down to make the next generation. I know if you were here you'd fill my head with caution and ask me about *agape* and *eros*, sexual chemistry, and get me all confused in my head so that I cannot obey an impulse which seems more solid than any other I've had until this moment. Anyway come to our wedding a week next Saturday (oh, I can hear you clucking), please do this for me and Fred! Sorry, I'm just too tired to ask you, *exquisitely*.

P.S. Matthias, don't dress or act too gay at my wedding; you know how *conservative* mother is and how much weddings mean to her.

Matthias was angrier than he had ever been in his life.

The Virgin Becomes the Bride

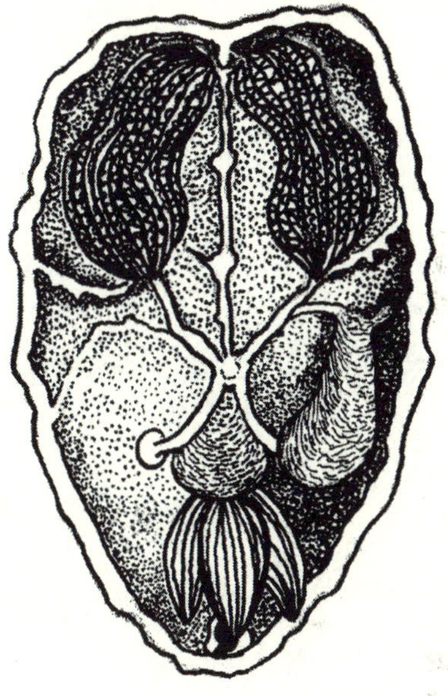

Friday June 8, 1963
Vancouver, B.C.

Dear Matthias
I'm not sure why I must write you so frequently, but I had a dream last night that the thread was broken. It came about in a curious way – this rupturing of the silken thread – for no wind troubled my dream, not even the delicate movement of my spoken breath. I was silent as I recalled the manoeuvres in our *war of murmurs.*

'My sea is ravelled up like grey silk,' you said.

'My lens reflects the Midas riches of the sun,' I replied.

'My waves could broil and surge to the beacon of a perfect moon,' you insinuated.

'Ah! But somewhere there are faerie lakes who have no greater lover than the wind,' I replied.

And my dream eye saw your mystic smile as we hugged our truce; my inner eye rejoiced in the recollection of our displaced espousal, our devotion to this land of gentle showers and peaceful greyness, where the viscid webs of spiders are hung with crystal drops, each morning; chains as delicate as gossamer, as strong as steel. So imagine, my friend, the sorrow that I felt when my dream brought me such a web, a bejewelled parabola between two dogwood blossoms that broke the silence with a *snap* so powerful that the tree shuddered its despair. I awoke in tears and the tears abraded my flesh like uncut diamonds. You are the only person I know who would understand me if I cried:

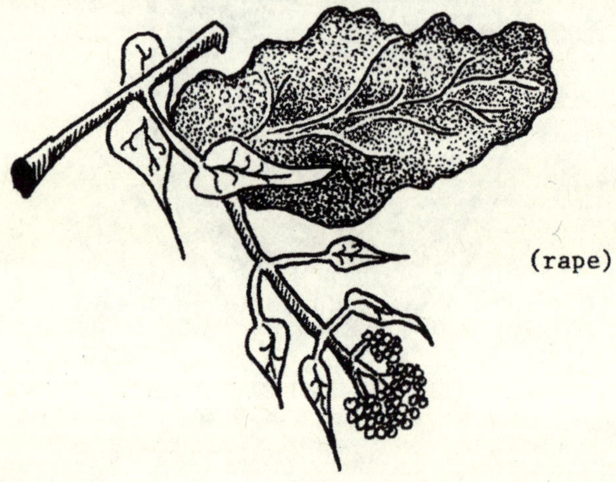

(rape)

For though I am yet an unravished bride, situations are being *forced* upon me. And I hope that just as our 'INVESTIGATIONS INTO HIVE ABNORMALITIES' brought and brings us a shared pleasure, especially the socio-biological bits that we amused ourselves with, that a similar delight might be found in comparing the habits of the *normal hive* with the heterosexually based mores of society. Despite your natural aversion to the topic, for the sake of science perhaps you would be willing to develop an interest. *Let me tease you.* You remember how we used to joke about what the queen bee could be doing as she lived through the interval between the time when she crunched her way out of her cell to dispatch her rivals and the moment of her wedding? Now I will give you some hints about the activities of her brief maturity.

In my case, Fred dispatched the other queens. There was no stinging, just a series of three phone calls to women with whom he was not seriously involved. The third was the most difficult for although Fred had come to Jordan River on business he had arranged to meet surreptitiously with a single lady whom he had been seeing for some time. His parents didn't approve of this match because Inez had a baby and when we are married he promised that he will see her no more. I know you'll be wondering 'Why not?' but I think that society is right when it insists on *mono-gamos* unions for, if you will forgive the pun, games played with the same partner are likely to improve the quickest!

In the last several days, however, I've been so frantic that I have scarcely had a moment *to think,* let alone to argue with myself. I have devised a Monday to Thursday account that will give you some idea of the ways in which I have seen the typical events and how I am experiencing a loss of ego which I'm sure will be repaired after the wedding when Fred and I are alone and I can be myself.

Do keep this 'play' I have written for your amusement against the day when we might wish to write a paper on the *Normal Hive.* I use the *third person* for an objectivity I don't quite feel. Enjoy! Enjoy! I think that fatigue often induces a distorted but otherwise correct perspective.

DRAMATIS PERSONNAE:

A BRIDE Habella Cire

A BRIDE'S MOTHER Mrs. Pilar Cire

A BRIDE'S FATHER Mr. Louis Cire

A MOTHER-IN-LAW Mrs. Martha Smith

A FATHER-IN-LAW Mr. Henry Smith

A BRIDESMAID Renata

THE GROOM Fred Smith

FEMALE CHORUS:

GREAT AUNT LUCINDA

THREE NEIGHBOURS

TWO GIVERS

A SISTER TO THE MOTHER-IN-LAW

A GOOD FRIEND

A CHILD

MALE CHORUS:
EIGHT BACHELORS
(the ninth is FRED SMITH)

Act One: Scene One

THE SETTING: The obligatory meeting between two pairs who have nothing in common except children intent on marriage takes place on a Monday afternoon at the home of the bride's parents. The home is a convenient box in which synthetics figure prominently in the furniture and decorations. The first scenes occur in a split-level stage where the upper part is 'living room' and the lower part is bar. An aluminum screen door decorated with a beaver is prominent at stage left. The action begins with Mr. and Mrs. Cire doing the last touches of the requisite tidying that precedes formal entertaining – emptying ashtrays; dusting the knick-knacks that cluster the false mantelpiece, the otherwise empty bookshelves, and the plastic vines in the planter under the glass-brick room divider. The style of the chesterfields, the coffee table is briskly and unrelentingly blond-wood no-style (floral covered). Wall to wall drapes in a maroon and green jungle pattern are a prominent feature and they are tightly – hermetically – drawn, for it is evening. A cabinet stereo plays Mantovani softly. The bride paces about smoking nervously. Steps are heard approaching the door. A five-bell chime calls loud and high. The parents hide their instruments of cleaning behind the curtains as the bride makes a falsely-leisurely way to the door.

HABELLA WITH MOCK SURPRISE (and speaking like a textbook on polite conversation): 'Ah, you must be Fred's mother and father, come in, *come in.* Mom and Dad, let me introduce you to Mr. and Mrs. Smith. Mr. and Mrs. Smith, these are my parents, Mr. and Mrs. Cire. Please excuse me now while I bring the tea and cookies ...' (She exits stage right through a plywood door.)

The two sets of parents now awkwardly shake hands. The men are dressed in sport coats and jackets and wear identical white shirts and ties. The women are wearing printed polyester in garish colours and sensible shoes. They have identical blue-rinsed *perms* (so freshly done that they smell). Mrs. Cire is very fat and Mr. Cire is very thin; Mr. Smith is very fat and Mrs. Smith is very thin.

Jack-Spratt-could-eat-no-fat-and-his-wife-could-eat-no-lean.

MRS. CIRE TENTATIVELY TO MRS. SMITH: 'Fred's such a good boy, I'm sure he and Habella will be very happy!'

MRS. SMITH TENTATIVELY TO MRS. CIRE: 'Habella's such a clever girl, I'm sure she and Fred will be well-suited!'

MRS. CIRE WITH ANXIOUSNESS IN HER VOICE BUT A SMILE ON HER FACE: 'It's a quick decision, so it won't be the nice proper wedding I'd have liked.'

MRS. SMITH WITH AN EDGE TO HER VOICE BUT A SMILE NEVERTHELESS: 'I think girls ...'

MR. SMITH INTERJECTS DRYLY: ' ... these days have the upper hand. They always did, Martha. *They always did.*' MR. CIRE LAUGHS HEARTILY AT THIS UNTIL HE IS BOWDLERIZED BY A GLANCE FROM PILAR. NEVERTHELESS HE VENTURES TO OFFER THIS REMARK FOR CONSIDERATION: 'In the old days when we were young courting took so long, too long – you never know someone until you marry ...'

MRS. CIRE TESTILY: 'Louis, that's a stupid thing to say, if I hadn't *known you* I wouldn't have married you, and I think that people of our generation have good marriages and stay together because we *did* know each other.'

MR. CIRE RETREATING UNDER HIS EYEBROWS IMPLIES THE REVERSE OPINION ON BOTH SUBJECTS.

The two pairs lower themselves now on the two couches. They take a good deal of time getting their legs arranged just right – for comfort and for modesty. In this period the women wear their skirts quite short but still have to contend with girdles and stockings or garterbelts and stockings and so it is very difficult to appear socially presentable, particularly if one is plump. The four face each other earnestly, now, over an empty coffee table. After a shuffling pause, Habella appears stage right with *tea* and places the elaborate filigreed service on the table. As she passes her mother she whispers to her anxiously.

MRS. CIRE LOOKS VERY OFFENDED THEN MOVES TO CENTRE STAGE

WHERE THE AUDIENCE BECOMES THE EAR FOR HER SUBJECTIVE OUTPOURING WHICH IS DELIVERED AS THOUGH IT IS ONE SENTENCE WITH A MARVELOUS COMBINATION OF HYSTERIA AND EARNEST REASONABLENESS. THE SPEECH IS VERY LONG AND MRS. CIRE MUST CONSTANTLY TUG AT HER GIRDLE, AND FAN HERSELF AGAINST HER SELF-IMPOSED HEAT:

'Yes I will tell little-girl stories if I want to, you'll always be my little girl and when you have children of your own you'll understand and anyway you were so cute when you were young and wore your hair so nice, not long and untidy like you do now, and anyway I was just about to tell Mrs. Smith about the day you tried to revive all the dead bees in the house by giving them honey and how I sent a photograph to the newspaper and how *The Sun* printed your picture with the caption *Bee Mother Gives Honey to The Dead* which made you angry though lord knows why, for I'm sure Mrs. Smith would love to see it and I'm sure she'd be interested because it was the first indication that *I* had that you were going to be a scientist and I said at the time and I'm sure Mrs. Smith would understand, "Why don't you train to be a nurse because it'll give you some practice for being a wife and mother," but you wouldn't hear of it then, though you may regret it now and I was going to show Mrs. Smith the picture of you dressed all in pink when you played *Sarabande* at the concert – I made the dress myself and it really did drip dry, just as the saleslady at Eaton's promised when I bought it, Habella got chocolate or something all over the skirt never did understand how she could have sat on chocolate at a concert for we never allowed her to eat candy it was one of the rules in the house, one of the many rules that taught her the discipline she needed to get through college and I'd like to show Mrs. Smith the nice pictures of you in all your classes when you were a little girl smiling so nice and being so pleasant to everyone, and the photos of you at the cottage with your friends – you remember Ned, the boy who was always raking the leaves and how you enjoyed swimming all the time and bringing me tadpoles, the awful wiggling things, and I can tell you Mrs. Smith, Habella has had the benefit of a really close family, a loving family and so I do think that Fred is getting a real bargain, a wife who really knows how to stick at things to make things work just like her father and me have stuck at our marriage and learned together how to grow vegetables and how to make do like all good couples must, and though I'm not sure how Fred will manage to cook for himself if Habella insists on taking a job but I'm sure the family will come along soon to take care of that question, though I suppose nursing would have been a better thing to fall back on if times get rough again or if Fred's father's business falls apart but I suppose if that happens they'll cope just as we have all done through thick and thin making compromises and sacrifices and saving our pennies and taking the good with the bad and helping our young ones not to make mistakes, so that it is a relief, Mrs. Smith, to have our daughter marry while she is pure we just never liked it that Habella moved out to her own place with her friend Renata, so we followed her here just to keep an eye on her and I'm sure if you'd had a daughter you'd have done the same and fortunately Mr. Cire could transfer to a different branch of the company where he has worked for so many years and do the same job here that he was doing in Ontario ...'

Mr. Cire mumbles something that can almost be heard about the *ancient regime* of boredom, as he ushers Mr. Smith downstairs to the 'bar' where they can be alone to have a little drink and a man to man chat. As Pilar excuses herself to bring the photo album, Mrs. Smith has ample opportunity to note, touch, feel, show signs of amazement at the correct accoutrements of the bride's home: the Simpson Sears' 'oils' in ornate frames with individual lights, the wall to wall acrylic broadloom, the dark-green and blood-red drapes, the artificial wood grain panelling on the wall behind the mantel and the tasteful glow of the artificial fire that Mrs. Cire switched on as she left the room to 'make things more cozy.' When Mrs. Cire returns with her naugahyde book of photos, Mrs. Smith is feeling 'kindly disposed' towards her and they sit knee to knee like schoolgirls twittering and giggling. Then words like 'darling!' and 'dimples,' phrases like 'awful little boys' are answered by 'pretty,' 'sweet,' and 'boys will be boys' from Please-call-me-Martha and Please-call-me-Pilar. And while the rumble of jovial male voices is heard from the 'bar' below, it is time for Martha to deliver her centre-stage monologue on the upbringing of boy-children to which Pilar listens with as much attention as she can spare from the examination of her painted fingernails.

MARTHA SPEAKS IN SUCH A WAY THAT INDIVIDUAL WORDS HAVE LITTLE IMPORTANCE. HER MESSAGE IS REALLY THE ACRONYM OF THE WORDS SHOUTED WITHIN THE FRAMEWORK OF HER NON-LOGIC:

'I think that BOYS are more difficult. We GALS even as tiny girls never dARE to talk so loud. Fred rARElу picks up his clothes. I've MADE a real point of being SUGAR sweet when he asks but I'm OF course not able to make AND do just every thing. He's a PUPPY, really, so he hopes to SPICE up his life by marrying. DOGS have more respect for hANDS than Fred's got for gals. TrAils his dirty shoes over EVERYTHING NICE I have. Some GIRLS are workers and then GUYS depend on it. I know we ARE similar gals and housetasks ARE our lives we are SUGAR in our men's coffee. I MADE a decision to help Fred AND Henry with the books, I OF course don't let it stop SPICE cake from being made. SNAILS are part of the soil AND I don't mind business AND books as long as I can get EVERYTHING NICE and keep PUPPY DOGS' TAILS clean.

In front of the bar on the lower part of the set, the men's voices become audible as they proceed with mutual inquiries. The women have returned to their knee-to-knee examination of the photo album in the living room above.

MR. SMITH ADDRESSES MR. CIRE OVER THE RIM OF HIS GIN AND TONIC: 'I understand that Habella's background is Spanish and French. *Cire* ... hmmm ... unusual name that! Not from Quebec, are you?'

MR. CIRE TO MR. SMITH WITH THE CONFIDENCE OF ONE WHO HAS THE RIGHT ANSWER: '*Cire's* quite a common name in Tournai where my family came from two generations ago. They were candlemakers. And Pilar? Well, her family came from Barcelona in 1910. She was born here.'

MR. SMITH TO MR. CIRE: 'I understand that you've been with the same company for thirty years. *Wesson Wesson and Pinkum,* the insurers?'

MR. CIRE TO MR. SMITH AGAIN: 'Yes, I had to make a commitment to the first job I could get. Things were difficult after the war, but I've worked my way up – office boy to manager of the typing pool and in another twenty years I'll be retired. I call my job my second marriage. Gardening's my real interest, and yours too from what I've heard ...'

MR. SMITH TO MR. CIRE LOOKING QUITE HAPPY NOW: 'Not exactly an interest, a *business* you might say. I took the little property my parents left me and sold it; went into peat moss and rape weed with a little soil-mixing on the side. Martha helps me a little with the books when she's not polishing and scrubbing and Fred's learning the ropes. He's got a degree in business management but what really matters is the weather. If it's rough, business is rough. He's a good boy, a friendly puppy of a boy, and it's the experience that counts when you're running a small firm.'

Mr. Cire touches his rye and water to the rim of Mr. Smith's gin and tonic. They together inspect the guppy tank near the bar then walk slowly (reluctantly) to join the womenfolk upstairs where discussion is turning to the wedding itself. Habella hovers on the edge of this 'conversation' nervously awaiting Fred. Her opinion has no place in these deliberations.

MRS. CIRE ASSERTIVELY: 'Habella wanted an outdoors wedding, but we said *no* to that, after all it's not traditional and we want things to be done just right so we've booked St. Amboise where we know a priest who knew Habella when she went to St. Paul's who did not ask her whether she'd been to church since then, and of course she'll wear white and a veil and her friend will wear pink and so that leaves us with a little time to colour-co-ordinate, I was thinking of wearing pale green with white flowers and I suppose you could wear whatever you want but I personally think that a darker shade of green with red flowers would be the only thing appropriate because Habella insists on carrying red roses although I've told her that they don't go with pink, so perhaps you could make it look planned by introducing a spot of red? And we've rented the church hall for the reception and we're not having a real band, we can't afford it and the men, of course, will wear tuxedos – *black* ones and Martha I'll be sending the invitations out today. Oh, it's been a rush to get things done in the proper way. Just look over the list to see if there is anyone you'd like to add and do be on time, please, because there is another wedding booked for twelve-thirty and I'm wondering if Fred can be counted on to be on time for he's half an hour late *now.* Habella, where is that boy?'

Fred ignores the door bell and knocks instead. Habella rushes to the door and flings her arms about him. He disengages her in deference to the present company and soon Mr. Cire leads him to a couch in order to make him more comfortable.

MR. CIRE IN A FATHERLY VOICE: 'Tell me, my boy, did you meet Habella at college? I've forgotten to ask how you two got together?'

FRED BLUSHING: 'No, I just bumped into her in the woods at Point-no-Point. I was doing some business for my father at Jordan River ...'

MR. CIRE HEARTILY: 'Wonderful! Wonderful! The woods are as good a place as any to meet. Your father tells me you play bridge. We can all play bridge together!'

FRED CORRECTS HIMSELF GOOD-TEMPEREDLY INTO THE MARRIAGE MODE: 'Sure, I'll ... we'll play. Sure. After the honeymoon.' Mr. Cire turns to Mrs. Smith, now, with a conviction that is amazing and warmly shakes her hand.

MR. CIRE OFFERS HIS CONGRATULATIONS: 'Mrs. Smith, you've got a fine boy there and Mr. ...'

MR. SMITH INTERJECTS: '*Henry.* Call me Henry.'

At the end of the evening all is sweetness and light. The parents learn to call each other by their first names: Henry and Martha; Louis and Pilar. It does not matter that Henry calls Louis *Lewis* or that Pilar calls Henry *Henri*. The first exercise in the polite formulae of weddings is complete. The next follows with unmerciful swiftness.

Act One: Scene Two

THE SETTING: It takes place in the same 'room' but the decoration is changed slightly to give the effect that it belongs to a neighbour of grandmotherly age. Crocheted afgans are thrown over the chesterfields to protect them from use. The coffee table is draped with a lace runner and decorated with a large bouquet of red and yellow plastic tulips. The wall-to-wall drapes are drawn back to reveal wall-to-wall venetian blinds, tightly clenched shut. The mantlepiece is unrecognizable now under a clutter of doilies and family photographs. The room is festooned with crepe-paper ribbons and Kleenex flowers. It has a different aluminum screen door with a design of rampant moose.

When the action begins several women are seated already on the chesterfields. They are of varying ages and physical types but all wear the same polyester pant suit in different colours – even old Aunt Lucinda who sits in her wheelchair by the fireplace. Four women rush in from the kitchen door (stage right) bringing the chairs from the kitchen chrome set. They place them in such a way that the chesterfields are now a part of a ring of seats. Finally, the last woman emerges from the kitchen, bearing a rocking chair whose splats are covered with aluminum foil. All the women cheer and clap. The preparations for the Tuesday shower are complete.

The suspense builds as the women group and regroup themselves excitedly. Suddenly there is a slam of a car door and the sound of stiletto heels clicking up the walk and then, up the stairs to the door. The women scramble quickly for their seats in the circle with cries of, 'She's here! She's here! Turn off the lights! Turn on the tape!' The bride is ushered into the centre of darkness by her maid. *The Wedding March* peals forth. The lights go on. The bride is led to her tinsel throne of-the-empty-hearth. She blinks stupidly in the sudden brightness. There are cries of 'Ohhhhhh' and 'Ahhhhhhh' as the bride removes her shawl revealing a low-cut, high-waisted, very short floral print dress. Her maid is wearing a black sheath. Both wear pointed-toed high-heeled sling-backs. The women squeal and gather around as if to sniff the virgin flesh. The hug and pinch them both. They retreat to the circle of seats and as the bride sits upon her throne, she pulls her skirts down against the glint of ten pairs of curious eyes.

GREAT AUNT LUCINDA SPEAKS IN A RASPING LARYNGEAL CROAK, HER FALSE-TEETH LISP TRANSPOSING THE 's's' to 'f's', EIGHTEENTH CENTURY STYLE: 'Here, Niece, take my Handkerchief, prithee now, if you can find nothing elfe to cover your Nakednefs. If you knew what a Fulfome Sight it was I am fure you would not go fo bare: I can't abide your Naked Breasts heaving up and down; it makes me Sick to fee it.'

HABELLA INSTINCTIVELY PLAYS THE PART OF ANTONIA FROM MANDEVILLE'S 'THE VIRGIN UNMASKED', REPLYING WITH THE BEST LOGIC AVAILABLE: 'Oh, Auntie! 'Tis so hot, I can't endure a thing about me neck!'

GREAT AUNT LUCINDA PERSISTS IN SOTTO VOCE: 'Harkthee, Habella, thofe little pretences won't pass upon your Aunt, t'int the Heat of the Weather, 'tis the Heat of your blood, your Wantonnefs, and Lafcivious Thoughts, 'tis they, that are the Caufe of your immoderate Behaviour ... Fafthion and Cuftoms I know have alter'd with the Times; fometimes People have worn long Cloaths, fometimes fthort ones; but never have I heard or read of an Age before this where they did not have fome Cloaths to cover the bofom. Now-a-days, the very Virgins that fhould be the temples of Modefty, flaunt their bodies half naked....'

HABELLA RESPONDS IN KIND: 'Desist, Auntie! When fashion dictates veils, I'll wear them!'

GREAT AUNT LUCINDA PERSISTS IN KIND: 'Fuppofe your stays were cut as low as your Navel, pray would you fhow it? Women in ftrictnefs fhould never appear in Publick but Veil'd; at leasft Young Women fhould never fhew their faces to any Men, just their neareft Relations. You're getting like Betty with her great Dugs broiling over the Fire, fhe would hide them if fhe could! And another thing, your mother tellf me the Groom has a Beard, I hope he'll cut it off before ye are Church'd!

HABELLA ASKS THE ONLY POSSIBLE QUESTION: 'Would ye exclude, Auntie, Moses and the Prophets from me wedding?'

To the bride's throne now come three contingencies of women who make the identical speeches in trios, making sure that the names that identify their individuality are audible:

TRIO ONE: THE WIVES 'It's wonderful that you're marrying a man who's in his father's business. When I got married SAM PETER JOHN was unemployed, we didn't have two cents to rub together. Marriage is just great, you'll see. There's always someone to come home to, to share things with.'

TRIO TWO: THE GRANDMOTHERS-BEFORE-THEIR-TIME 'So you're getting married now! Never thought you would. You're so much later than the other girls we know. Why, in about ten years I'll be a grandmother the way LINDA SUSAN MARY is growing up so fast! I guess we'll meet your young man later, after the honeymoon. Your mother's just tickled pink and oh so busy, poor thing.'

TRIO THREE: THE RELATIVES 'So glad you've found someone reliable to marry. You'll be glad you don't have to go out on dates looking for the right man. Oh, it's so exciting, I'd give anything to be in your shoes but never mind, I've had my fun!'

A small child comes and sits on the bride's knee. Her face is flushed with the pleasure of being included with the adults. She kisses the bride and goes back to her place in the circle. Now the white basket overflowing with gifts is placed at the feet of the bride and the women caution her to open each offering with care, being careful in particular to preserve the ribbons. The bride knows that she must betray only pleasure as she receives each gift. She must 'Ohhhhhh' and 'Ahhhhh' then pass each around for individual inspection. She must fail to respond to the undercurrents of envy the rite inspires. The circle of women grows quiet and their eyes glimmer as they await the first selection; as they await the snip of scissors, the sound of scotch tape being ripped from reluctant cardboard, the rustle of tissue paper, the first ×+−← of delight.

Silence now, as the first gift is opened. It is a copper ashtray.

THE BRIDE (TENTATIVELY): 'How nice, How N I C E!'

THE BRIDESMAID (INAUDIBLY): 'How awful. How perfectly awful!'

A NEIGHBOUR (CHEERFULLY): 'Pretty! Just like the one I have at home!'

THE GIVER (UNGRACIOUSLY): 'Hummmph! Expect you to use this. You smoke too much!'

A NEIGHBOUR (CURIOUSLY): 'Doesn't copper smell when you use it for an ashtray?'

THE MOTHER OF THE BRIDE: (Takes offence).

THE-MOTHER-IN-LAW-OF-THE-BRIDE BRISTLES: 'It's rude for women to smoke!'

GREAT AUNT LUCINDA: (IN SOTTO VOCE) 'Fmoking if Lewdnefs!'

A NEIGHBOUR (PEEVISHLY): 'I'd like it in blue.'

THE MOTHER-IN-LAW'S-SISTER WHO IS HOPING TO LEARN WHETHER HABELLA IS PREGNANT INQUIRES OF THE BRIDE'S MOTHER: 'Does your daughter always have such high colour?'

A GOOD FRIEND WISHES THE SHOWER WAS OVER.

THE CHILD SINCERELY: 'I like the wrapping better than the prethent!'

There is silence now as the second gift is opened. Everyone gasps and giggles as the bride reveals the precious relic. It is a cloth diaper folded into a correct triangle. The crotch is smeared with mustard. It is passed.

THE BRIDE THINKS 'HOW CRUDE' BUT SHE SAYS HEARTILY: 'H O W FUNNY. H O W *V E R R R Y F U N N Y !*'

THE BRIDESMAID GRUNTS (SOTTO VOCE): 'I'd like to throw up.'

A NEIGHBOUR (JOKINGLY): 'Just like the ones I've got at home, only mine stink!'

THE GIVER (TEASINGLY) WHO IS THE MOTHER-IN-LAW'S SISTER: 'Thought I'd show you what you'll be needing soon!'

A NEIGHBOUR (CURIOUSLY) 'I thought paper diapers were *in* now?'

THE MOTHER OF THE BRIDE PUFFS UP HER FEATHERS LIKE AN ANGRY BIRD.

The mother-in-law of the bride is the seventh person in the circle and the recipient of the magic gift. The diaper tells her she will be a grandmother soon and she hopes it won't be sooner than she expects.

GREAT AUNT LUCINDA (GROWLINGLY): 'Thif if obfcene.' (And she is right.)

The third gift is passed in reverential silence. It's a *lazy susan.*

THE BRIDE (CURIOUSLY): 'How does it work?'

THE BRIDESMAID (CONDESCENDINGLY): 'When you twirl it, silly!'

A NEIGHBOUR (ABSENT-MINDEDLY): 'Pretty!'

THE GIVER (PROUDLY): 'It's just the latest thing!'

A NEIGHBOUR (WICKEDLY): 'Why didn't you get one with *a motor?'*

THE MOTHER OF THE BRIDE (HAPPILY): 'I'd like one of those!'

THE-MOTHER-IN-LAW-OF-THE-BRIDE WISHES HABELLA WOULDN'T SMOKE IN PUBLIC AND SIGNALS HER DISPLEASURE BY MAKING FRANTIC WAVING MOTIONS IN THE BRIDE'S DIRECTION.

A NEIGHBOUR (HONESTLY): 'I'd have preferred it in red.'

GREAT AUNT LUCINDA (ADAMANTLY): 'I know Lazinefs to be a fin againft God, but who if thif Fufan yer fpeaking about?'

The next gift that's passed is anonymously given. It is a marriage manual by Jan Echenlöbe published in 1961. It has already sold 500,000 copies 'so it must be good.' The ladies who can bear to touch the book exclaim, 'Who could have thought of *such a thing* when we were young!' or, '*We* had to learn things the hard way!' But the bride knows that her maid, always concerned with her sexual education, bought it at the drug store under the Manhattan Apartments and she is grateful for she would not have had the nerve herself and she looks around her satisfied that everything is going according to custom, knowing that showers are as important to society's recognition of her impending change of state as are the banns published in the churches and suddenly as the voices of the women mingle (for no one was talking to her) she visualizes the progress from Lemur to man and wonders if it *was*.

COMPARATIVE TABLE OF INDIVIDUAL DEVELOPMENT IN PRIMATES

Species	Length of Pregnancy	Status at Birth	Period of Dependency on Mother	Learns To Walk	Suckled for:	Capable of Social Independence	Sexual Maturity	Social Organization	Longevity*
Lemur	111, 145 days (two species); multiple births; other primates usually single	Relatively very large, mature, with senses functional	A few hours or days	Within first week, usually	Several days or a few weeks	Within a few weeks	Within a year	*Tarsius* in pairs; but some lemurs are gregarious	25 years
Monkey	Marmoset, 150 days; macaque, 163 days; rhesus, 166 days	Relatively large, mature, with senses well developed	A few days or weeks	Within first month, usually	Several weeks	Within 2–4 months	Within 2 or 3 years	Mostly gregarious; harem-forming in some baboons	15–45 years, depending on species
Ape	Gibbon, 209 days; chimpanzee, 235 days	Relatively very small and helpless, with senses partly functional	3–6 months	Within 6 months, ordinarily	Several months	Within 12–18 months	Within 8–12 years	Gibbon: family bands; orang: ?sexes apart except at mating; chimp: bands of 4–14 (av. 8.5); gorilla: groups of 2–4 nests; maximum known 16	25–45 years, depending on species
Man	266 days	Relatively small and helpless, with senses partly functional	At least a year	Within 18 months, usually	1–2 years	Within 6–8 years	Within 10–14 years	Exogamous family groups within larger societies	Depends upon time† and country; in U.S. a male born now may expect to live 67 years; a female, 72 years
Trend from lemur to man	Lengthening of the period of gestation	Smaller, more helpless and immature	Dependency increases	Longer time needed to learn to walk	Length of suckling extended	More time needed to achieve social independence	Puberty progressively delayed	Tendency for family to emerge in higher primates	With human culture, longevity distinctly increases over infrahumans

TABLE 2
Lift-histories of the Castes

Weeks	Days	QUEEN	WORKER	DRONE
	1	egg laid	egg laid	egg laid
	2			
	3			
	4	hatch	hatch	hatch
	5			
	6		diet changed	diet changed
1	7			
	8			
	9	sealing	sealing	
	10			
	11			sealing
	12	5th moult		
	13			
2	14		5th moult	
	15			
	16	emerges		
	17			5th moult
	18			
	19			
	20			
3	21	mature		
	22		emerges	
	23	mates		
	24			
	25			emerges
	26			
	27			
4	28			
	29			
	30		flies	
	31	begins to lay		
	32			
	33			
	34			
5	35			
	36		mature	
	37			
	38			mature
	39			
	40			
	41	stale if not mated		
6	42		foraging begins	
8	—			dies, if not already slain
			foraging for 5-6 wks. (rough average)	
12	—		dies	
		dies after several years or is replaced		

(It was too late to be *infra-human,* and the life-style of the bee was beyond question.)

Upon her now impinge a dozen remarks:

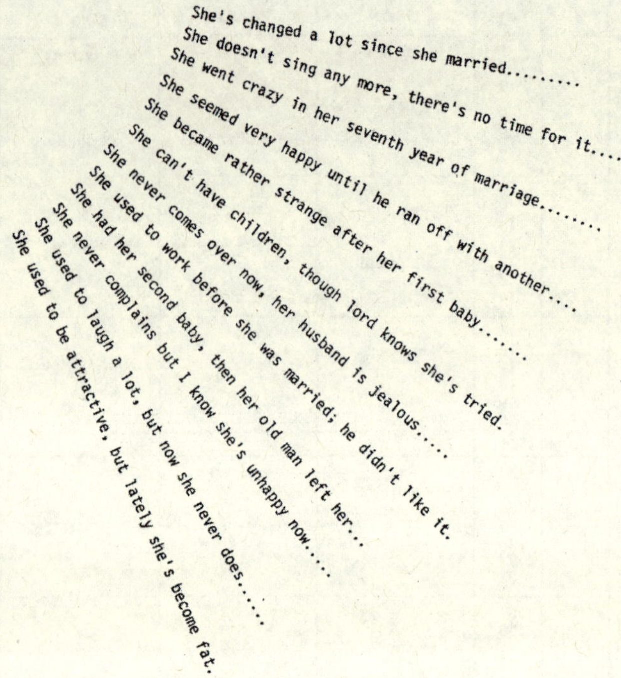

She resented her future being discussed. For she knew, Matthias, that you were probably right and the play that grew in her mind was not very playful.

Matthias, please help me. I am struggling to understand the impulses that I dared not act out. Suddenly, as I sat in the midst of the riches – the towels and the sheets, the ashtray and the lazy susans (oh yes, there were two), the Waterford crystal casting rainbows on my hands as I poured nervous tea from the Sarabande service that was the surprise gift of the group (a terrible allusion, my friend, one that I could *not tell even you*) – I had the impulse to strip off my clothes and descend the staircase of my mental set Duchamp-style creating:

Act One: Scene Three
THE SETTING: A Spotlight is on the brief steps to the lower stage.

The women crouch in the darkness below snuffling and grunting like wolves, licking and smelling each other. Howling and gnashing their teeth, growling and panting in exaggerated anticipation:

arrahhhh, arrrahhh, hrhrhrhrh, arrahhhh, arrahhh, hrhrhrhrhr

rhkrhkrhkrhk, huh huh huh huh, rhkrhkrhkrhk, huhuh, huhuh, huh,

graak, grrh, gruhrak, grgrgrarrah, uhrrraah, uhrraaah, hi hi hi ...

The snarls and graaks now keep time to the burlesque tune of your choice:

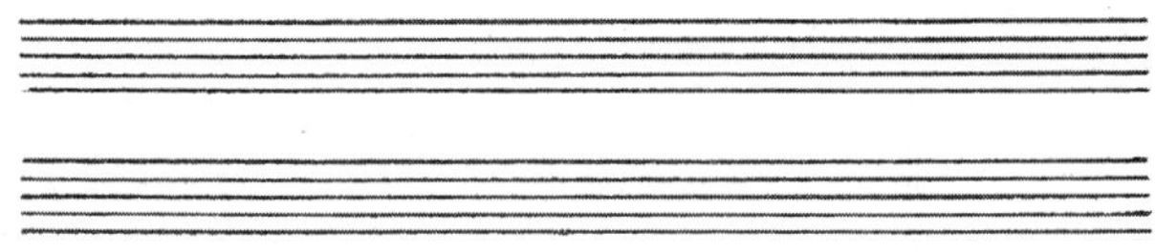

The Bride's legs are illuminated by the spot-light as she begins her journey downwards, she tosses her stiletto heels to the pack below at just the right moment to emphasize a bump, the garterbelt and stockings next to the beat of a grind. Her necklace, earrings, her dress, her stole follow in the right rhythms. (The panting and grunting of the beasts changes into pathetic whines and moans

nninininnai, grai, grai, mmmmmmai, n-n-n-n ai, Nai, mmmmmmmmmmmm,

grgrgrmmmm, mmmmmmai, n-n-n-n ai, hiyiiiiii, hiyai, Hyai, n.n.n.n.,

nninininnzi, grai, hiyiiiii, n.n-n.n-n., aiai, NNNNNGRRRRAI III

as the climax of the striptease comes) with the tossing of the underpants, and a tossing of each leg as preface to a jerky descent to the beat and bounce of more

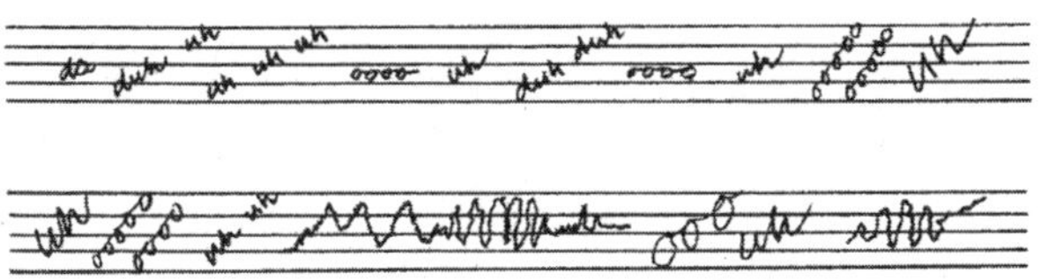

THE BRIDE SCREAMS:
'I will be for you HEXAPODA, the winged membrane.
I am THE MECHANICAL BRIDE. BRING ME MY ROBES, oh maiden.'

(And out of the darkness comes the maid in funeral black bearing an elaborate costume.)

The women sit in a semicircle at the bride's feet.
The maid assists her first with her veil;

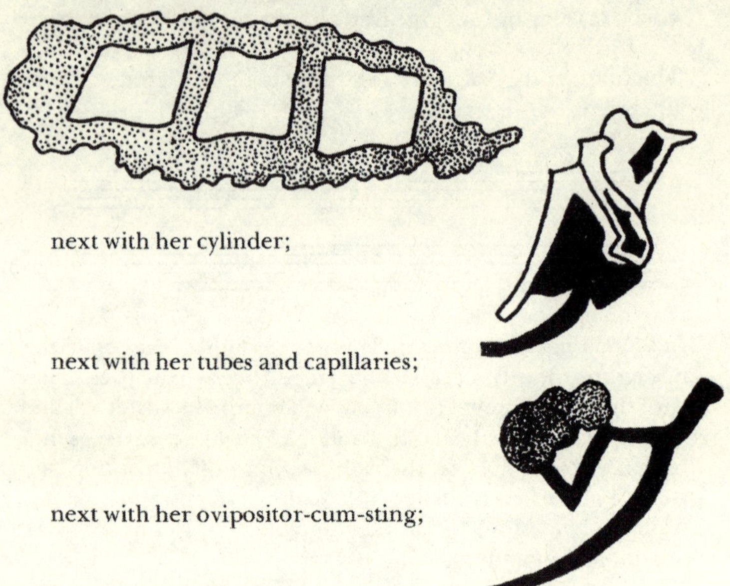

next with her cylinder;

next with her tubes and capillaries;

next with her ovipositor-cum-sting;

finally with the mask to make her costume complete.

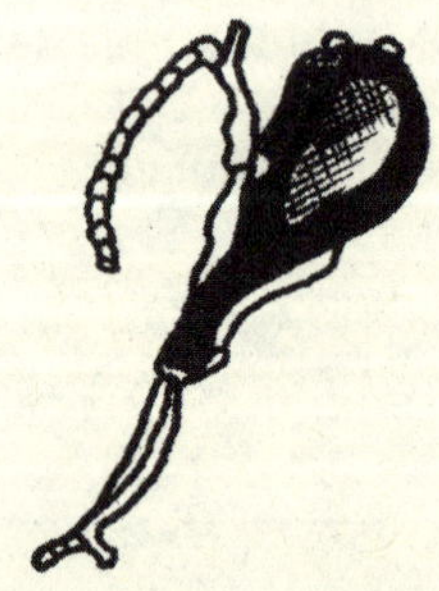

(and the beasts grovel before the mistress of fear.) A heraldic flourish which you can supply:

THE CHORUS OF BACHELORS ENTERS, RIGHT AND LEFT STAGE, EACH CARRYING A TOY GUN. (ONE OF THEM IS THE GROOM.) THE BEASTS SCATTER TO THE EDGES OF THE STAGE SO THAT THE BACHELORS MAY KNEEL IN A CIRCLE BEFORE THE BRIDE, GUNS IN FIRING POSITION.

They each go through a personal, elaborate ritual of fear in preparation for a 'shot' at 'the bride.'

The first bachelor rubs his gun, he shoots and misses.
'Rggrahhh, rggrahhh,' snarl the women.
The second bachelor kisses his gun, he shoots and misses.
'Hyiiiiii, hyiiiiii,' whine the women.
The third bachelor caresses his gun, he shoots and misses.
'Frrruhhh, frrruhhh,' grumble the women.
The fourth bachelor murmurs to his gun, he shoots and misses.
'Rrraaaggr, rraaggr,' caution the women.
The fifth bachelor pulls on his earlobe as he shoots and misses.
The sixth bachelor crosses himself after he shoots and misses.
'Graaagrhh, graagrhh,' cheer the women.
The seventh bachelor clears his throat after coming very close ...
'Graagrhh, graagrhh,' jeer the women.
The eighth bachelor rubs his knees together as he shoots and misses.
The women are too tired to comment.
The ninth bachelor who is Fred shoots
and
HE HITS.

another fanfare

as he carries the bride offstage.

(SUDDEN BLACKNESS AND SILENCE)

In real life, of course, I simply poured the tea over my knees and over Mrs. Hanover's best carpet that she bought with the help of green stamps. I helped her clean it up and went home with Renata, who I must say has been really kind and soothing and through her gift of that little book, *informative.* But please Matthias know that I really am having second thoughts. Perhaps you could be the first man in history to give 'just cause why this woman should not marry' – we could pretend that I'm having your baby and go off happily into the night. Would you dare? Do you care that much for me? I'd love it. Do it for me.

Your anxious friend, Habella.

NOTE: But the letter went to Vancouver as Matthias was on his way to the country and the next stage of the pre-nuptials followed cruelly on Friday evening with the dress-rehearsal (or dry-run). The procedures were marred, briefly, by a telegram (presumed congratulatory) from Kamloops.

Habella didn't know anyone there.

It was read aloud, naturally, to everyone present for society's customs allowed matters usually kept private to be made public.

HABELLA STOP FULFIL THE DESTINY YOU HAVE CHOSEN STOP I WISH YOU MANY CHILDREN SOON STOP

('How nice! How nice!,' murmured the listeners.)

I CANNOT AND WILL NOT MEET FRED STOP

('Too bad! T O O B A D !' commented the listeners.)

I CANNOT AND WILL NOT REVISE MYSELF TO APPEAR AT YOUR WEDDING IN THE WAY YOUR MOTHER WISHES STOP

('Oooohhhh! W H O *is* this?' wondered the listeners.)

THE TELEGRAM SIGNIFIES THE END OF OUR FRIENDSHIP AND THE END OF OUR MIXED METAPHOR STOP

('RREEAALLLY! Have you ever? At a dress rehearsal, too!')

MATTHIAS HARP

POST SCRIPTUM: THE MATING OF HUMANS IS NOT ACCOMPLISHED IN THE SAME WAY AS IS THE MATING OF QUEENS AND DRONES OR WOODSMEN AND LITTLE PRINCESSES STOP

(Oh, clearly some nut from Natural Science. Never did understand academics. He's probably jealous. What a *poor loser* ...)

Habella, crying now, could be heard through her tears to sob:

CHOP ... CHOP ... CHOP ...

STOP ... STOP ... STOP ...

Her mother comforted her with the words:

'He always was a queer duck, just couldn't stand to have him around why he used to make Mrs. Gimble's flesh crawl when she saw him at the door for those pot-roast dinners we used to give him once a month, could never get you home at all unless you could bring *him* or that Renata you prefer to live with – imagine her nerve turning up at a dress rehearsal in a pant suit because she didn't have time to change after work and that priest Father della Bono didn't say a word. He was such a thin thing, always hugging himself and folding his hands and dressing in dark clothes and babbling on in strange languages and showing me and your father charts and telling us foreign stories so that we never did understand why you found him good company and so queer, so *obviously queer* the way he crossed his legs so dainty and said 'New theynk yew, Mrs. Cire, I won't have another slice new' after he'd just about cleaned us out of house and home in front of Great Aunt Lucinda who would have been glad to take the leftovers home, so little attention her family pays to her, and you never noticed his accent because you learned to talk like him yourself in Ontario when you were at college and where you got a liking for odd ducks like him and thank goodness he won't be there in the front row oogling the choir-boys, and wearing those black pants so tight he'd split them if he sat down for you've at least had the sense to choose a normal boy to marry, one of our kind, and certainly Fred's a better choice than that other fly-by-night that made you cry so much, oh you know, *Sam* S..eth, *S..aul,* what *was* his name?'

The wedding would take place next noon at St. Amboise's Catholic church – he of the three-lashed flail, symbolic of his verbal scourging of non-trinitarian heretics; he of the bee-hive, symbolic of the honey smeared miraculously upon his lips at infancy, presaging his easy-flowing, honey-like rhetoric. This allusion escaped Habella who was busy with the others.

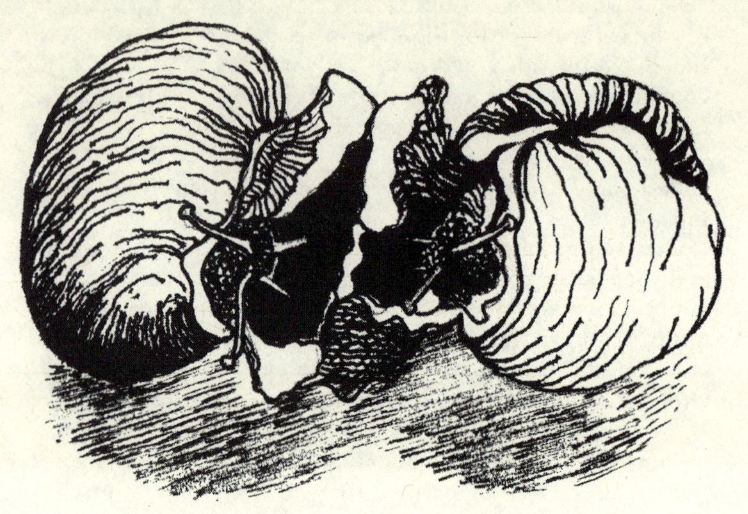

The Nuptial Flight

Under the veil that covered her tulle dress
like the cocoon that envelops the imago
the moment before it is torn apart –
her face was pale; her eyes were bright ...

She came forth tremblingly on the arm of her father to meet the other she'd known as a child – good Father della Bono whose breath was alive with onion. Renata before her, in unaccustomed pink, tossing the red petals of roses upon impassive green carpet to the beat of the Wedding March and to the smiles of relatives and friends. The groom turning towards his bride knew nothing of her fear and misread the tears that glinted through her veil as tears of joy.

The service was brief and Latin intensified the mystery of the occasion. The moment in the mass when sin is jointly confessed:

quia Peccavi omnis cogitatione, verbo, et oper
that I have sinned exceedingly in thought, word and deed,

(STRIKE BREAST THREE TIMES SAYING)

mea culpa, mea culpa, mea maxima culpa ...
through my fault, through my fault, through my most grievous fault

so quickly followed by the equation of marriage with repression and bondage:

Thou didst foreshadow the union of Christ and the Church. O God, Thou dost join woman to man, and Thou dost endow that fellowship with a blessing which was not taken away in punishment for original sin nor by the sentence of the flood. Look, in Thy mercy, upon this Thy handmaid, about to be joined in wedlock, who entreats Thee to protect and strengthen her. Let the yoke of marriage to her be one of love and peace. Faithful and chaste, let her marry Christ. Let her follow the model of the holy women: let her be dear to her husband like Rachael; wise like Rebecca; long-lived and faithful like Sarah. Let the author of sin work none of his evil deeds within her; let her keep the Faith and the Commandments. Let her be true to one wedlock and shun all sinful embraces; let her strengthen weakness with stern discipline ...

Habella quivered under the steady eye of the priest who knew her as a child reluctant-to-learn the catechismic rules, reluctant-to-embrace the concept of guilt. But the very moment that his gaze touched her core, she sailed away from him triumphant down the aisle on gauzy wings under a tempest of rose petals and rice, 'flesh of one flesh' inspiring her flight into the evening reception with its menu of scalloped potatoes and gravy, apple pie à la mode for dessert between the guests divided ruthlessly into two camps: *His* and *Hers*.

The church-hall was a-glitter with the glimmer of the aurora-borealis jewels on the necks of the women, their gold lamé 'dickies' and sequined glasses, the plastic chrysanthemums in bowls on the thread-bare tablecloths added 'additional' colour. But there was nothing more radiant and *pure* than the scarlet of the bride's cheek as she greeted the guests who approached her table. For at this moment she was happy that she had obeyed society's conventions and relieved that Matthias had not come after all.

The crowd's expectations mounted with an excited buzzing as the microphone was put into position beside the bride. A wonderful letter had been sent by Miss Kelly who was too ill to attend the wedding. Some bogus telegrams were read from the Queen and other figureheads. Then, the traditional speeches: the first, a toast to the bride delivered by an uncle who had enough liquor in him to publicly confess his lust for Habella:

'I understand Fred is an expert at handball, well tonight, ladies and gentlemen, he will have a new partner, I know that she'll do well, I used to find excuses to diaper her when she was a baby. Yes, I've known her, in a manner of speaking, that long ... longing to be, as it were, in Fred's shoes so-to-speak (laughter). Please, this is no laughing matter! (more laughter) It's rare to find a woman who is intelligent (laughter), who is also pretty and when we do, by god, we don't know *what* to do (laughter) so I guess that rather than wish Fred luck, because he'll certainly need it (a pause for more laughter), I'll tell you two true stories about this young bride that will be best interpreted by each of you after you've had two or three more drinks.

Habella at thirteen was already discovering sex (laughter). Never mind, Fred, not in the usual way – she was *too well protected* for that! (more laughter, but not from the family Cire). She used to bring home hamsters and at moments when her mother and father were giving their regular bridge parties and things were getting rather dull (concerned mumbles, mixed with embarrassed laughter) she would bring the little beasties into the living room to do their thing with their things and things would develop awkwardly, as it were, until her mother would remove her and them to their beds (suppressed giggles). And the next thing I knew, Habella was blooming and seventeen and asking me if you get pregnant from kissing and I said no, if only your mouths do it – you know that from watching the hamsters. So my guess is, m'boy, you've got a virgin to play on tonight. Remember the rules of the sport, keep the ball bouncing, keep it clean and swift.... Rise and Toast the Bride....

CLINK ... CLINK ... CLINK

(Uncle was ushered rather unceremoniously and unsteadily out of the limelight and banished, along with his wife, from future events of the family Cire.)

The groomsman arose with the Toast to the Bridesmaid(s):

'I've known Fred for as long as I can remember and feel safe in my commendation of your physical charms which he can no longer, being married, pass on to you himself. I am happy to be part of this occasion ...'

CLINK ... CLINK ... CLINK

The groom arose and with unrestrained genuineness thanked the parents of the bride and no sooner had he finished than a darkhaired cherub – stuffed into a suit two sizes too small – wrested the microphone from him and launched into a barely comprehensible ode to the institution of marriage:

'Habella, mia, itsa gooda to see you witha youra huomo buono, *spero,* I hopa lo Dio bringa you botha multi bambini. Mia Luisa exulta, spera unire di nouva retro la *luna di miela* ma oggi, thisa giorno, this a very die avera bambino nell'ospedale and she saya me, 'Avanti, go Gino, give la sposa novella, lo sposo, la damigella d'onore, l'amico della sposo – tutti, le bacie affezionate' so Ima hera to kissa you and youra grooma, your amica Renata, youra

Maminia, youra papa, Ima so happy for you. Grazie lo Dio! Youra bono sposo, looka hima, he giva you multi ragazzi e ragazze e lo matrimonio givesa you permissione fora sesso regularizzarato, non higgleta-piggleta – rinfusa, çatafascio, chaotico but molto punctiglioso e per consequenza le uove e gli spermi knowa whatta to do, anda they getta bambini, grazie Dio qui crea concupicenza armonioso ed amore per consequenza. Attrazione del sesso, amonge le ragazze e ragazzi like they do negli filmi – Sophia and Marcello, Sophia e *tutti* thatso no gooda – withouta la marriaga, senza la dispenza di matrimonio, senza la testimonanza, la *prova* ina the churcha have only sexa, thatsa alla and thatsa affronto di Dio, uno hieroglifico di disperazione, deconsolazione, divestazione e cosi di sequito, et cetera, begga you to considera la diferenza fra l'amore di Zeus per Hera – difficile ma pio – e quale di Venus, sua concupiscenza erotica – cosi maligno, cosi effimero, cosi *barbaro*. Mia Luisa ed io ara felice, contente e fruttifere. Luisa she makea me a boy righta now, so Ima going backa to hera ... Grazie, Arrivaderci, bona fortuna....'

Gino the waiter with a philosophy for a happy life departed into the night.

The records and the dancing. The new pair who had not waltzed since their respective (and different) dancing classes one-two-threed tentatively until it seemed appropriate to dance with the mother/father that produced them in recognition of the continuity through genealogical chains hat stretched back in time beyond Adam. At midnight, according to custom, the bride and groom appeared *changed* from formal virgin-white and black to regular (irregular) garments – she in hat with sequins; he in a three piece business suit that the peat-moss rape-weed industry did not require. And soon in canberattled 'Chev' to a hotel room where *hieros gamos* in-reduced-form would be enacted as it is on every Saturday night (especially from May to September) by new couples from Sidney to Bamfield, from Hong Kong to Istanbul (formerly Constantinople and before that who knows or cares) and as weddings go, this one 'didn't go off badly.' And Habella, 'God bless her' was still – despite the skirmish with Saul and somewhat contrary to Fred's hopes – technically and mentally a virgin.

When they were, at last, alone together, Habella burst into tears. Fred thought that something like this might happen and so he wasn't really concerned (bride's nerves he had been warned about) and yet even after a sleep, and even after breakfast Habella seemed tired and fretful, not the least bit anxious to begin their married life.... Conversation grew difficult:

'Come on, Habella, let me love you....' (He kissed her.)

'Fred, you're such a good man, I know it will be OK....' (She consented.)

Hand on her breast now, his mouth on hers, he recalled the warning of Jan Eichenlöbe, for he had been given a book by his buddies at the *stag* on the Thursday before the wedding:

> As a beginner you will find these specific directions for dealing with the virginal membrane useful as you will also find these suggestions for building sexual desire in women who have not yet developed full sexual sensitivity or responsiveness. Remember your objectives in the first few encounters are *modest.* I suggest that if the new husband is unable to freely insert two fingers to their bases when sex play begins, he should probably avoid sexual contact even if his wife cries for it....

He groped for her under the covers and under the cover of her nightgown he found her dry and tight, so unlike Inez, Irene and several others. His fondling did little to induce her interest and nothing to increase, as the good book put it, her 'feminine fervor.' She pushed his hand gently away and said:

'Let's talk!'

He was not sure that talk was required at a time like this, *action* was what he had in mind. He asked, rather sadly,

'What is there to talk about?'

She responded with a smile, and a chaste peck on his cheek,

'Where we are going to live after we come back from the honeymoon?'

'Oh, wherever you want, but let's *have* a honeymoon first....'

His voice trailed off as he kissed her ardently and his hand strayed once more to where it had not, at first, been welcome as he tried to make her

> sexually aroused, to bring to the glands in and around the vagina the mildly lubricating juice which unfortunately remains within the vagina itself – at least until the changes which follow childbirth relax the vaginal outlet. The tissues at the vaginal opening (especially the two inner folds in front of the vagina) badly need lubrication to make caresses feel silky and to prevent discomfort during intercourse.

Ordinarily the husband can use the moist vagina as a source for lubricant, transferring the female juice to the surface with dip and stroke caresses several times during genital play. With the new bride who has had too little sexual stimulation in the past to make anticipation awaken her glandular responses, artifical lubricant such as Vaseline or K-Y Jelly....

as he reached for a jar on the bedside table, as he kissed her and murmured endearments to her, he recalled the headings under *honeymoon*:

delights of, 128-9
female organ preparation, 64-7
hymen (virginal membrane) 13,64-66
lubrication, 65
position summary, 82-5
sex-play for beginners, 59-61
synchronizing movements, 195-7
time table, 214-18

and wondered why conventional wisdom had required him to marry a virgin. He enquired gently of his bride (who was certainly not warming to him quickly),

'Habella, I thought that you had done this before?'

'Yes, n-oooo, I don't know... just once but not v.v.v.very...'

'Then this is going to take some work, just relax, it'll be over very quickly...'

'Fred, I know you're not trying tooo, ... I j.j.just thought it would be e.e.e.asy ... it's not y.y.your fault ... kiss me some more I'll be alright ....'

(He remembered with confidence)

Surfacaine ointment has advantages over others, in that it numbs the genital area. Remember in any event that your objectives in the first few encounters are *feminine comfort* and *masculine control. Couple effort* for *couple satisfaction* – that's the key to *harmonious* sex play...

Soon with Habella's co-operation the hymen was broken for once and for all. She emitted a whining scream:

'HIYIIIIIIIIIIIIIIIIIIIII'

'Did it hurt?' he whispered.

'Noooo, not really. It was l.l.like a bee sting ...'

'A bee sting?'

'Yes ... It burned a little, and stung, but I couldn't feel the location ... It could have happened *anywhere....*'

'Oh,' he sighed, rather disappointed, 'That's too bad.'

'Well I guess that's the way it's going to be....'

She had never given words to a more truthful insight. Habella rolled over and went fitfully to sleep. Fred, whistling to himself, dressed, and went off to find the weekend paper. He paused good-naturedly at the door and said:

'We'll do just fine. We've got fifty years to practice!'

That the country near Squamish was beautiful helped to restore the humour of the young couple as they searched for a place to spend the first five days of their married life. The mountain shed its morning mists like an ancient coquette, layer after layer falling, vanishing, baring wrinkles as wry as they were elderly, lichen in her hair and a bush for her beard and waterfall trickles for moisture. In the forest nearby, they found a cabin with a woodstove and windows upon the trees. As they cooked an evening meal Fred's practicability won over the poetics of Habella as surely as his amiable nature invaded the reticence of his reluctant young wife. Soon in a bed too narrow for comfort, the flickering fire of the woodstove conjuring ghosts on the birch plywood walls, they searched for the means of sexual communication so fundamental to their decision to marry and when they had finished she said:

'Well, Fred, I guess that was better.'

And he said: (without believing it) 'Yeah, that was pretty good!'

. . .

'*Fred?*'

'Uuughhhh?'

'Do you know what I like about you?'

'No, what?' (now suddenly interested)

'You're so *normal....*'

... ('Oh fuck, what have I done?' he thought) but he said:

'That's nice. Go to sleep. We'll talk in the morning.'

... In his dreams that night he was a high school hero riding herd on the cheerleaders who cried, 'More, Fred! More!'

... In her dreams she was a lily on a vast northern lake. A beaver came to her and sank his teeth into her shoulder s h e f e l t n o p a i n. *She commanded him to 'sink in deeper'* s h e f e l t n o p a i n. *She told him* 'harder' *and he sank in deeper* s h e f e l t n o p a i n *only a burning in her knee and so she held him under the water until he drowned.*

No matter how they tried, their patterns did not fit.

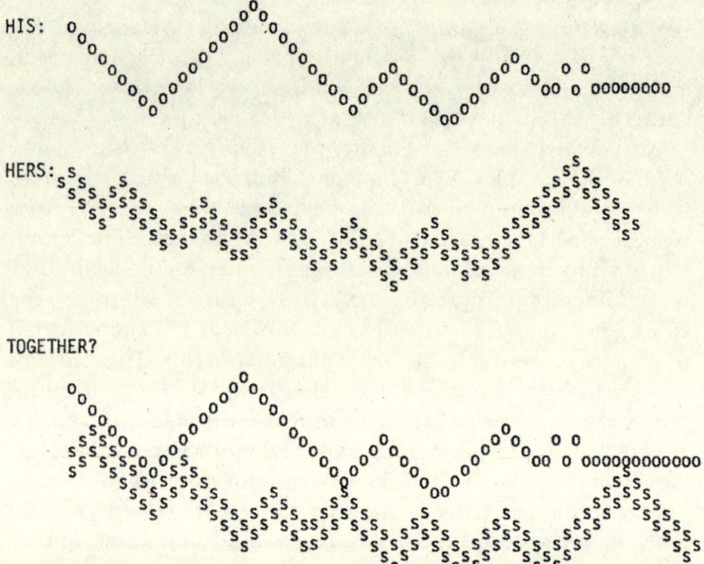

They were hopeless and they knew it. The missing ingredient was *lust.* Yet they listened to the words of Dr. Itchinglobe (as they now both called him) when he insisted that:

You do not have to be in *the mood for sex* before your partner can bestir your interest, but you do have to be in a passively cheerful state because only a calm or happy emotional state leaves every needed fibre free for its sexual function ...

They took for wisdom his remark that:

The wife (or husband) who is always searching to see whether passion is developing only builds anxieties which impair or actually wreck responsiveness....

They agreed that:

The availability of the wife builds in her husband's mind an image of her sexual appeal because every memory is nourished by the memory of past successes and is not impaired by the memory of past rebuffs, and certainly the sexual activity that never leads to disappointment is an ego builder for the husband. Sex is a *perfectly regular* function.

During the week they lay side by side unasking and unsatisfied. *Except* on Friday without fail (unless a menstrual 'holiday' was necessary) and Sunday morning if they had not been out too late the night before.

Just as he required that the same breakfast be served at 7 o'clock promptly so also he required his sex regularly and without fuss. And after he had gone she would begin her ritual of cleanliness. First she would polish the taps that were smudged with his fingerprints; next she would straighten the towels that succumbed to his impulsive disordering; then she would make the bed; then she would clear the table and wash the dishes; then she would reward herself with the morning's papers being careful to avoid the classified ads, for he did make enough money to support them both. After ironing his shirts and making his dinner, she was more tired than she had ever been in her life and even though she called him 'her strong man' (as the good book suggested) and he called her (likewise) '*Tumblebun*' she was not convinced that this *was* a life and even the arrival of Harry – who most certainly added to the routine and who was from the beginning a pleasure – could not dissuade her from feeling that she had made a mistake.

Although they never fought, they had nothing whatsoever in common. Although there was mutual respect and even good will, it was a vacuum punctuated by regular meals and predictable entertainments, especially the bridge games that they played with their parents on every second Saturday evening when they were not at the movies. The conversations at these games were totally interchangeable: the two sets of parents would come over and the couples would take turns in forming a table of bridge, leaving two free to talk.

'Fred, my boy,' said Louis heartily, 'Peat business OK? Pass me the garlic dip and I'll say, just for fun of it, 2 no trump.'

'Ah, Pop, you always do that and you always lose, but that's OK, if you want to. Rape is going better than Peat this week but that's to be expected, weather being what it is. My ace has taken your king, but your turn anyway Dad....'

'See, the boy *is learning*, Louis, *everything* depends on the weather – Oh lord, these corn chips are fattening,' exclaimed Henry tossing down a three of clubs to follow suit, 'I'll bet Harry is going to be good-natured just like Fred was, what do you think Martha?'

'Well I hope he learns to pick up his socks, unlike you and Fred, if Habella can take the time to train him he'll be a good clean boy, but I think' (in a quiet voice now) 'the birth has left her a little depressed, she's not the housekeeper she *was* – I noticed a little dust on the coffee table – but that's to be expected I suppose but she still puts together a good dip so I guess everything will be alright. Here, I'll put down a 2, no loss, no loss....'

'If you don't mind me saying so,' whispered Louis, 'I think Habella should take a job, she's a little bored, and I don't think this has anything to do with you, Fred, see what you can do with this?'

'Oh for heaven's sake, you got me *there*. An ace of diamonds, but don't throw out the good ones at first, your partner might....'

'This partner *can't*', said Henry....

'Henry you always give *everything* away, you men are all alike! Careless, no long-range planning, why if I ran my house like you run your business, if I ran your business like you play bridge we'd never have two dimes to rub together but Habella has nothing that she can do at home, so I think she should be *here* with Harry... university education, Natural Science, for heaven's sake! What a waste of the taxpayers' money....'

'Martha, it wasn't a waste, nothing is. Have another corn chip and *watch me go*,' as he tossed the king of diamonds onto the table (totally ignoring Fred's good advice) 'and another thing, I don't think we can expect our children to live like we did....'

'Pop, that's not true. You've done very well, had good marriages and raised responsible children, I just can't see how Habella can find the time to work, she's always *so tired*,.... I'll let you have this one, *cheap*.'

In the kitchen Habella and Pilar were having their bi-monthly set-to as they prepared the ham and the cheese:

'No child of mine ever had a diaper rash ...'

'But mother, you only had one child ...'

'That has nothing to do with it, what would the neighbours think?'

'I don't know my neighbours ...'

'Don't be saucy with me, and don't make excuses, here you are surrounded with the luxury of modern conveniences, why I had to wash diapers out by hand! There's just no excuse for dirt and if you can't get them clean use Pampers, they're on sale now at Fedco ...'

'Mom, I want to go back to work ...'

'Work?! You can't even organize your house and your baby ...'

'Yes I can, in the ways that *matter* ...'

'I've seen you spoiling him, talking to him, picking him up, why when you were young I had a routine ...'

'Routine. Routine. That's all I have ...'

'Then why does Harry have a rash? If you had a routine he wouldn't. Bluing. Old fashioned Bluing will do it. Get some, then everything will be fine. You can get the economy size at Safeway tomorrow – better yet, I'll get you some and I'll see that you use it. Diaper rash, well I never, and neither did your Great Aunt Lucinda who said to me the other day that you were reminding her more and more of Alicia, that ungrateful daughter of hers ...'

These ennervating evenings had elements of obscure humour and Fred and Habella recounted the highlights to each other as they cleared the dishes. But there were times when they were alone together and simply had nothing of consequence to say; there were the times when they left each other notes on the kitchen bulletin board that neither of them could understand.

Habella, m'dear,
You forgot to put lettuce in my bacon sandwich. I know it is a small thing, but it ruined my afternoon. Please don't do it tomorrow. I'm counting on you for a smooth day!
Fred.

Fred,
Please don't ask me to put lettuce in your sandwich. I have breakfast straight, I cannot cope with lunch. Isn't it better to wonder whether there will be lettuce or not, rather than *knowing* that bacon predisposes lettuce? I think Persephone probably had more creativity in the life of her mind before she knew that *every* summer she would be free to visit her mother, able to escape Hades.
Habella.

Habella,
Who is Persephone? Who is Hades?
Fred.

Fred,
If you don't know who they are, it's your tough luck. I think that we have a Hades/Persephone marriage. So if you're interested, look it up.
Habella.

Habella,
I wish you'd look it up for me, and at the same time darn my socks, because mother is complaining that you don't look after me, and you know I can't argue with *her*.
Fred.

Fred,
Learn to argue and perhaps we would be closer.
Habella.

Habella,
Arguments give me indigestion and so do bacon sandwiches without lettuce.
Fred.

In the twelfth month of their marriage she began to tell stories of animal and insect matings to his friends. They would laugh and feel terribly embarrassed and on a particular evening she embarrassed even herself.

'Well,' she said brazenly to the young man Fred had introduced as 'new staff in the office,' 'What can *you* tell me about slugs?'

'Er,' mumbled the young man, 'Not much. They eat plants and mushrooms, and are real pests to the serious gardener ...'

'Do you know how they multiply, they're all over the place? Chocolate brown, piebald yellow and brown, Banana slugs, if you'll forgive me – how is it that there are always more and more and more?' Moving close to him on the wings of her glass of honey wine, 'How do they *make* it?'

'Um,' blushed the young man, 'I dunno, never watched them, have you?'

'Heavens no!' said Habella with a great sense of affirmation, 'I'm not a voyeur. But,' she continued with a dramatic whisper, 'I've read once about the Great Grey Slug (European) and I know that a slug imported inadvertently in 1948 in an English trouser cuff arrived in Vancouver and I suppose that our slugs proceed-in-the-same-way....'

'Well,' said the young man (growing rather interested), 'perhaps you'd better tell me in case I'm ever asked....'

'With pleasure,' she said assuming her *lecturing posture* that always reminded Fred of the many times he had fallen asleep during class. 'The Great Grey Slug is eight inches of hermaphroditic charm who insinuates himself through the landscape parting the grasses with a blunt nose, oozing himself along the ground in the slime that is the by-product, the rheumy extension, of self so that it is impossible to decide where this creature's definition lies, just as it is difficult to declare where the fish mucus becomes the water or where the water becomes the fish....'

'Go on, go on,' murmured the young man (fascinated)....

'The slug is looking for a mate, a paradigm. The creature is not Narcissus who must love his mirror-self in a sylvan pond and who, if he had found a living mirage of self somewhere in the forest could never have experienced a simultaneous like-love, nor could Narcissus have found completion with Echo so unlike himself. The creature is he/she/hir and seeks to mate with a he/she/hir knowing that every sensation that reaches its sluggish system slowly will be matched exactly by ganglia transmitted feelings elicited from and in the sexual partner. The slug need not wonder how it feels, as we do in human congress, imagining what is prick and what is cunt, for the slug, my dear, has/is both....'

'Hruuumph, Hraack,' mumbled the young man as he cleared his throat, 'go on! go on!'

'The Great Grey Slug,' she paused for emphasis, 'is hermaphroditic, an advantage nature gives the lower orders so that they may know more about themselves than we do, as we lie in bed contemplating an opposite and unequal, and that knowledge of our birth-in-slime may have prompted Socrates' vision of the hoop-man, rolling a ring of harmonious self-completion with another on the ancient reedy plains....'

'Uhh?' inquired the young man, oblivious to Fred's black looks before he left to prepare the evening's coffee.

'Yes, think about that as you imagine the Great Grey Slug who, as I've told you, is eight inches of friendly fun as he parts the grass, munching upon flowers and other delicacies, looking for a mate and the mate is looking for him/her/hir, feelers extended wide, slime leaving a tracery upon the earth thinking (as clearly as that impulse that travels along an *excuse* of a spinal column *can*) of reciprocal mating....'

'Aren't we *all*,' sighed the boy, gathering about himself his too-tight jacket....

'Yes, you've got the picture. We're all looking for the same thing, but we cannot find it even though our impulses travel at 400 feet per second from our brains; we are less fortunate than the slug who ruminates as slowly as the cow takes down grass into the first of her seven stomachs, for although we seek we do not know what we will find and when we do, we don't know what the discovery will bring....'

'OK. OK,' said the boy, anxious to get on with the story. 'How do they find each other?'

'That they find each other is a miracle of sorts for their territory is the earth; they have no natural reticence, as the cat does, for crossing boundaries....'

'So how do they meet?'

'Well, they bump into each other just like Fred and I did in the woods a long time ago, but they kiss for a very long time....'

'H O W L O N G?' asked her eager student.

'Oh, a V E R Y L O N G time.... How long do you suppose?'

The boy said thoughtfully, 'About the length of a Bergman movie?'

'And how long is that?' asked Habella.

'Oh, about two and one-half hours,' he responded.

'EXACTLY,' affirmed Habella.

'So they kiss for two and one-half hours, is that *all*?'

'Not, quite. They circle around each other in a puddle of yellowish/greenish slime, quite iridescent if you look at it on a sunny day, touching and feeling every orifice, kissing and stroking every aperture, tasting and feeling *everywhere*....'

'That's PASSION!' exclaimed the young man.

'PRECISELY,' confirmed Habella.

'But you've not told me *how they mate*.'

'I'm coming to that. After two and one-half hours of circling and stroking and kissing and rubbing, which is so prodigal, so much in excess of the necessary, depending so much on the charity of strangers that....'

'It's just a lot of trouble to take with someone you'll never see again....'

'POSITIVELY, and maybe that's why they feel so free....'

'It's just like the leather-jackets I saw mating the other day. It took them so long to transfer the sperm to the ovipositor, handclasp-motion, their eyes glazed over with blue that I was quite bored before they finished. Their nervous systems were so overtaxed that I thought that perhaps they had died, although I knew that the male rather than the female was redundant at this point, yet even when I touched him I couldn't determine if death had occurred....'

'So true of leather-jackets and so *boring* not to know if you're dead and yet if I'm allowed to continue I will show you that the Great Grey Slug is ingenious – a genius – compared to that ...'

'Oh, do continue,' said the boy.

'Well, obeying some secret signal that only they can understand, the Great Grey Slug Couple ascends, by mutual consent, a tree, an ancient crumbling wall such as one finds in Essex and this act takes a very long time for you have observed how the slug swims along so sedately on the impulse of his/her/hir own secretions, the peristaltic perambulations that are akin to our own digestive process, but I digress.... It is important to note that they climb a tree, a wall, a *whatever* and when they do, when they accomplish the ascent, they know the time and the place where it is appropriate to begin *suspension*....'

'Suspension?' queried the lad.

'Yes,' hissed Habella. 'They hang down, you know.'

'Like a brave couple from a chandelier?' asked the boy wise beyond his years.

'EXACTLY. They cast then a thread of co-mutual slime from their lofty perch and descend it and when the moment is ripe, they mate.'

'*Mate*?' exploded the lad, 'I thought that's what they'd been doing now these last hours....'

'It's all been a leading-up-to-that,' demurred Habella.

'Really,' marvelled the boy. 'T E L L M E M O R E.'

'It's not that simple,' stated Habella. 'I do not know a slug's mind, I only know that he/hir is thinking that he/hir is mighty attractive and that it's time to get down to *serious business*....'

'What business?' asked the boy who was barely familiar with the rape seed/peat moss industry.

'The business of *screwing*,' asserted Habella,' and did you know that Fred and I have agreed only to do it on weekends, whereas the slug will do it any time he/hir finds a willing participant? You'll have to admit *that* is the trick ...'

'I'll admit that,' stated the boy, 'If only you'd tell me more.'

'Good,' remarked Habella, 'a willing listener unlike Fred who says I remind him of his geography professors....'

'NEVER! What *then*?'

'Well, the thread of slime rocks back and forth as they copulate. Each Great Grey Slug has a penis that grows to a length of two inches which means that you, proportionately, would have a penis 20 inches long if erect, and you couldn't under any circumstances could you?'

'N-o-o-o-o-o-', shivered the boy.

'Well neither can Fred and he's a lot older than you, though he tries. For with the slug it's *sprezzatura,* effortless grace and their erections come from the place where you suppose you could grow horns (if only you knew how)....'

And the boy touched the place between his ear and his eye, the place from which Michelangelo, in error, gave Moses *cornuu* through a misreading of the Vulgate which misinterpreted the Hebrew....

'Good!' expostulated Habella who knew the right place when she saw it.

'So they are finished,' said the lad (sadly).

'Not quite. What do you think they do then?'

'Ascend?'

'*Precisely*. They ascend as Hillary did at Everest with instinct (not Sherpas) for guidance, up the slime and later....'

'Down the wall, the *whatever,* and then?'

'They return to the verdant emptiness from which they came.'

'Whewww,' sighed the boy.

'Now, I suppose, you'd like to know how the snails do it.'

'Yes. Show me.'

'Here is a picture....'

'Wow', cried the boy, 'They're really going at it!'

'And furthermore, they're *enjoying* it.'

'Don't you enjoy it? I mean, you have a baby now....'

'Let me put it to you this way, even snails need help to achieve full satisfaction.'

'They do?'

'Yes. Here they are rocking together in hermaphroditic bliss, but they could not mate at all without the introduction of a painful, acute stimulus which they themselves generate....'

'What *is* it?'

'They form in their genital tracts calcareous darts, 20 millimetres long and these they thrust deep into each other as they mate. They are called, euphemistically, 'love darts' and our unconscious brain may remember them as the *vagina dentilis,* and myth celebrates them as the arrow of cupid, the necessary pain before the pleasure of love....'

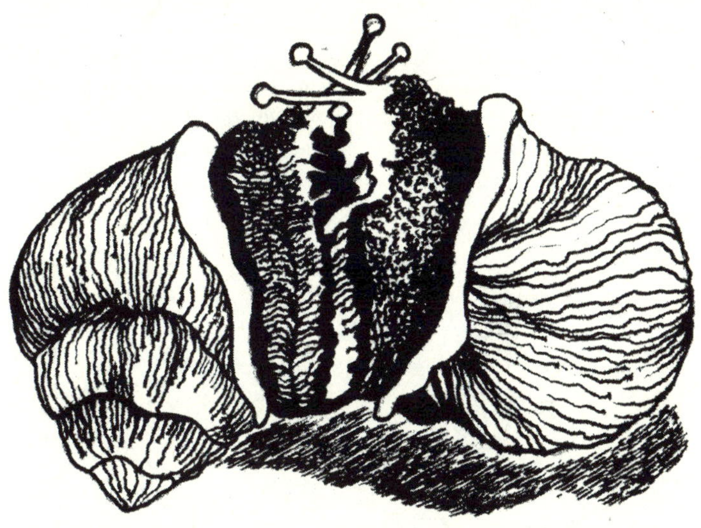

'Surely,' whispered the boy, 'you don't want Fred to *beat* you....'

'No. I want him to *affect* me, so that I can become aroused.'

Fred, who had been busy making coffee returned in time to catch the tenor of the conversation and seeing *Natural History* open at 'A Conjugation of Snails' he knew more than he wanted to. The evening was terminated in stiff politeness. The 'new employee' sensed that he would have a difficult time repairing relations with his boss's son. His ears glowed red in the subdued light of the dying fire. He bade 'goodnight' in a dry voice.

As soon as the door was shut Fred turned furiously upon Habella. Unaccustomed rage made him stutter:

'Habella, I I won't have you telling our unhappiness to others. I I won't have you flirting with men through your dirty stories and pictures.... I I'm out of school now, and I don't want you lecturing in the living room, why can't you amuse yourself with what's under your nose, put your head to work on saving a little of the money I make, getting my lunch made properly? Look I'm just an ordinary guy, with ordinary expectations, I just want to be warm, comfortable and cozy, I don't want to talk about things, I just want to do them. I don't want arguments, I want peace and quiet and it's Saturday, so tonight I want to take you to bed, we've hardly had any fun since Harry was born.... It t makes me mad h how little I want and h how unwillingly y you give. C come on, now, Tumble-bun, l let's go to....'

She followed him quietly up the stairs knowing that he was absolutely right, yet knowing that the little he expected was more than she had to give. And as they made restrained and careful love, all she could think about was the spermatozoa of the drones:

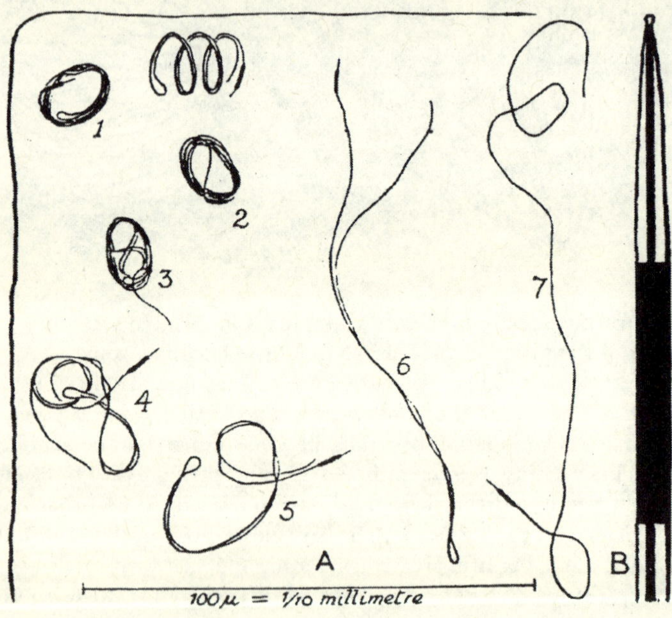

Fig. 30. A, spermatozoa, as they appear in a stained smear: 1, 2, coiled, inactive; 3 to 7, stages in uncoiling. The total length of a spermatozoon is about ¼ mm.; the head is about 10μ long and 0·5μ in diameter. B, structure of the head and part of the tail. (A, drawn from smear; B, simplified after Rothschild.)

Kamloops, May, 1965.

Dear Habella,
I was shocked to receive the letter you wrote in the form of a play. On the day that you sent it to Vancouver I was enroute to the country and as I wished at that time to cut ties with everyone I knew in Vancouver (even you, my dear, dear friend) I did not submit a change of address form to the post office until rather recently. In the meantime, of course, the Natural Science department has been forwarding the communications regarding our joint thesis and I have longed to discover in your excellent findings some small personal note. I would have celebrated a 'Matthias, you're a bastard,' for it was really mean of me to send that telegram, that temper tantrum by wire on the eve of your wedding but I was really terribly distraught over your pending marriage and I struck out in a way that brought us both pain.

I took the liberty of calling Renata the moment the letter was 'resurrected from the dead' to ascertain what your feelings might be if I contacted you directly again. She told me that you have never talked of me since that dreadful moment at the dress rehearsal when my tactless telegram was read aloud, but she felt you were so locked into the necessities of your life especially after the birth of a son (my congratulations) that you just might forgive me and welcome the chance for an intelligent correspondence. I would be so happy if you could find it in your heart to forgive me. Please know, however, that you are communicating with a different person from the one you knew.

I reacted to your marriage violently because I saw you were succumbing to a pattern that would limit you and exclude me. You teased me about the homosexual role I was falling into and that hurt me because it was very true, and I hated the superficiality of it or at least the superficiality in me as I practiced it. In the interim I have been training to become a Jesuit with permission to work in the world, and in this choice I am conscious of several factors: the long tradition of scholarly monks, who may even immerse themselves in the study of sexual matters; the respect that is given to the order that will facilitate any research that I wish to do; the celibacy and poverty that I require, which I need no longer invent excuses for. Such relationships as I permit myself do not preclude physical intimacy and yet because I am almost a priest my friends open themselves to me without fear that self-confession will presuppose sexual attachment. Sometimes it is almost impossible to practice self-restraint for I am a man with passionate feelings and a high degree of sensual appreciation and yet what I would lose by a moment of forgetfulness is greater than the brief pleasure I would gain. I can cradle to me the curly heads of sleeping babes, listen to the lisps of children's learning, acknowledge the clear eyes and gentle embraces of the mothers, accept the camaraderie of husbands and youths. I suppose that I have chosen to practice the art of friendship.

My work at Kamloops is going well. I am studying the life cycle of the wood tick. Enough of me, who, familiar with the customs of insects may never experience the full range of human habits first hand. I count on you, Habella, to tell me about the birth of your son.

In the year that we have not communicated, I have been thinking deeply about the tribes that I was beginning to tell you about on the last evening we had together. In my spring holiday (very brief, but most illuminating) I visited them for the first time. I didn't spend more than a day with the Koutomi who are really very well-adjusted, good-natured folk, living on the shores of a fairly hospitable portion of the Amazon River where food, trade and transportation are fairly easy. Just like ancient Egypt – a wonderful, serene and just society. Further upstream where the jungle thickens into an impossible tangle, where the poisonous snakes hang from the trees ready to spit venom and blindness into an innocent eye, where the insects proliferate like maggots in a carcass – there, with barely enough space to construct the village huts live the Suazi, whose very name means misery.

It is as though they desire extinction, for even birth, which in most societies is a cause for rejoicing, brings punishment to either parent. After the birth of a boy-child the wife/mother is taken into a hut and beaten with wild irises to remind her of *hirtutu-lemani* rite the boy child will grow to. The irises leave on the mother's back stripes of orangey-yellow pollen. She is tied down in the grass outside in the tiny clearing and bees come to load their pollen baskets. She is required to show no fear for expresson of felt emotion is forbidden in this society and after the ordeal is over she is put on a five day fast. It the child is a girl, the husband/father is taken into the hut and beaten with light nettle branches. Then he is tied to the centre-post with the marriage chain through his nose for three days. Afterwards he is humiliated by his wife.

The new words I learned are interesting in their reductiveness. And the vocabulary, which is severely limited, suggests the restrictions the environment makes upon the villagers. There is no verb *to go* because there is nowhere to; consequently there is no *there,* and since the *here* is omnipresent and small, no need to have a word for the concept. There are only three verbs in the entire vocabulary and one of them, *lemani* (to fly, to make love) you already know; the other two are *tampani* (to do, to be in the action of) and *verani* (to see, especially to witness). No verb for dying? No need. *Habella tampani-le.* If Habella no-can-do, she dead! There is no use for pronouns because there are only thirty Suazi left and one simply supplies the name of the person referred to. The present tense is indicated by their word for this day, today, *taliteri* (or lighttimes) and 'Harp is doing ______ now' is *Harpu tampani-taliteri 'X'.* Similarly *blateri* is darktimes, night and the past; *ralenteri* is tomorrow-times, the future, a possibility. The most fascinating words, however, have to do with falsity. *Mneneki* is soundless grief; *glaneki* is laughless joy. *Suazi,* misery, is the concept that needs mythical definition.

In blateri *there was grass as far as Pelimu could see. The land was full of* riniki *(food that walks) and* trillimi-le *(things that fly that were not yet considered evil). In lighttimes darktimes Pelemu* verani *(witnessed) watersnakes* lemani *(making love) Watersnakes-do-tie-knot. Pelimu do open-mouth-and-make-noise:* 'Hyah, Heyeh, Hajh.' *Watersnakes* lemani-li *(stopped copulating); do tall as* hirtuti-lemani *(grownups), do taller like trees-in-tangle, and do* initi *(children) so-many-no-count. Lighttimes Pelimu* verani *(see) snakelikes (everywhere). Pelimu do water-from-face:* 'Cryah, Creyeh, Crajh.' *Snakelikes* (sinui, *tree n.) do* 'Featu, Featu *(all evil upon you) Pelimu* 'Hyah-Heyeh-Hajh' sinui-lemani, sinui tampani *(do) Pelimu* SUAZI *(misery)* MNENEKI *(soundless grief)* GLANEKI *(laughless joy)* [*sinui is the infinite jungle.*] This makes the Christian ethic look like beer and skittles.

Anyway, Habella, I beg your forgiveness. I long to hear from you. Matthias.

Habella wore a smile for three weeks that didn't dim when she discovered she was pregnant. She decided to let Matthias wait for his letter and with the Suazi on her mind she resolved to give words to her feelings.

'Fred,' she pronounced at next Sunday's breakfast, '*Habella tampani-le.*'

'What?' mumbled Fred, who was chewing his bacon.

'If Habella doesn't work, she's dead.'

'God, don't be so dramatic; don't talk nonsense! What are you *really* trying to tell me.'

'I'm going to get a job teaching film criticism and I don't want to hear you say no.'

'Habella,' sighed Fred, '*anything* to make you happy. Do what you like....' (sarcasm invaded his voice).

'Fred, you just don't know what it's like being here *alone*....'

'Alone? You're not alone, you've got me and Harry... and soon....'

'I *am* alone. You're never here and when you are you hardly talk to me and Harry's just too small to be real company....'

'Look, be reasonable. We keep things going, we get things done. That's all that counts. I work. I don't see the fun in that. Get up, get going, push a few papers, fill a few orders, hustle a few new clients, come home, eat supper, play with Harry, go to bed, get up ... If you take a job, you won't be able to make mead for the folks and my friends. I just said the other night *Honey will make more,* so Honey, do it....'

Into her mind raced the South American myth they enacted in their brief courtship:

In olden times bees' nests and honey were very plentiful in the bush and there was one man in particular who earned quite a reputation for discovering their whereabouts. One day while chopping into a hollow tree in order to extract honey from it, he heard a voice calling:

'Take care! You're cutting me!'

He discovered a beautiful woman who told him she was called:

'Maba, Honey-Mother, the Spirit of the Honey.'

She was quite nude and he asked her to be his wife. She consented on condition that he never mention her name and they lived together for several years. And just in the same way that he became universally acknowledged as the best man for finding bees' nests, so she made a name for herself in the way of brewing excellent honey-wine. No matter the number of visitors, she had only to make one jugful and this one jugful would make them all drunk. She thus proved a splendid wife.

One evening when all the drink was finished, the husband went round to the guests and expressed regret that there was no more liquor. He said to his wife the next day:

'Honey make me more.'

The mistake had been made and the name of his wife uttered. The woman changed at once into a bee and flew away, although he put up his hands to stop her. And with her his luck flew away, and since that time honey has been more or less scarce.

(This coincidence was too complex to mention to Fred, yet she knew the spell was broken). She simply said:

'There will be time to make mead, but it will contain less of your Honey-mother.'

'OK. That's a deal. See you later, I'm late for my golf game with dad.'

Before she knew it, the familiar knot gathered in her abdomen. It came and went at regular intervals; it raised rhythm to a conscious level; it made a hymn of pain. She called her mother to care for Harry who at one and a bit could lisp:

'Mommy's pwengat, going to make thister or bwother....'

Her mother arrived scarlet faced and out of breath:

'Oh, you poor thing, I was just saying to your father last night how will she ever, ever look after two? She spoils the one she's got, carrying him around like a baboon on her side, letting him play in the dirt and put things in his mouth, talking endlessly to him about nature and old stories from foreigners, and sometimes even in other languages as though he could understand when he doesn't even know the word *no*, and doesn't know not to touch things that aren't his and to stay off other people's grass and even Great Aunt Lucinda knows he has diaper rash, for I told her by mistake the other day and she said, 'Thatf obfcene,' and I forgive her for she's right, and your father said, and whatever he could know about this I've yet to discover, 'Let her alone, she'll do alright.' And here I am having to cancel my bridge club for the week to look after that boy who can barely walk but knows you're pregnant and I think that's wicked of you to fill that innocent mind with such filth when he can't even tell you that he needs to go *number one* and *number two* and so I'll be changing a child who knows the facts of life before he can control his bowels like a good boy on a routine, and now you're going off to have a rest in the hospital, I'll be needing one myself when you come home. I suppose they'll black you out for the whole thing, I certainly didn't want to know anything about it. Nowadays I hear even the fathers can watch. Disgusting. I'm glad Fred's out of town ... Well, don't stand there, kiss Harry goodbye, let him enjoy this time for when you get back you won't have time to spoil him so much. Get into your Taxi. Don't forget to call when it's over....'

The room was mint green and the curtains freshly flowered. The sheets were white and crisp and she sank down upon them with a grateful sigh. Childbirth had been for her the only pleasure of her biological life; its sensations swept over her and took away her predilection for conscious thought. First of all the contractions transforming her mid-section into a giant accordion with her lungs for bellows; next the voicing of the breaths between pulses of knotted pain:

'Ah haaaaa' # 'Ah haaaa' # 'Ah haaaaa'
'Ohhhhhhhh' ## 'Ohhhhhhhh' ## Ohhhhhhhh
'Uuuuuughh' ### 'Uuuuuughh' ### 'Uuuuuughh'
'Oooooooo #### 'Ooooahhhh' #### 'Oooooooo
'Ahaaaaaa' ##### 'Ahaaaaaa' ##### 'Oooahhhhh'
'Uuuugh' ###### 'Uuuugh' ###### 'Uuuugh'
'Ooooh' ####### 'Ooooh' ####### 'Ooooh'

(sensations e l o n g a t i n g, breath/time/shortened)

############ 'ah' ############ 'ah' ############ 'ah'
############### 'ah' ############ 'ah' ############

(cords of muscle pulling in, cords of muscle pushing down) and suddenly the music ceased and upon her forehead was written

PUSH
(in beads of sweat.)

She called.

They came.

They said, 'You're ready.' And, knees up to her chin she bore down triumphantly on each impulse and soon from her slithered a tiny being in a rush of water. Covered in blood, smothered in protective wax, he smelled as pungent and as acidic as spoiled milk. She pulled him to her and called him James. It was the second time in her life that she was at peace with herself. She knew that Matthias would understand an abstract account of her, birthing.

Sitting in a bed of flowers, babe in arms, she looked for all the world like a normal wife.

Propolis, Venom, & Other Substances

The bees manufacture constructive and destructive substances. First of all, the honey.

Honey is the by-product of apiculture and we know how willingly a bear will endure a hundred stings upon his nose to sweeten his tongue with it. We know that honey flavour depends upon the specific nectar on which the bee has supped; we know that the different species of bees produce varying kinds of honey – some so savory that one doesn't know if one has eaten or succumbed to the burning fire of love; some, indeed, so putrid that a maggot would pass it up.

Honey is sweet. Very very sweet. Its sweetness comes from these sugars: levulose, dextrose and sucrose mixed with water and embellished with the traces of sodium, sulphur, magnesium, phosphorus, pollen, manganese, aluminium, calcium, copper, albumen, dextrine, nitrogen, a hint of protein and acid. It is prepared for us, predigested if you like, in the honey stomach of the worker bee so that upon our ingestion of it, honey supplies instant energy. In the matter of *caloric* energy honey outdistances any other kind of sweet. Honey has the power to turn polarized light to the left; honey has the power to make the ill well. Honey is wonderful in cooking. It was the essential ingredient of the mead that Habella was preparing for the summer picnic:

1 gallon of water
4 pounds of honey
6 cloves
2 sticks cinnamon
the juice and peel of 2 lemons.

As she boiled the components for half an hour, waiting to strain them into her grandmother's earthenware crock, waiting to add just enough yeast at just the right moment, she was composing a fairy tale for her four children:

The princess lived in an ancient castle guarded by two grizzly bears. The king and queen knew their daughter was ready for marriage but they didn't want anyone to steal her away. Her yearning, her anticipation, her eagerness for love was rung through the *stanzas* of a ballad she sang daily (in subtle variations):

Come to me my honey love,
your brilliant treasure bring,
and I'll sing like a pearly dove,
gossamer for wings.

Bring to me my honey love
the pleasure of the spring
and I'll live as your wedded wife
not needing anything.

Give to me your honey love
that radiant measuring
and I'll give you a splendid life
within my golden ring.

When the king and queen overheard her, they sighed: 'She's ready for love but how can we be sure she'll choose the right man? We must create a test. If the young man knows how to pass the grizzly bears, he may enter the castle. If the young man enters the castle we will make him answer riddles. If he answers the riddles correctly, he shall be Inconsolata's husband and our own beloved son.'

As the castle was far away from everywhere, it was a long time before the first suitor came, drawn to the place by a golden thread of a maiden's voice that drifted over the silver aspen. As he started up the walk, the bears ate him up.

As the castle was far away from anywhere, it was another year before the second visitor came. He had heard rumours of grizzly bear guards and sudden deaths and so he brought with him a honey comb. He was hoping to sell the king and queen some magic potions. He did not wish to win a wife. As he started up the walk, he tossed the honey comb to the bears. They ate it up.

Within the palace garden, he heard a maiden's song as lyrical and light as rain on an April window:

Where are you my honey love?
I long to make you king;
I'll prance you a fairy dance,
rose petals I will fling.

Bring to me my honey love
the porcelain of the Ming,
all blue and white, a magic night
imprinted on each brim.

I must know thy honey love,
if I'm to have a life;
within this green and ferny grove
lust cuts me with its knife.

After he had sold his healing drinks, he agreed to answer the king and queen's questions.

'What sings like a bird by day and flies to the moon at night?'

'A maiden.'

'What creature will give its most precious gift for a word of praise?'

'A virgin'.

'What being exchanges freedom for a golden ring?'

'A wife.'

'Do you need one?' they asked anxiously.

'No, I've got one and one's enough.'

As the castle was further away than you could imagine, it was three years before the next stranger came. He had heard about the bears from the vendor of potions. He brought honey in a jar to drizzle upon their muzzles and as they happily licked it, he killed them for their pelts. He did not wish to visit the maiden although he heard her faint voice over the rustle of the reeds beside the moatpond.

Come to me my honey love,
my heart's an empty thing;
the weather whispers to the dove,
the bee prepares its sting.

Give to me redemptive love
like Christ has for his Queen
and I'll bloom as your wedded wife
not wishing anything.

Crystal waters I do lave
upon my troubled brow,
If you don't come oh honey knave,
I'll be dead, I vow....

She rubbed her nose a little as she threw the yeast into the brew. Sad stories always made her cry, especially the ones of her invention. But she knew that Harry and James would like it and perhaps when they were older they would sense the meaning of it.

Fred came through the back door to the kitchen and the door-slam made her start. He kissed her absentmindedly upon the ear and said:

'Great. Honey's making me more mead! Where's my golf cart? I want to get in a few rounds with dad, before he comes over to talk business. I tell you, things are really booming. I think I'll clear fifteen thousand this year, great huh?'

'Terrific,' responded Habella as she remembered that *A drop of honey catches more flies than a barrel of vinegar.*

After he had gone she began the next task, murmuring to herself these lines from Sir Isaac Watts' 'Against Idleness and Mischief':

How doth the little busy bee
Improve each shining hour
And gather honey all the day
From every opening flower!

How skilfully she builds her cell
How neat she spreads the wax
And labours to store it well
With the sweet food she makes.

In the words of Abraham Lincoln,
'If you want to gather honey, don't kick over the bee hive.'

The honey in food, the honey of gentle words, the honied pleasures of love sweeten the cake of life. But what of the other substances manufactured by the bees? The whole world of the bee is dependent on wax. It is the material out of which their storage cups are made. Without them, there could be no food for winter nor cradles for the young. Beeswax is a fatty acid – cerotic admixed with a large proportion of palmitic, with traces of other ingredients. It is formed between the fourth and seventh sections of the worker's abdomen. To Habella's mind *wax* was a practical substance akin to plaster of paris, something to do things with, something that almost always worked. And as I saw her involved in the routines of her life, I could think of her best as a wax-making worker. She had an amazing facility for creating cookies all the same size without apparent thought and she would always know the *exact* temperature when they were cooked. We had been friends since our schooldays at St. Paul's. I knew her almost as well as I know myself (or so I thought).

'Where's Fred?' I asked, sniffing the air for cookies and mead.

'It's Saturday, so it must be golf,' she answered. 'It's OK, Renata, because it gives me time for my fantasies. I've just been thinking up a children's story; let me tell you about it....'

'Christ, Habella. Here you are an old married woman with four kids and you're still a romantic, dithering around in the realm of ideal love. I thought that side of you was dead. You're very down-to-earth, always knowing what to do, always knowing where to find the lost socks, invariably able to insert the right phrase into an unfinished sentence, always able to hold your tongue....'

'Renata, while that's true, there's another side of me that you haven't seen much since I was young, mainly because I hardly ever visit with you alone. But today everyone is out, at least for a while. It's just that my life is so perfunctory, so predictable and while Fred is pleasant, he's...'

'No turn-on.'

'Right,' sighed Habella....

'Well let me tell you, a week with anyone and the chemistry vanishes....'

'Does it? I'm not so sure. With Matthias the *mental* chemistry survives....'

'He keeps in touch with you?'

'Yes often, though Fred doesn't know it. He writes me at the college where I work....'

'And what does he say? Does he still love you?'

'Yes. I'm sure he does, he doesn't need to say so. He writes about things I understand and we communicate in esoteric languages. It is always new, always exciting.... It's just like when Miss Kelly taught us – she's pretty frail, you know...'

'Well, I do understand what you're saying, but I'm just pleased to see a warm body across the breakfast table. I've no illusions about perfection, maybe I live at a lower level and so from where I sit, Fred functions better than Matthias because he's a man and he's here; a great puppy of a man, patient and well-adjusted. He doesn't have a single obsession as far as I can tell. Boy, I've been out with some weird ones....'

'He just never thinks....'

'Maybe he's content just doing. Hey, come on, I'm playing Devil's Advocate. I want to hear about you....'

'I'm the waxen mask that I wear daily; it will melt one day and leave me naked. I can build the nest and feed the brood, and clear the feces from the hive, fan the air when it's warm, cluster with others when it's cool, facilitate the mating of queens and drones....'

'Habella, you're not a bee! You're giving me goose pimples....'

'No, Renata, I'm becoming a metaphor and that is worse.'

'Maybe you need a holiday?'

'No. I want a change.'

In the afternoon, we went to the Natural Food Store. I hadn't realized that Habella was concerned about her health. She pored over the packages and was particularly attracted to those containing nutritious delicacies produced by the bees. She pulled from her purse an advertisement from *The New York Times:*

ASTONISHING
VALUES SAVE OVER 70%

B COMPLEX 100 — 69¢ 500 — 3.25
ZINC 10 mg. 100 — 49¢ 1000 — 3.99
VIT. C 500 mg. 100 — 90¢ 500 — 4.25
VIT. B-6 50 mg. 100 — 70¢ 300 — 1.85
VIT. B-12 25 mcg. 100 — 49¢ 1000 — 4.45
LECITHIN 19 gr. 100 — 1.39 300 — 3.95
VIT. A 10,000 U. TAB. 100 — 69¢ 500 — 2.90
DESICCATED LIVER 100 — 79¢ 500 — 3.45
BREWERS YEAST 100 — 65¢ 1000 — 1.85
HERBAL LAXATIVE 100 — 90¢ 500 — 3.50
NATURAL GARLIC CAPS 100 — 79¢ 500 — 3.85
GARLIC & PARSLEY TABLETS 100 — 75¢ 500 — 3.25
ALFALFA TABLETS 100 — 49¢ 500 — 1.95
DOLOMITE TABLETS 100 — 49¢ 500 — 1.85
PAPAYA ENZYME 100 — 79¢ 500 — 3.80

VI-STRESS COMPARE TO STRESS TABS-600 60 — 1.75 240 — 6.10
TIME RELEASE VITAMIN C 500 mg CAPSULES 100 — 1.65 500 — 7.90
ORIENTAL GINSENG TABLETS 100 mg. 100 — 1.95 500 — 7.35
SUPER GINSENG 250 mg. 100 2.98 500 — 12.95
BEE POLLEN TABLETS 500 mg. 100 3.75 300 — 10.25
LIQUID PROTEIN CAPSULES PREDIGESTED 500 mg. 100 3.75 500 — 17.25
FORMULA "4" KELP, LECITHIN B-6, CIDER VINEGAR 100 89¢ 300 2.39
MULTI-MINERAL TABLETS 9 NATURAL MINERALS 100 — 98¢ 500 — 4.50

GERIVITES
COMPARABLE TO GERITOL 100 — 5.95
GERIVITES 100 — 95¢
300 — 2.75 SAVE 5.00

She was happy to discover, in addition to several tablets mentioned in the clipping, a fine, Korean Royal Jelly Tonic with its careful list of contents:

ROYAL JELLY (王乳) .... 1,250 mg
Ginseng Radix (高麗人蔘) .... 50 g
Angelicae Gigantis Radix (當歸) .... 35 g
Atratylis Rhizoma Alba (白朮)............ 12.5 g
Aurantii Nobilis Pericarpium (陳皮) ... 35 g
Mel (中煉蜜) .... 50 g

(I would have bought it for the very handsome package.)

'What is Royal Jelly?' I asked, feeling rather ignorant.

'Produced by the forehead glands of young workers; it's the whitish food that creates the queens and it's given as well to all larvae during their first three days of life. It has a pungent smell to human nostrils and it's bitter to the taste....'

'There's not much of *it* in this tonic.'

'Just knowing that I'm drinking *a little* makes a difference.'

'And the bee pollen tablets?'

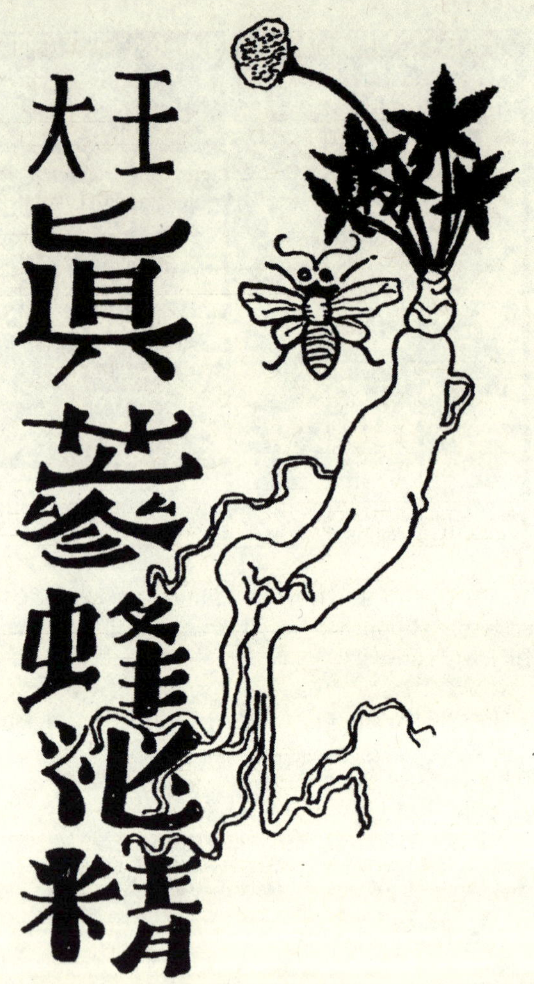

'Oh, high protein supplement. Just the thing to take with desiccated liver and ginseng radix, when you're down. And while I'm here I'll get a little propolis....'

'Propolis?'

'Yes. Bee glue.'

'They make glue?'

'Yes. Propolis is a dark brown substance made primarily from the resinous oozings of trees and plants which the bees collect and bring back into the hive. They use it to repair the hive, when cells are cracked; they use it to bury invaders that they can't remove. If a mouse comes in they sting it to death then they build it a propolis coffin. In southern countries when someone dies, the bee keeper raps upon the hive so the insects will follow a new coffin for the resin varnish. The custom is called *'Knocking the Bees....'*

'Oooooh, that's rather weird. What do *you* use it for?'

'To fix my china. "Sarabande" is broken.'

I took leave of her and was glad I had not asked about the venom.

When the worker bee stings you, the venom her torn-out poison sac injects is actually a water-like liquid. It smells like over-ripe bananas and tastes like bile. When the bee stings you – and she surely will under the following circumstances:

If you step on her as she nuzzles clover;

if you are standing by her as a sudden rain begins;

if you impede her entrance into the hive, her sacs loaded with pollen;

if she mistakes your perfume for the fragrance of honeysuckle and becomes entangled (in your hair) –

do not pull out the sting.

F. Fleury, a toxicologist at the University of Würzburg discovered that the bee venom contains tryptophan, chlorine, glycerin, phosphoric acid, palmitic acid, a fatty acid that won't crystallize and an unknown non-nitrogenous substance that causes the trouble. But as he put it so wisely:

Wenn die Biene Irnen steicht, müssen Sie, 'Oh weh!' sagen. Und dann müssen Sie herumspringen und herumtanzen, und müssen sagen, 'Ach Gott!' Das Gift trifft Ihr körperliches System vie ein Lantwagen Ziegelsteine. Es macht einen Schmerz so gross wie ein reisiggrosses Wienerschnitzel.

If you are allergic to bee venom, after the third sting you may be dying:

face an immutable white;
blotches migrating over skin;
throat muscles paralysed;
tongue swollen and purple;
pulses thready in the deep mystery
(of shock).

If you're not allergic and chances are you're not, the poison invades your system peacefully. With each encounter the immunity grows so that a bee-keeper, for example, senses the stinging as a brief pin-prick of fire, a pleasure not a menace. In Russia bee venom is a highly prized treatment for rheumatism and arthritis. But I digress.

It is clear that there are analogies to be drawn between the life cycles of the bees, the substances they produce and human affairs. Many writers have attempted to give words to the similarities that may be found between the bee-colony and human society:

For so work the honey bees
Creatures that by rule in nature teach
The act of order to a peopled kingdom
They have a king and officers of sorts
Where some, like magistrates, correct at home,
Others, like merchants, venture trade abroad,
Others, like soldiers, armed in their stings,
Make boot upon the summer's velvet buds;
Which pillage they with merry march bring home
To the tent-royal of their emperor;
Who busied in his majesty, surveys
The singing masons building roofs of gold,
The civil citizens kneading up the honey,
The poor mechanic porters crowding in
Their heavy burdens at his narrow gate,
The sad-eyed justice, with his surly hum,
Delivering o'er to executors pale
The lazy yawning drone....

as Shakespeare – unaware the hive was ruled by Queens – expounded in *Henry V*. But I feel he catches our attention more firmly in *The Tempest* with 'Where the bee sucks, there suck I ...,' for in that instance he connects the bee with human sensuality and forgets about the politics. Equally fruitful equations have been made in poetry or myth between the injection of venom with infatuation and/or unrequited love. I have read, for example, how Venus took no pity on her winged son who entered her golden palace snivelling over a bee sting, hopping up and down on his uninjured foot.

'Now you know what it feels like to be struck by one of your love darts,' she said coolly.

'Awwww, Mom! Knock it off,' grumbled the adolescent Cupid.

So much for the erotic connection.

Literature has failed however to make the link between slow poison and indifference. Habella's marriage was a testing ground for the toxic invasion that brings numbness of feeling, a fact which I, as a close friend, had many opportunities to witness.

'Habella, why don't we bundle the kids into the truck and go into the mountains tomorrow? I've got to make some soil-tests near Manning Park, and I know it won't take all day. We could have lunch near Hope and romp around in the hills. It would be fun....'

'Sure Fred, that's a good idea. But what will Mom and Dad say, they were counting on coming for dinner tomorrow afternoon....'

'Couldn't we cancel?'

'We could, but do you think we *should* at such notice?'

'Couldn't we *just have some fun,* on short notice?'

'Now, Fred, let's not go through *that* again.'

'Fred, there's this terrific Fellini festival on at the Varsity. It starts Sunday morning and finishes at four Monday afternoon. Your mom and dad could babysit. The climax is *Juliet of the Spirits*....'

'Oh lord, you go if you must. You're the one who likes monsters and freaks. If it was a Wilder festival I'd go, he's more down to earth. Anyway you'll probably be taking that eager beaver class of yours and everyone will be blathering away about gestalts, cuts, pans and symbols. I'd rather watch the kids....'

But while little stings beget impartiality, we shall see soon how the absence of stinging can bring death.

New Queens and Drones

In June come forth the new queens and the drones; their behaviour is predictable. They search the beach for mates.

The sun withdrew his flaming head.

Without the modelling force of his illuminating fire the hills across the harbour flattened themselves against the azure backdrop of the sky. Rendered in cobalt, details of green forest erased, houseforms collapsed in mist, the mountains were alive with the twinkled pointillism of a million lamps' unsteady amber and florescent blue. The ocean beneath them, an opalescent gem catching to itself on rippled facets the vestigial light, supporting with diamond toughness the hulking hulls of ships that lay black upon this richness like eunuchs. Along the near-shore pearly waters lapped gifts upon the edges, spilled necklaces of jewels upon the sand imprinted with the warmth of naked feet. Dark silhouettes piled log on log, dark silhouettes gave torch to fires that would cause the dusk to blush. And soon the air was thick with the pungency of flamed meat.

It was summer and the moon was early.
It was summer and the tides were late.
It was summer solstice and the sun paused
(in the eastern sky).

Habella brooded under the flickering gaze of the fire that rouged the pleats of her pewter robe; Fred piled on more wood. The guests singly or in pairs entered the circle bearing food, drink, and musical instruments. The party began.

It was very quiet really. Folksongs and ballads; the drinking rather light. At midnight the office boy brought a girl with dark and tragic eyes who reminded Fred forcibly of all the women he had loved before Habella. And soon they were sitting knee to knee, thigh to thigh, nuzzling and purring in the gathering blackness like hairless cats. Habella fled from their heat into the magic night.

Running through the silvery light, cool air invading her

parched throat, toes dappling the patterned sand, vaulting gracefully the fallen logs, tossing willow branches from her hair, darting between and over and among – *Sarabande* so far behind – she took refuge on a rock at the ocean's edge. Tears springing from her eyes like crystal beads, she regarded the moon's disc and searched there for her sister Selene, and the gift of everlasting sleep.

But all Selene could say was:

O O O O O O O

from a frozen mouth.

The chariots of her god were nowhere to be seen.

Out of the darkness came a voice.
'Are you alright?'
'Yes. y.y.yes, really I am.'
'No you're not, you're crying.'
'I'll b.b.be fine, really.'
'Shall I come to you?'
'Oh, please, please do.'

He sat beside her. She did not know his name.

His eyes were pale, mercurial;
his hair, an aureole of curls;
his voice, as distant as the stars.
He was naked
(to the waist).

'And what is your name?' he asked.
'Habella.'
'Ah little bee, mine's Paul.'
'What are you doing here?'
'I always come at night.'
'Always alone?'
'Yes, always alone.'
'Do you always talk to strangers?'
'Yes, if they're in trouble.'
'Do you have friends?'
'Oh yes, but I'd rather hear about yours. Ladies first ...'

'Well, I guess I don't have many. There's Renata whom I've known the longest, and Fred (my husband) is sometimes a friend, and my children and my students, though really they're more like acquaintances.... But I had a friend who's on my mind tonight, an old lady called Miss Kelly who died a few days ago. She lived until she could no longer, until there was no one else to look after, until she'd outlived her usefulness. She didn't commit the sin of despair, against all odds, against her own affliction.'

'Was she your teacher?'

'Yes, and I am grateful.'

'What did she teach you?'

'That there is no limit to the human will; there are no boundaries. If only I had listened.'

'You're listening now.'

'I'm listening to *you*.'

'Tell me what you like to do.'

'Cook, play with my children, talk to people, make scripts that will never be made into movies, about the eye looking upon the world with its individual distortions.... And you?'

'I collect objects for my eye to feed on.'

'Do eyes need food?'

'You know they do.'

And in the night they conjured up mutual images that glowed like starcharts, like the blueprints of two identical minds. They knew that:

And that this

was the same as

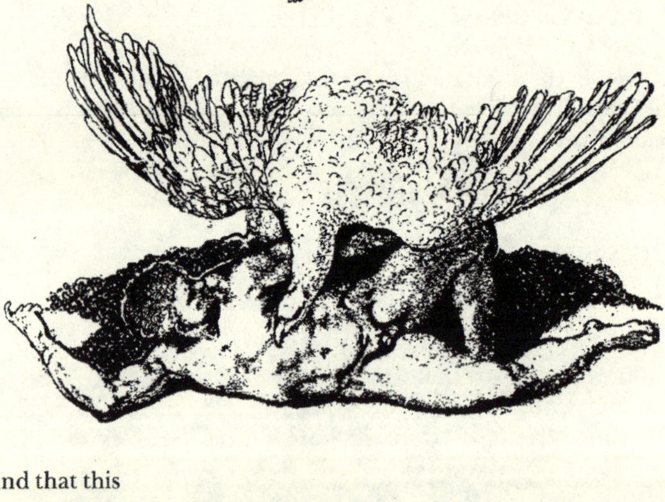

And that this

was to 

the same thing as the frog is to the prince, the cygnet to the swan. There were the myths they knew and the ones that they were living.

The tides feasted upon the rock and they were running hand in hand oblivious to the workers that streamed from the city at dawn. They were splashing each other with saline water and shouting with joy, the questions for which there were answers.

'Who are you, Habella?'

'I'm Art Woman, do you know her?'

'Yes, she is slim, coquettish, not highly sexed. Her organs have the scent of honey....'

'And you, oh Paul?'

'I'm not the scourge of the New Testament, I am a....'

'Pollo.'

And suddenly he said:

'I must go.'

And with one eloquent finger he traced the rings of the cartilage in her throat. He drew her to him, fingers clasped about her neck, thumb massaging the delicate bone that was her chin. He thrust his inquisitive tongue-tip (briefly) under hers.

He was going. Hair burnished fire in the orange of the dawn; slim body, diminishing.

He was gone.

He had opened to her the possibility of new life.

The Queen

There were nipples on her nipples, *nipple-ettes*. These were:

amusing to the first boy who liked her;

interesting to the only man who had ever noticed them (alas, not *so* interesting that he asked to see them twice);

unremarkable to her husband of many years;

unknown to the friend she thought she loved.

At another time and place, these breasts would have made her a venerable goddess of love, but few knew enough about *that* mythic creature to appreciate this Milky Way of nipples as an anachronism worth mentioning.

She had never before allowed herself to write under a heading that expects a frank list of *distinguishing* physical characteristics, 'Astarte Breasts', although she had been tempted by the humour of it. But she did so now in a structure of her own invention and the entry was answered in this by the 'Exotic Mole' in the ear of the man she had failed to win as lover. She wished to communicate the truth about the relationship through logical procedure and hence began the section called 'BODY' with a list of *general* characteristics that required no explanation. The provable facts were very boring:

HIS
medium tall
slight build
clear skin

HERS
medium tall
medium build
clear skin

The list of *distinguishing* marks that followed set 'the Mole in his left ear' *above* her 'Astarte Breasts.'

She noted down the fictions she had created around her breasts which allowed her to 'dismiss them from her mind as misrepresentative of her essential self.' She also recorded the fantasy he had created around his mole that 'transmuted it from natural growth to Sultan's Onyx so that it could rescue him from debtor's prison.'

That the mole he mentioned often he did not want touched or that the breasts she never mentioned she did want touched, that in different ways these remarkable features were not there or, at least, not as they appeared, she refrained from writing down. The metaphysical problems would be central to other portions of the structure.

The section called 'ROUTINE' was illuminating of their disparity. She arranged their social habits in the order of their importance. Those most essential to the survival of each individual were placed near the top of the list.

HIS
to live alone
to have free time
to collect objects
to enjoy strangers
to eat a little

HERS
to live in company
to fill her time
to give away objects
to analyse/make films
to sleep a lot

'SOCIAL NOTES' she couched in the *Language of the Bees* as a metaphor for their typical behavior in group or on private occasions.

He would arrive late in a yellow and black sweater. People of three sexes would buzz around him, quivering in a ritual, information-gathering dance. Each in turn sought the right to rub his back, stroke his legs, sense his senses. This solitary bee had the power to excite the hive.

As suddenly as he came, he would dart away. Alone. He did not participate in the building of structures nor did he care to gather pollen.

When he was gone each would buzz a communication of his ambiguous meaning to the other. Whatever he murmured begged clarification through the scrim of the real or imagined closeness each had to his vibrant presence.

'He inferred that he "could go on no longer" and was so on edge that I know he needed money for rent,' said his brother.

'He averred that he "could go on no longer" (without me),' sighed a lover.

'He said he "could go on no longer", but I know he can,' offered a friend.

The bee would also, habitually, express a need to 'be transparent.' Some understood this as an intention of frankness; others, as a confession of an inability to be frank; still others saw it as an invitation into his psychic layer. On these occasions no one would reconsider her or her words. She was as unambiguous as a Queen bee. And if she had cried, 'I can't go on any longer,' she would have explained *why* in order to set speculation to rest. She would never have confessed a need to 'be transparent,' because she thought she was. Her body communicated her function and told everyone that she could take care of herself. Only the wild bee sensed that she could not, that the eggs that dropped one by one from her body, one by one robbed her of energy.

On other occasions she would flee from her hive to invade the lair of the solitary bee. As she flew into the sun, her soft bristles would stiffen, her thorax would throb in expectation. His lair was always dark and, as befitting his kind, it had a cell for honey and a cell for wax. The entrance was difficult to find. In the honey cell there was fruit, frankincense, myrrh and nectar; in the other, candlewax, glazes and glass. In the first where he slept, he performed the asexual rites proper to his kind; in the second he received those who aspired to be his mate for life.

He would settle back on cushions to offer scented tea. Courtship, its rules long established, would languidly begin.

She would sit at his feet, her head close to his knees. She never took the liberty of stroking his thighs. She would drop a present of gold resin at his feet. Then his multifaceted eyes would glimmer in the candlelight and he would extend his feelers towards her. The space between them would electrify and a whispered conversation would begin.

Its structure was, invariably, a double hexagon that linked two sides out of twelve. The form remained the same however the content varied, just as bees transubstantiate a variety of substances into uniform waxen cells.

'I know your reaction to ____ would be the same as mine.'

'Well, why don't we see it together?'

'You would love its ____ and ____.'

'I'm free tomorrow.'

'It's too early for me to know.'

'If the sun shines, I must sit on the grass. And you?'

'It's impossible to know.'

'But you always enjoy doing ____ with me.'

'Yes.'

'Well?'

'I don't like to make plans so far ahead.'

'I'm sorry but I *have* to.'

The walls that touched recognized the force of a certain intimacy. The additional walls he inevitably built leaned away from hers with caution; the ones she constructed towards him were fabricated with desire.

The meeting would end with an embrace so light that their delicate hairs barely touched. He would lead her outside to give her a taste of the honeysuckle blossom.

The Queen bee made stupid in the darkness would fly away home.

NOTE:

The genus of the Queen bee, *Apis mellifera,* is the most familiar of the super family of hymenopterous insects, *Apoidea.* The Queen survives her diet of Royal Jelly to be leader to and progenitor of the hive after mating once with a male she kills in the process. She is attended by Workers who create new Queens on the sly. When a new Queen becomes ascendant the old Queen must leave and establish herself a new colony. The parable above explores the deviant course of a particularly intelligent Queen who foreseeing the future sought to upset tradition.

She embarked on a series of forays for a new habit *before* another Queen had been substantiated as usurper. She presumed not to start a similar hive elsewhere, ever. Hence she sought out the company of a solitary bee.

This bee belonged to the sub-genre, *Apis Aesthetica* and according to an Apiarist called Jeannie, was guaranteed to be asocial. He would live alone or he would share his lair with a life-time mate of his choosing.

The Queen bee in question liked the idea of this counter-productive move. She did not know he was capable of stinging.

Further information about encounters were discounted as banal. It would be of no use to say that they were often in the same place, unplanned; that they would phone each other at the same moment and wonder why the line was busy; that they would cook identical meals in two different places. She did think it valuable, however, to record two instances of 'EXTRA-COMMUNICATION', in case the younger generation became through law or moral evolution, disinterested in hallucinogenic experience. The lines in these conversations are interchangeable.

'I think we are at the end of famine because the ears in my backyard are growing tall. Anyway, you as pharaoh's advisor know more about that than I do.'

'Certainly I've been hearing things like that. Do you think I could eat your ears when they're ready? Meanwhile the scribes predict ...'

'My ears are *always* ready, but I know you won't and anyway if you did they'd be mis ...'

'tified and make something of me I can't cope with ...'

'I'm less frightened of Potiphar ...'

'than you ...'

and

'Make that cat turn into a panther, will you? I want to watch it leap.'

(The cat, obedient to their will grew long and black and flowed towards them in a bound.)

'My God, it's coming and its teeth are bared. Change it back into a cat! I'm frightened.'

(The cat grew small again.)

They had experienced a most peculiar relationship. There had been artificial intimacy, exhilarating but false, induced by drugs. There had been moments of *real* intimacy that occurred when unsolicited confession passed between them. At such times each would bare to the other feelings and fears, intuitions and perceptions that no other soul beyond the two would be expected to understand. To record these revelations would have been as serious a breach of confidence as a priest telling tales of adultery at a poker party.

There had been, mostly, events of one-sided intimacy that were impossible to discuss.

The following diagram might explain their path through the forest on the day *she* fell in love with him:

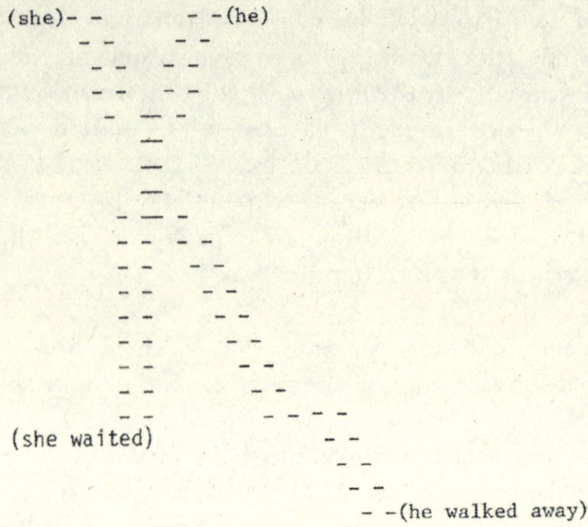

She included a photo of the site. It was nowhere special, but the ferns in the clearing were dappled with light and the dew drops shattered their reflections into fragments.

The children interrupted her. Harry, the oldest, fell through the door of her study first.

'*Mother,* you're always typing. James pushed Penny and everyone is crying. Help me stop them. What's for supper?'

(She gave her consideration to a typical complaint.)

'James pushted me and then he satted down on me verry hard and I ... hitted him, but not so hard as he hitted me. Lookit my bruises, see ... Where's a bandage and is James 'lowed some cake he was so rude to me? Is ther enny left from the other day? Do we have some, Mom, and can I eat it please?'

'Ma, don't listen to *her,* it was this way, *really.* Shee took my trruck then I hitted, ah, *hit* her but not so hard as she says. Maam, I had to sit on her to get my truck away ...'

'Ahaa, Wahaa, Awaa.'

(The fourth voice offered by Cecily in sympathy with Harry, Penny and James, came the closest to her inner response.)

It was not true that she was *always* typing, but at this time she was writing something of great importance that she wished to keep hidden even from her oldest child. It was the framework for the story that she considered her most personal, that she intended to work into a movie script. It had less to do with the intent of spoken language, than with the feelings even the most simple language could evoke given an emotional circumstance. The visualization was uppermost in her mind and this month of her husband's absence offered her an unusual opportunity for psychic privacy, a state rarely achieved by young mothers.

After ten o'clock this particular night, she prepared herself with special care. She brushed her hair and put on the white robe of a monk. She was hesitant to begin 'THE JOURNEY.'

The journey had begun, inauspiciously in thunder. The two women dressed in the clothes of innocence travelled to a distant island to visit a wizard who lived in an abandoned house. The journey was long and, fraught with error, it lengthened beyond their easy endurance. They arrived, exhausted at the stroke of midnight, to a party of elegant sprites their host had provided. The guests told true stories of magic to entertain them.

One young man with eyes of emeralds talked of *The Children Who Were not There.*

'It happened on the night of an unusual blizzard that beat about my tiny cabin, leaving a thick blanket of snow that glinted in the moon.

There was a noise at my door.

Knock, knock.

I answered the door and was not surprised to find two children. I asked,

"What do you want?" (there was no answer).

They ran about my house bumping over whatever they could. I saw that they had no shoes and no coats. A cold wind followed them around the room and suddenly, they were gone.

There were no footprints in the snow.'

The next speaker, a woman, had hair of fire and spoke of *The Tribe that Was not There.*

'One night, walking through the woods, I noticed that the sky grew bright with shooting stars of different colours.

I stopped short. It was as if an invisible barrier had dropped in front of me.

Then I saw a dozen or more people, young and old, walking across my path. They were speaking an unfamiliar language.

"Who are you?" I whispered. (There was no reply).

They vanished with a sigh into the darkness.'

The wizard told his tale last. It had no title. He drew his cloak around him and scratched his beard with a crooked finger. His eyes were closed.

'Some people, exercising their psychic powers, sent a message to say that I was to be in charge of a Fish Myth that had been lost. I would be able to draw it after I had communicated, suitably, with the Spirit who guarded it.

The message had not arrived.

We had been smoking and the guardians of this island who were against this practice came for an unexpected visit. A woman fled with the magic smoke into an empty room.

When the guardians left the woman returned to our circle, ashen.

"What is the matter?" I asked. (There was a reply).

"I have shared a room with a ghost of an old man."

Everyone went to bed and slept fitfully among silk hangings and mandalas. The next morning she sat alone before the wizard and communicated to 'him of all that was in her heart.' He revealed to her 'nothing that was not hid from him.' And, in the end, he had this advice to offer:

'Take charge of your dream, you only dream here once. You will have the friends you need if you allow fate to select them and direct you in friendship. Let me tell you this story:

I lived in a community of artists and seers. They advised me to consult the *I Ching* and to that end I carefully prepared myself. One day I cast my coins and opened the page to *Kan*:

— —
— —
———
— —
— —
———

Delighted with the advice, I ran to tell my initiate. He was painting the symbol *Kan*.

— —
— —
———
— —
— —
———

My nose bled with the shock of recognition. He offered me a pink tissue. My blood dried on it to the colours of the painting.

'Where did you get the colours in that painting?' I asked, expecting an indifferent answer.

"This morning I cut *my* hand," was his reply.'

The way back was long, but there was no error.

She embraced the message of the wizard to her soul.

Her eyes were red with crying when she appeared at the breakfast table. The dreams within the dream had obsessed her night. How could she have the friend she needed? Why could she not lead the chimerical existence of a child, for before her the children performed with ease the pyrotechnics of metamorphosis?

Girls could be boys and older ones could be younger ones. Bankrobbers could become princesses without so much as the intervention of a kiss; princesses could be aroused from a trillion years' sleep at the push of an elbow.

'Hey, Harry you count up to ten thousand and when you're finished, I'll be the king of Japan and you can be the mean prince.'

'You know you can't count *that* high, James, and anyway I don't believe you know enough about Japan to pretend you're king. Let's play something sensible, for heaven's sake ... Oh, play with Penny. I want to fix my bike.'

'I'll play with you, I can count up ten hundred thousand, are ya ready? one two three four five six seven eight nine I'm going real good, eh, ten eleven twelve when I get up there, I'll really be the mean prince even though I'm a girl thirteen fourteen fifteen ah *six*teen seventeen eighteen nineteen me n' my friends, we got artificial dinks in the graage sowecanbe BOYS nineteen, whoops, twenty twenty-one twenty-two twentythree twenty-four.... James, what comes after twenty-four? JAAMES! Where are you? Hey Mom. MOM! James won't play King of Japan and the mean prince!

'Waaa, awaaa, Wahaaa ...'

Cecily sobbed as she munched on the grass. If she had understood that conversation she would have thought twice about growing up.

She had learned when very young to eliminate the impossible or challenging from her conversation. Juvenile musings had to be carefully censored; frank answers were not expected. She remembered an exchange between herself and her mother.

'Did you lie beside Daddy, like it says in the book, to get me?'

(a silence most profound)

'Well, *did* you?'

(her face flushed purple)

'I gave you the book to answer your questions.'

'Why do you drop things when Mr. Smead comes over?'

(a silence most profound)

'Is it because you *like* him?'

(her face turned white)

'Don't think things like that. I'm married to your father. Go to your room.'

She had, of course, intended to be more frank with her children and she survived the first test well. Her own offspring hatched babies from pillows, grunting and pushing with glee, gesturing to the proper area of exit on their hairless genitalia. *They* knew who made them and *how.* The second test she had failed miserably, for she had been less than honest about her nervousness when he had appeared on the doorstep after a very long absence. The shock of discovery led to this 'NUPTIAL FLIGHT.'

She left her body and flew up into the air in hymenopteros joy. Up, UP beyong the trees where the air thins blue. Her form dazzled in the sun; the brown hairs glinting from her body like a nimbus of swords answered fire that expired from its substance like plumes. Her *halteres* hummed, drumming her vision of a dagger unsheathed and vulnerable to her reception.

But no w h i r r i n g w h i n e signalled *his* coming. The diamond sharp moment that would leave her evanescent with his viscera did not happen.

He did not follow. He would not follow her to this bright moment.

He was on the ground unaware that she had even soared above.

Her body plummeted to earth. She recovered enough to say:

'I missed you.'

There was no reply.

Her eyes, infirm before the gaze of 30,000 facets grew dim; her third eye (a little known phenomenon we share with the bees) shrivelled under his stare.

She supplemented this anguished memory with a visualization of the Queen bee in her quiet nest and the stages of marriage that normally ensued.

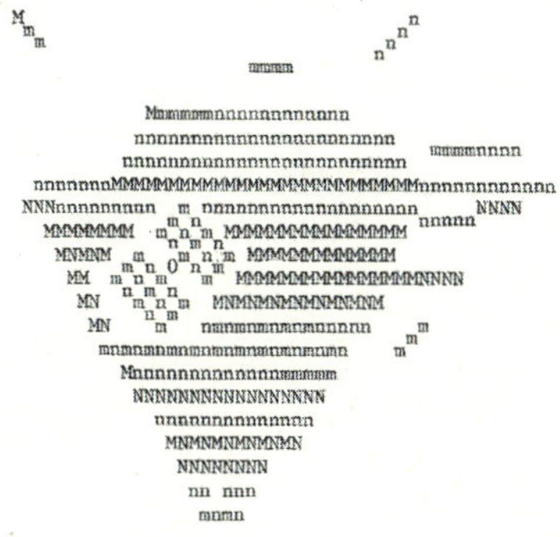

.
.
o
o
o
o
o
0
0
0
0
0
0
0
0
0
0
0
0
0
0
0
M
M 0
M 0 m
m
m
0 mnmnmn m
0
0 Mnmmmmmmmmmmmmmmmmmm
0 nnnnnnnnnnnnnnnnnnnnnnn
mmmmmmmm
0 m mnmnmnmnmnmnmnmnmnmnmnmn
m n
nnn 0 m n m NNNNNNNNNNNNNNNNNNNNNNNnnnnnnnnnnnnn
n m n
MMM m 0 m n m mmmmmmmmmmmmmmmmmmmmmmmmmmmmmmmMMMMMmm
m n 0 n m
m n m m MMMMMMMMMNMNMNMNMNMNMNMNMN
n m n
m n m NNNNNnnnnnnnnnnnnnnnnn
n m
m MMMMMMMMMMMMMMMMMMMMMMMMMMMMM
MNMNMNMNmnmnmnmnmnmnmnmnmnmnmnmn
MN mnmn MMMMMMMMMMMMMMMMMMMM
m
nnnnnnnnnnnnnnnnnnnnnnnnnn m
m
MMMMnnnnnnnnnnnnnnnn
NNNNNNNNNNNNNNNNN
mmmmmmmmmmmmmmmmmm
NNNNNNNNNNNN
MNMNMNMN
nnnnnn
mmmmm

.
.
.
o
o
o
o

o
o
o
o
o
o
o
o
o
o
o
o
0
0
0
0

MMMnnnnnnnmMMMNNNNNN *

. . . . . .
0
0
0
0
0
0
0
0
0
0
0
0
0
0
0
0
0
0

piiig

piiinng

NOTE 1

Figure 1 shows the Queen at peace with her hive as o.

Figure 2 shows the Queen rising for the purpose of mating as a diminishing o. Drones p i i i n n g against her.

Figure 3 shows how the mate meets the Queen with the mnnn, MMMMM, Mnmnmn of sexual desire. They mate in an o, each for the moment the / the other was. The sated Queen takes the Drone into her spermatheca and he falls dead

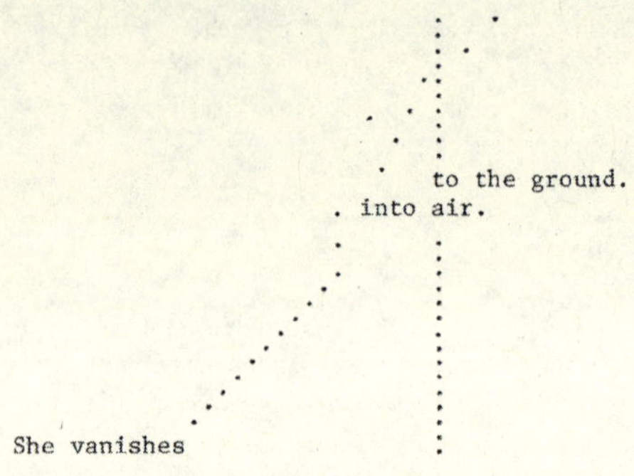

His impassivity stung so horridly that the next day so long ago, she met with a friend to determine her fortune. They huddled before the fire and cast their coins with reverence. They were very close and sought to live through the wizard.

Renata chose her symbol first. It was *Kwei Mei* and gave no answer. Hers was *Kien*, the opposite, and gave her the answer she did not wish:

Kien suggests to us the marriage of a young lady, and the good fortune attending it. There will be advantage in being firm and correct.

By the last day in May it had become difficult for her to know whether she was *in* her structure or *out* of it. But she took her class, as promised, to see *Cries and Whispers*. It was her policy to teach from only those films that wed illuminating dialogue to visual brilliance; she was concerned with the directors who *realized* the life of the emotions. This movie unfolded before them a chronicle of indifference and when it was finished, a buzz of consternation reverberated through the audience.

At coffee the class pondered on the meaning of the servant who had cradled a corpse like the Virgin of the *Pietà*. And because a peculiar humming had arisen in her ears, she was unable to bring her own experiences to bear upon the film analysis as was her custom. She half-listened as each student spoke through the veils of bias.

'The servant was Bergman's candidate for Sainthood,' said an ethereal young man. 'She was the only one disinterested in self ...'

(One who is interested in self impinged on her mind.)

'Yeah, she was the woman liberated from the usual roles of Wife, Mother, Sister. She alone could befriend,' stated a robust young woman.

(Bee-friend, Bee-friend, BeeOffend, grew in her.)

'She Wazz Sooo Waarm, a Great advertizzzment furr the biiisexual Liife,' said another.

('Mmnnnnn, mnmnmnmn,' murmured the teacher.)

'Aah, that's crap. You're just putting yourself in the movie. She was, in fact, Mary Magdalene. Get serious, willya! She was also a Proletarian in a hive of the Bourgeoisie, obviously Bergman's ideal of the Christian Socialist,' said the last to speak.

'I'm at odds with my Social Hive,' said the teacher.

Everyone laughed without knowing why. The class had ended.

She drove home in a *Fury,* erratic in her speed and direction, the sound of the movie track whirring in her brain.

h
S S s s H
I S S S s s s
S I H S i s s h h
I H i i s s S s S H I
I H S s s ish H I S
S H S h H s S s H H s H I
H S S s H s s s S s s S s S
H S S s S s H s s s s S s s S s S
S s S s s H u sh s sh s H s S s H
H S S s S H S s H s S H s H H
H S s S H s S s H i H H S S H
H S s S H H i h s s s S S s S
H s s s S S H h i h H S S S
s h S H i i s S S S S
s H s S S S S s S s S
S s H H S S s S s S
S s H H i h s s S s S
h i s s h s s s
H s S s h S

[A concrete poem of scattered typewritten letters — S, s, H, h, I, i, u — arranged in a diamond/honeycomb pattern; spatial arrangement approximated line by line.]

It took on the configuration of a hive of bees about to swarm. She kept hold on herself long enough to phone the wizard.

Brrrrnnnnng, Brrrrnnnnng, Brrrrnnnnng,
Brrrrnnnnng, Brrrrnnnnng, Brrrrnnnnng,
Brrrrnnnnng, Brrrrnnnnng, Brrrrnnnnng,
(a sleepy voice answered)

'Who is it?'

'I just had to talk to you. I'm writing a script and you're in it. What was the meaning of 'THE JOURNEY'?

'Oh yes, I remember now. You came to one of our story-telling sessions. That was a really fine evening, lots of good tales. How have you been? How are the children and your husband?'

'Were they true? Those stories, I mean, were they really true?'

'Sure they were. Phenomena like that happen in the country and to people who are disposed, open, in touch with the Moving Spirit ...'

'Well, why can't I *create* my own dream and *choose* the people who live it with me? Why can't I become *in charge* of my reality?'

'You mean you phoned me at the dead of night to ask me that? You know damnwell you can only dream with those who are like you and you can only choose those who show a willingness for being chosen. What's really on your mind for Chrissakes?'

'When I saw you, I repaid your insights with *Social Notes in the Language of the Bees* ... I ... O ... I ... O'

'Well, I could have told you that that solitary bee of yours was not the one for you. But the stories were great. But just keep the reality of the situation in your mind. He, the bee, is entitled to be in charge of himself; he will not be recreated through you, nor will he tame at your desiring. I thought you had better sense than to phone the wise in the middle of the goddam night to talk about your love hallucinations. Be what you are destined to become and be happy with it, Honey.

Click.

End of conversation.

She flew upstairs and that very night constructed a hexagon in her room with one side open. It was so elegant that no one questioned her about it, at least not at first.

Into it she retreated to feed herself on Royal Jelly.

For a long time she seemed to be as always. The children still made their conversations and found her responses to them apt.

When Harry announced for some reason with ten-year-old earnestness that he would build a colony where workers shared equally in the labour and where there would be no sexual rivalry, she sang the structure of a perfect colony without strife:

MMMMMMMMMMMMMMMMMMM
MMMMMMMMMMMMMMMMMMMMMMMMMMMMM
MMMMMMMMMMMMMMMMMMMMMMMMM
MMMMMMMMMMMMMMMMMMMMM
MMMMMMMMMMMMMMMMM
MMMMMMMMMMMMM

Harry giggled at her whimsical reply. Then Penny who was especially fond of riddles asked her, 'What happened to the man who fell into slush?'

'HSSH, hssh,' he said, 'Hssh, hussh, hush,' was her answer.

She had such a foolish look of surprise on her face that they doubled over with laughter. Then she rose and did a curious hexagonal dance accompanied by a song.

I dont think Ill ever see a thing as lovely as a bee I dont think I
I'll ever see a thing as lovely as a bee, I don't
dont think Ill ever see a thing as lovely as a bee I dont thini I'll

This number delighted Cecily in particular who gurgled: 'Ahee, heehee, Mama's a bee, Mama's a BEEEEEEEEEEEE.'

With increasing frequency, however, she locked herself into her room to be alone in the hexagon which she elaborated daily. It was arranged like the set of a film so that it would arouse no suspicion and give no offence. Its open entrance was guarded by two fine medieval warriors (a gift from her late French aunt) and the six walls were covered externally with grey, watermarked silk. Inside where she would permit no one to come, there were lush yellow carpets and ochre velvet cushions. Alabaster lamps were suspended from the ceiling. When lit, they revealed mahogany chests filled with the translucent vessels containing the sweet substance on which she fed. In the centre of the cell was a prie-Dieu on which her writings were raised between two golden candlesticks. The text's most recent addition was her Order of Service for which explicit directions were given.

The structure of writing that had been a recent obsession, she immolated in her shrine. Echoes of the destroyed notes lingered in the 'Bible' under the heading, 'BEE CELEBRANT.' This section was decorated with an illustration of the three-lobed mask that crowned the Queen during the ceremony.

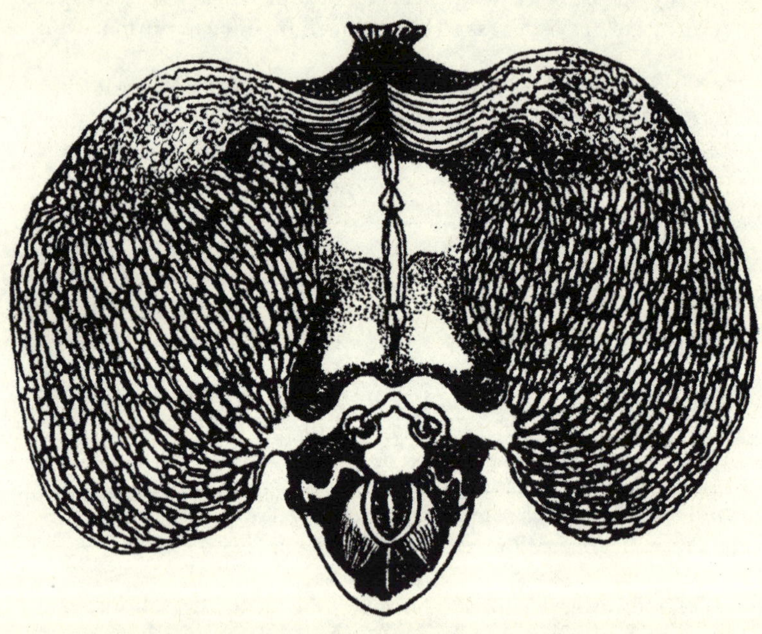

Let the Celebrant approach the Hexagon with head bowed low. Let her touch the Scabbards of the Warriors with gentle hands. Let the Celebrant unsheath the Swords. Let the Celebrant kneel to kiss the feet of the Warriors for they alone can permit entrance into the Mystery.

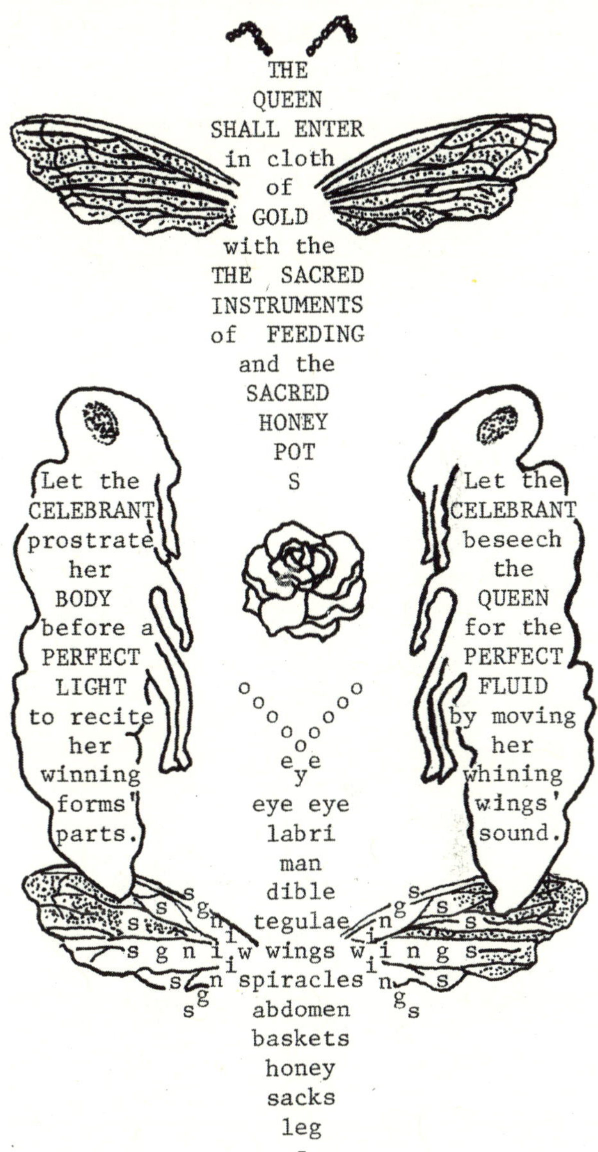
THE
QUEEN
SHALL ENTER
in cloth
of
GOLD
with the
THE SACRED
INSTRUMENTS
of FEEDING
and the
SACRED
HONEY
POT
S
Let the
CELEBRANT
prostrate
her
BODY
before a
PERFECT
LIGHT
to recite
her
winning
forms'
parts.
Let the
CELEBRANT
beseech
the
QUEEN
for the
PERFECT
FLUID
by moving
her
whining
wings'
sound.
eye eye
labri
man
dible
tegulae
s g n i w wings w i n g s
spiracles
abdomen
baskets
honey
sacks
leg
s

They together will sing this sooong waving their
wings.

BEEEEEEEEEEEEEE B B B EEEEEEEEEEEEEEB

BEEEEEEEEEEEEE B B EEEEEEEEEEEEEB

BEEEEEEEEEEEE B EEEEEEEEEEEEB

Let the Celebrants prepare for the Rite of EXTRA-
COMMUNICATION by drinking the Magic Mead with the
QUEEN
and let them communicate in mellifluous voice the
WISDOM OF THE
BEE

BEATITUDES

Beloved is the Bee who beguiles those who are beneath the wind.

Beloved is the Bee who bestows belief on those who bemoan their fate.

Beloved is the Bee who begrudges nothing and who behaves without belligerence.

Beloved is the Bee who betrays no one she befriends, who bewilders by her beneficence.

Beloved is the Bee who besieges no one and who waits for her betrothed without the beehive.

Beloved is the Bee who is begotten between the branches and the sky.

LET THE CELEBRANT PREPARE TO MAKE HER NUPTIAL FLIGHT.

By the height of the summer, nothing could conceal her madness and no doctor could cure her bizarre symptoms. So she soared one day from her window, leaving a note that read simply: *'I have flown to mate with Apis Africanus.'*

The hexagon revealed to them a shambles of gold ornaments, broken furniture, soiled pillows and a flood of honey on which bees had gorged themselves to death. The Bible of her sect was taken, by some, to be proof of irredeemable mental disorder.

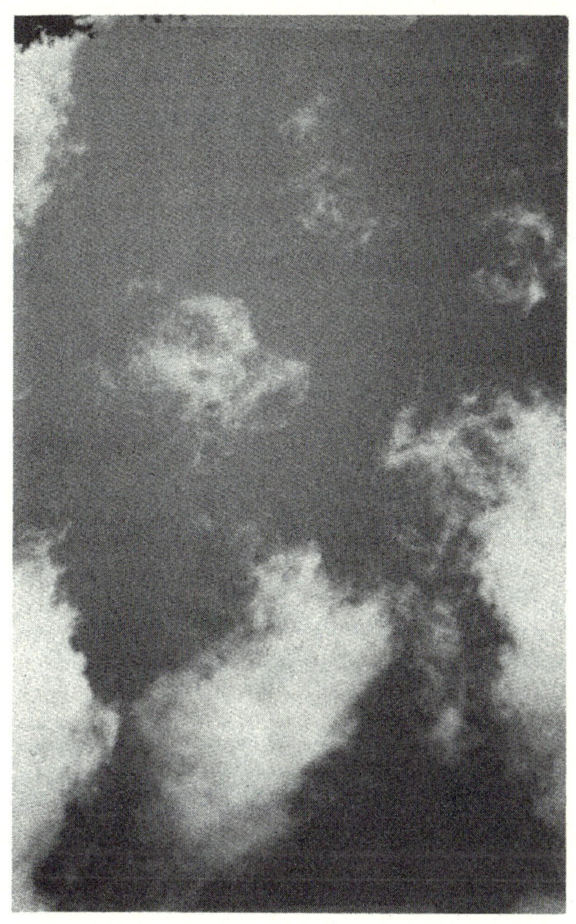

THE THROWBACK SERIES operates on the premise that books have more than one season. Spanning the twentieth century, we aim to republish out-of-print books that we think have something to offer a contemporary readership. The Throwback Series has re-published books that are diverse in style and tradition: books from the decades of the modern realist novel to books of late-twentieth century experimental fiction. We aim to surprise and reacquaint. Each book comes with a short introduction written by people who have both creative and academic chops. Our introductions provide context (but never spoilers!) as they attend to the life of the original authors and the flavour of their writing.

Invisible Publishing produces fine Canadian literature for those who enjoy such things. As an independent, not-for-profit publisher, we work to build communities that sustain and encourage engaging, literary, and current writing.

Invisible Publishing has been in operation for nearly two decades. We released our first fiction titles in the spring of 2007, and our catalogue has come to include works of graphic fiction and nonfiction, pop culture biographies, experimental poetry, and prose.

We are committed to publishing writers with diverse perspectives. In acknowledging historical and systemic barriers, and the limits of our existing catalogue, we emphatically encourage writers from LGBTQ2SIA+ communities, Indigenous writers, and writers of colour to submit their work.

Invisible Publishing is also home to the Bibliophonic series of music books and the Throwback series of CanLit reissues.